THE COURTS OF IDLENESS

THE COURTS
OF IDLENESS

BY
DORNFORD YATES

WARD, LOCK & CO., LIMITED
LONDON AND MELBOURNE

First Published	.	.	.	.	1920
Reprinted	.	.	.	.	.	1922
Reprinted	.	.	.	.	.	1923
Reprinted	.	.	.	.	.	1924
Reprinted	.	.	.	.	.	1925
Reprinted	.	.	.	.	.	1926
Reprinted	.	.	.	.	.	1929
Reprinted	.	.	.	.	.	1930
Reprinted	.	.	.	.	.	1933
Reprinted	.	.	.	.	.	1936
Reprinted	.	.	.	.	.	1940
Reprinted	.	.	.	.	.	1941
Reprinted	.	.	.	.	.	1942
Reprinted	.	.	.	.	.	1943
Reprinted	.	.	.	.	.	1944
Reprinted	.	.	.	.	.	1945
Reprinted	.	.	.	.	.	1947
Reprinted	.	.	.	.	.	1949

MADE IN ENGLAND
Printed in Great Britain by The Whitefriars Press Ltd., London and Tonbridge

CONTENTS

BOOK I.—HOW SOME PASSED OUT OF THE COURTS FOR EVER

INTERLUDE

BOOK II.—HOW OTHERS LEFT THE COURTS ONLY TO RETURN

To the countryside of England, the hanging forests of Austria, and the tilted, flower-starred meadows of the Pyrenees.

BOOK I

HOW SOME PASSED OUT OF THE COURTS FOR EVER

BERTRAM PLEYDELL

(of White Ladies, in the County of Hampshire)

```
                    BERTRAM PLEYDELL
          ┌────────────────┴────────────────┐
        BERTRAM                            DAPHNE─JONATHAN MANSEL
          │                                  │
  BERRY ─ DAPHNE                        ┌─────┴─────┐
          │                           JONAH       JILL
        BOIS
     ┌────┴────┐
   DAPHNE     BOY
```

CHAPTER I

WHAT'S IN A NAME?

"THIS," said Fairie, " is too thick."

It really was. From a leaden sky snow was beginning to fall. The draughts—for there is no wind in London, only draughts—caught and flung it insolently in the faces of passers-by. These received it, some dumbly, most with an ill grace, much as once lords and gentlemen-in-waiting endured the horseplay of the King's fool—with crooked smiles. A veritable prince among jesters, the weather. Never had monarch's fool so ample a licence.

From a club window Bill Fairie surveyed the scene gloomily. By his side his brother-in-law, Marlowe, busied himself with the delicate operation of piercing a slim cigar.

" Snow's all right," said the latter suddenly. " Very seasonable. It is this sort of weather, brother, that has made us Englishmen what we are."

" I believe it is," said Fairie. " Incidentally, d'you know we've had twenty minutes' sunshine in the last thirteen days ? "

Marlowe reached for a match with a frown.

" I can see you've been reading the papers," he said.

" And that the average rainfall for March has already been exceeded, with another twenty-two days of the month to go ? "

" Twenty-three," corrected the other pleasantly.

" Don't you remember ?   ' Thirty days hath September, April, June, and Nov——' "

" There are times," said Fairie, " when I feel that I could offer you violence."

" Not really," said Marlowe. " Your better self ——"

" At the present moment, for instance, I could witness your immersion in a horse-pond unmoved."

Marlowe sat up and laid down his cigar.

" The existing climatic conditions make that remark peculiarly offensive," he said. " You've made me feel cold all over. Only an old brandy . . ."

His companion grinned.

" You shall have one," he said, beckoning to a waiter. " And now replace your cigar. It does much to relieve the monotony of your face."

Bill Fairie was thirty-one. Nice-looking, clean-shaven, lazy-eyed, he strolled unconcernedly through life, to all appearances a leisured bachelor. Yet he adored his wife, with whom he had slipped into matrimony when he was twenty-eight. Between the two there existed a perfect understanding. Never far apart, they were seldom alone together, preferring to make two of a party. Their cousins, the Brokes—brother and sister—shared a house with them. The four pulled together excellently.

" Why don't you and Betty clear out ? " said Marlowe, after a pause. " Just now Biarritz——"

" Is probably rather colder than this, and gradually filling up with the sort of people one leaves England to avoid. Besides, we're hanging on for the Grand National."

" That, of course, settles it. Aintree ought to be rather nice if this weather goes on. Got your panama ready ? "

Fairie leaned against the wall and regarded his brother-in-law.

"He would be humorous," he said musingly. "I suppose it's being so much with me. Well, well! As I was saying, we both want to see the race, if only because——"

"Give it a miss and clear out," said Marlowe absently. "Pretty legs that kid's got. Over there, getting out of the car." He pointed across the street. "Awfully like Dolly Lair's. By Jove," he cried, springing to his feet, "if it isn't her! And I knew her little ankles at thirty paces. I must go and tell her."

The next moment he was gone. Fairie looked after him. Then :

"I don't think this is quite decent," he said. "However." With that, he moved to another window, the better to observe what took place.

The car had stopped at a corner. For a moment the girl had been speaking with someone inside ; now she turned to the chauffeur, clearly giving an order. The next second the great doors of an Insurance Office had swung to behind her. The car slipped away from the kerb into the line of traffic. Only a bull-dog in a blue coat remained, a lead trailing from his collar. Seemingly, while the door was open, he had scrambled out of the car unnoticed. He had not seen his mistress pass through the tall doors, so now he stood bewildered, looking slowly about him, suddenly lost.

Marlowe appeared upon the scene hurriedly ; it had taken a few seconds to find his coat and hat. From the club window his brother-in-law watched him amusedly. Quickly he glanced round for the car, by this time out of sight. Seeing it nowhere, he scanned the pavement carefully on either side. Fruitlessly, of course. So, by a process of exhaustion, he came to the buildings. It seemed certain that one of them must contain the lady. The question was, which had that honour. After a critical survey, he rejected the Insurance Office, naturally enough, for a doorway which admitted—so ran the superscription—to some temporary Exhibition of Water-Colours. After a moment's hesitation he passed in.

A slow smile spread over Fairie's countenance. This was an opportunity not to be missed, and it had stopped snowing. Besides, the bull-dog, poor fellow, was getting worried. . . .

A minute later he crossed the street and picked up the trailing lead. The animal blinked up at him curiously.

" Lad," said Fairie, " be of good cheer. She of the pretty legs will come again. We're going to wait for her, and I simply love your coat."

Thus addressed the bull-dog regarded his friend with big eyes, snuffling inquisitively. Fairie smiled back, stooping to stroke the broad brown head. With a sigh of relief the bull-dog accepted the situation.

The pair had not long to wait. In fact, they were still regarding one another, when my lady emerged from the building as suddenly as she had entered it. Very smart, if you please, in her fine mink coat, which swathed her from neck to knee in an odour of luxury. From knee to ankle she went naked, as women do, unless a rose-coloured lustre may be accounted clothes. Her hair was hidden under a small blue hat, but gaiety danced in her eyes for the world to see and be glad of, and on her lips hung a smile no winter could take away. As though to mock the rough weather, her slight patent-leather slippers made light of the dripping steps : the huddles of snow could not muster refulgence like theirs.

As the bull-dog surged forward, an exclamation of surprise broke from his mistress's lips. Fairie raised his hat.

"You are careless, you know," he said, with a smile. "It's one thing to leave your sponge in the bathroom, but it's quite another to leave your bull-dog on the pavement."

"But how—I don't understand," said the girl, her voice full of laughter. "I didn't leave him."

"Oh, but you did," said Fairie. "I saw you. And he's very upset about it. You should have heard him sigh just now."

My lady bent over the bull-dog.

"Peter, dear, you know I didn't mean to," she said. "But why did Peter get out of the car ? Oh, naughty Peter."

The familiar expression of reproof appeared to afford its target immense gratification. He wagged all his hindquarters and squirmed with delight, snuffling furiously.

"I'm forgiven, you see," said his mistress, looking up at Fairie.

"I think he's very tolerant," said the latter. "I wouldn't have forgiven you so easily."

"Ah, but then he's got a nice nature "—with a mischievous glance.

"Ungenerous," said Fairie aggrievedly. "The re-mark, I mean. Not the look. I loved that."

The girl smiled. Then :

"It was splendid of you to take care of him. I'm awfully grateful. And now . . ."

She put out a hand for the lead. Fairie looked at her.

" Er—Peter and I were just going to have some tea," he said. " Over the way there. At Rumpel-mayer's."

" Were you, though ? "

" Fact," said Fairie, with an anxious glance at the entrance to the Water-Colours. " We were wondering if—er—if you'd join us."

My lady raised her eyebrows ever so slightly.

" If you can get Peter across the street without breaking the lead," she said slowly, " you can have tea together."

" And you'll join us ? "

The girl hesitated. Then !

" And I'll join you," she added, with a faint smile.

" Done," said Fairie, turning towards the kerb.

Directly he felt the strain on his collar, Peter looked up at his mistress. Clearly she was not proposing to move. Enough. Without giving an inch, he screwed his head round and gave Fairie an apologetic look. The strain continuing, the look became one of surprised protest. Another moment and the brown eyes turned contemptuously away. You would have sworn the dog had shrugged his broad shoulders.

" Oh, Peter ! " said Fairie reproachfully.

A grunt of disgust and indignation answered him. The girl looked on amusedly.

" The silent knight," said Fairie, loosening the lead for a moment. " What's his horse-power ? "

" I'm not sure. But he's pulling very well this afternoon, isn't he ? "

Fairie nodded.

" An obstinate fellow," he said musingly.

Once more the girl put out her hand.

" Try ' determined,' " she said. " Good-bye."

Fairie shook his head.

"No," he said simply. "Obstinate. That's the difference between us. I am determined. And now let's go and have tea. If you stand here any longer, Miss Dorothy Lair, you will catch cold."

With that he picked Peter up in his arms, settling him on his back like a baby, paused on the kerb for a break in the stream of taxis, and then walked easily across the broad street. After a moment the girl followed him. As she stepped on to the pavement :

"I didn't know I knew you," she said coldly.

Fairie set down his charge and looked at her.

"I don't think you do," said he, "or you wouldn't have spoken like that. And now good-bye."

So saying, he held out the lead. She took it hesitatingly.

"Don't you want——"

"To give you tea ? My dear, I should have loved to. So long, Peter."

He raised his hat and turned on his heel.

"I say," said the girl suddenly.

"Yes ? "

"I know you don't forgive people easily, but as we did arrange—I mean, I shouldn't like to disappoint Peter."

"I'm not at all sure," said Fairie, "that I don't adore you."

"Thanks very much," said Dolly, with a little laugh. "And now, please, how did you know my name ? "

*   *   *   *   *

Marlowe emerged from the Exhibition of Water-Colours looking inexpressibly bored. Instead of the attractive Dolly, he had lighted upon an old friend of his father's, who had been abroad for three years

—an encounter which, for all his cunning, had cost him ten slow-going minutes.

He crossed the street moodily, reflecting upon his infamous luck. Of course, the delay had spoiled any chance he had had of catching Miss Lair. Listlessly he began to make his way up the pavement, looking idly into the shop-windows. Looking idly . . .

The sudden spectacle of Dolly and his brother-in-law engaged in obviously light-hearted converse over a dainty tea, behind the plate-glass of Rumpelmayer's, filled him with an emotion too deep for words. For a moment he stood as if rooted to the spot. Then :

" Hullo, old chap," said a soft voice.

His sister, Elizabeth Fairie.

Marlowe turned to her.

" Look at him," he said, pointing a shaking finger at the unconscious delinquent. " Look at the brute."

" Where ? Who ? " said his sister calmly. " Oh, it's Bill. And Dolly Lair. She's a dear kid. I wish they'd look round."

" So do I," said Marlowe grimly.

Within, the pair were holding high festival.

" If you'd only said you were Mr. Fairie," Dolly was saying.

" What's in a name ? " replied her companion. " The Doll by any other name would smell as sweet."

" Will you be serious ? " said Dolly, bubbling with laughter.

Fairie regarded her.

" How you dare have a mouth like that, beats me," he said. " Hullo ! There's Betty. Oh, and Marlowe, too. Now, isn't that nice ? "

Coolly he beckoned them to come in. With a smile Elizabeth turned to comply with the request. Marlowe took off his hat with awful deliberation.

His brother-in-law nodded genially, and Dolly bowed.

" How strange he looks ! " she said.

" Always like that when he's been looking at pictures," Fairie explained. " He's been to some exhibition or other this afternoon."

" I never knew he cared about art "—surprisedly.

" Practically all he lives for," said Fairie, rising. " And here's my helpmeet. I suppose I must get her a chair."

Elizabeth Fairie was a great beauty. More than that. There was an exquisite charm about her that was irresistible. Talk with her once, and you would remember it for all time. You might forget the big brown eyes after a while, but never the soft light glowing behind them, forget the proud curve of the mouth, but never the faint smile playing about it. The odds are, you would remember all four, probably with a sigh. The easy grace of her movements, her speech, her manners generally, was remarkable. With it all, she was perfectly natural. Sporting, too, and always ready for anything. She sat a horse better than most women sit a sofa, had no nerves, and usually wore a little air of amused gravity, which argued a strong sense of humour.

" Well, children," said Betty.

" Child yourself," said her husband. " You see in us a man and woman of the world."

" As bad as that ? " said Betty, raising her eyebrows. " Any way, you looked very sweet. What were you discussing so cheerfully ? "

" Agriculture, if you must know," said Fairie. " Yes, some further tea, please. I suppose Pip's coming."

" I expect so. He seems rather bored with you about something."

"Dear, dear," said her husband composedly. "But here he is. Now mark how a soft answer shall turn away his wrath." He turned to greet the gentleman in question. "Hullo, old chap. How are the Water-Colours? Any gems?"

"I will deal with you," said Marlowe, "at some future time." Here he drew up a chair. "Probably on a dark night, when there is no moon. I ought to have warned you about him," he added, turning to Dolly. "His sheepish exterior conceals a wolfish heart."

"How awful!" said Dolly.

"Yes," replied Marlowe with unction. "Beneath a thin veneer of——"

"Oh, look," said his sister. "It's beginning to snow again."

"Hush," said her husband. "Wherever were you brought up? Never direct attention to indecency."

"Idiot," said Betty. "All the same——"

"It is my firm belief," said Marlowe, "that there is a curse upon this unhappy land."

"I agree, brother," said Fairie. "This weather is, as it were, a foul plague. Presently we shall have frogs. Stacks of them."

"Yes, and then blains," said Marlowe.

"How many frogs go to the stack?" said Miss Lair.

"A hundred and forty-four," said Fairie. "Don't you know your tables? One man one vote, four votes one gallon."

Dolly broke into silvery laughter.

"Don't encourage the fool, dear," said Betty. "If you knew him as well as I do——"

"Let me put it like this," said her husband. "To know me is to love me. How terse! But to the weather. Pip says we ought to clear out."

" Leave England ? "

" Certainly," said Marlowe. " Give the 'orse-race a miss and leave England. England," he added ecstatically, " this precious stone set in the silver sea (Bacon)." With a rapturous wave of the hand he indicated the scene outside—the dark, wet street crowded with scurrying traffic, uncertain gusts driving the fine snow hither and thither, what dull daylight there was, failing. . . . Could he have seen it, old John of Gaunt would have turned his face to the wall.

For a moment they all sat silent. Then :

" Have another *éclaire*, Peter ? " said Fairie.

" You haven't been giving him *éclaires* ? " cried Dolly, horrified.

" This," said Fairie, " will make his fourth."

" No, no ! He mustn't have it, Mr. Fairie. He'll be awfully ill as it is. Three *éclaires*. Oh, Peter ! "

The latter seemed greatly moved by their attention. After sneezing twice, he sat quivering with expectation, looking from one to the other eloquently. His mistress gave him a piece of bread-and-butter. Nothing could have been more elegant than his acceptance of the morsel, unless it were his almost simultaneous expulsion of it as unworthy.

" You see," said Dolly. " You've spoiled him. Ah ! Naughty dog ! "

" Don't misjudge him," said Fairie. " Perhaps he's giving up butter in Lent."

" Of course," said Betty, who was still regarding the whirling snow, " of course, I know it's rotten stopping here, but even if we decide to give up the Grand National, where are we to go ? "

" Where indeed ? " said her husband. " Ireland is priest-ridden, Heidelberg's full of smells. There's really only Bruges left."

"What about Rome?" said Marlowe.

His sister shook her head pensively.

"No," she said. "And Biarritz appears to be like this. The Ludlows are back already, and they only went there last week. Jean says they never went outside the hotel for three days."

"Which, as is usual in these cases," said Fairie, "reduces us to the Riviera."

"Unless you go to Rih," said Dolly suddenly. "It's only four days, and you'd love it. Both of you."

"Oh, Bill," said Betty. "That's an idea."

"Yes," said Dolly, waxing enthusiastic, "and it'll be priceless just now. The flowers'll be so lovely. What with the bougainvilleas and jackaranda trees ——"

"I beg your pardon," said Fairie.

"Jackaranda."

"Hush," said Fairie. "Not before the dog."

"Fool," said his wife. "Go on, Dolly."

"Oh, and the great blue sky and the hot sun and the lizards and bullock-cars——"

"The fauna!" said Fairie excitedly.

"Will you be quiet?" said Betty.

"And the dear warm slopes and cobbled roads and everything . . ."

Dolly stopped suddenly and looked round. Then :

"I was very happy there," she said simply.

The others looked at her.

"You darling," said Betty with a swift smile.

"I agree," said Fairie. "But about this sun—hot sun. Is there any question about that?"

"I don't think so," said Dolly, a little flushed. "Somehow, it's just there—day after day."

"Give me strength," said Fairie brokenly. "Day after day?"

Dolly nodded amusedly.

" All day long," she said.

With infinite care Bill Fairie pushed back his plate. Then he turned to his wife.

" My dear," he said, " much as I would like to witness the hustle for the Blue Riband of the steeplechase world (sic), I feel that this phenomenon should not be missed."

Thoughtfully Betty regarded him.

" I was wondering," she said, " whether I'd take Falcon."

Now Falcon was Mrs. Fairie's maid.

*   *   *   *   *

An hour later the two passages had been booked. Also, a cable had been sent engaging rooms at an hotel—the hotel, according to Cockspur Street 1 they should know there. Bill and his wife were to sail in four days' time. So easily, sometimes, may strange steps be taken. Creatures of Impulse, the Fairies.

Impulse is a queer counsellor, too little honoured. There are those who will ever rank him close after Gluttony and Sloth, counting him one of the Vices. Such are the regular-lived. And very nice, too ; only . . . Habit digs deep grooves sometimes, almost graves, for his creatures. Others soberly suspect his advice, as a matter of course assuming it to be evil, until deep reflection suggests the contrary. And even then they are not quite comfortable. " Can there any good thing come out of Nazareth ? " But it is too late then, for the counsel of Impulse must be followed amain, or the charm of it is withered. So that only the reckless and irresponsible—undeserving heretics who make few plans, neither abide by those they make—may know the fresh air of excitement short notice lends to an affair ; the spice, very tasty, with which sudden resolve garnishes a holiday.

*   *   *   *   *

The Fairies leaving together, it was for Marlowe to see Dolly home—naturally. And before home, to Bond Street to choose some gloves. Whilst they were in the taxi :

" What I want to know," said Marlowe, " is how you and that serpent got into touch."

" Ah," said Dolly.

Her companion sighed.

" You know," he said, " I believe your life is one long series of indiscretions."

" Doubtless," coolly replied Miss Lair. " But what were you doing at the Water-Colours ? "

" I went to look for a picture which wasn't there."

" How tiresome for him ! " she murmured.

" Yes, wasn't it ? Such a sweet picture, too. The softest colouring. However, I found it in the end."

" But I thought you said——"

" It wasn't there ? Nor it was, Dolly. When I struck it, it was having tea with the serpent."

" O-o-h," said Dolly. " Then that was how——"

" Precisely. You see," and Marlowe explained.

" The one redeeming feature about the whole affair," he concluded, " is that you have persuaded Bill to leave the country."

Dolly gave a little laugh. Then :

" I think Betty's very fortunate," she said.

For a moment Marlowe sat silent. Then :

" You're right," he said quietly, staring out of the window. " She is. Bill's one of the best, straightest, kindest——"

" Dear old Pip," said Dolly, slipping a warm

arm through his. "But I wasn't thinking of her husband."

*   *   *   *   *

At eleven o'clock the next morning Bill Fairie entered the library, an open letter in his hand.

"I have here——" he began.

"Hush," said Betty. "If you talk, I can't hear. Will you say that again, please ? "

She was at the telephone, very intense, very adorable. Kneeling sideways upon a chair, she leaned far over the writing-table, propping herself upon her elbows, one white hand holding the receiver, the other's fingers about the mouthpiece. One little slipper had fallen off while she was talking, and now and again a pale pride of silk stocking would thrust out and down over the edge of the chair, till the toes of a shapely foot touched the ground there to grope vainly for the elusive foot-gear.

The conversation proceeded.

"Yes, will you send . . . No, no. As well as the other pairs. Then I can see if I like them . . . That's right. Five o'clock will do. Yes. Good-bye." As she hung up the receiver :

"What assignation is this ? " said Fairie.

"Shoes for Rih, old chap. What were you going to say ? "

Her husband displayed the letter.

"From Robin," he said laconically. "Listen.

"DEAR BROTHER,—Thank you for your letter. I pass over the fact that so much of it as is legible appears to be couched in studiedly offensive terms. Were your intellect less stunted, I would give you a short but telling word-picture of the malignant weather which has prevailed here for the last six

days. But it is, as you know, one of my rules
never to cast pearls before swine. The fact that
my sister, but for whose importunity I should not
have made one of this ill-starred house-party, has
contracted an appalling and, if I may believe her,
most painful cold, affords me some little consolation.
At the same time, the mental and physical dis-
comfort which I myself have suffered, owing to
continuous rain and an incredibly low temperature,
has, I feel, done much to undermine a constitution
more or less sound, perhaps, but never robust.
Under these circumstances it will not surprise you
to learn that we are curtailing a visit which we
should never have paid. In short, the snow-ploughs
have been ordered, the coroner has been informed,
and I have already decided what is the least I can
give the second footman. We shall make King's
Cross to-morrow at six-fifteen. You had better be
there with the car, as William is stupid about
luggage and it is well-known that two fools are better
than one.—ROBIN."

Betty threw back her head and laughed.

" They seem to have had rather a doing," she said.
" Back to-night, too. Well, they'll hate it here, won't
they ? "

With a shudder, she glanced out at the driving rain.

" They won't stick it for half a week," said Bill.
" Robin's evidently fed right up, and, according to
him, Fay's got one of the colds. I bet you they come
with us."

" To Rih ? " said Betty, coming across to the fire.

" Every time," said her husband. " You see."

Here a servant entered with a telegram. Fairie
opened it unconcernedly. Then :

" No answer," he said. " At least not now. How very untoward," he added musingly.

" What's the matter ? " said Betty from the club-kerb, where she was sitting with her feet in the grate.

Her husband handed her the flimsy sheet.

" Peter ill all night long," she murmured.

" Yes," said Bill. " Poor old Peter ! Must have picked up something, I suppose. That's the worst of these well-bred——"

" Nonsense," said his wife. " It's the *éclaires* you gave him, of course. And poor Dolly's been up with him all night. She must be wild with you to trouble to send a wire."

" I don't see why she should be wild with me. The dog shouldn't have eaten them. Supposing you went to the Billows' and ate a lot of boiled mutton and——"

" That's enough," said Betty. " What are you going to do about it ? "

" Do ? " said Bill, lighting a cigarette. " What d'you expect me to do ? Take the animal some grapes ? "

" You'd better ring her up."

" And get told off properly ? Not much. No," he added airily. " I shall compose a discreet wire, in-dicative at once of my esteem, anxiety, and remorse. Tears will start to the eyes of all who see it."

" Dear fool," said his wife, putting up her face to be kissed. " I do love you so. And now I must go and get ready. I ordered the car for half-past."

" Wearing apparel ? " said Bill.

Betty nodded.

" Just a few things, you know. Summer things. Don't forget you've got to get——"

" Chorus," said her husband. " He forgot to get what he'd got to get together to get to Rih. Pom."

"Idiot," said Betty. "Some tennis-balls, I was going to say. And, if you're going to get any clothes, do see about them to-day. You know what it is if you leave everything till the last minute." And she moved towards the door.

"All right, m'dear. Let's see. What do I want? Gent's half hose, fancy neck-wear, flannel trouserings—which reminds me . . ."

But Betty had gone.

For the next two hours Fairie busied himself with correspondence. A large estate in the country took some managing and a lot of time. Also he was a vigilant and conscientious trustee. For a man of leisure, he worked unusually hard. Indeed, his labour was worth a good six hundred a year. More than that, really, for no one else would have done the work so well.

It was past one o'clock before he laid down his pen. Suddenly he remembered the telegram. Quickly he reached for a form and wrote a reply. Then he crossed to the fireplace and rang the bell. To the footman who answered it:

"I shall be in to lunch," he said. "And let that wire go at once. Perhaps it had better be telephoned."

"Yes, sir."

"And tell William to come upstairs. I want to see him about my clothes."

The telegram was very short. It ran:

"Bowed with grief."

*　　*　　*　　*　　*

By the time he had been to his tailor's, purchased two dozen tennis-balls, and bought twice as much hosiery as he had intended, Fairie was getting cold. After a moment's hesitation, he decided to go to the Club. There would be vast fires there, at any rate:

once warm, gentle exercise about the billiard-table for, say, half an hour . . . Clearly the idea was a good one. He quickened his steps.

As he passed into the Club, the clock of St. James's Palace proclaimed the hour. Four o'clock. Five minutes later he was in an easy chair before the smoking-room fire.

Suddenly the door opened, and Marlowe came in—excitedly rather. For a moment he looked round ; then he saw Fairie and came to his side.

" Well ? " said the latter expectantly. " Let's have it."

" You shall," said Marlowe, drawing up a chair. " What about a hundred and thirty-five pounds in one afternoon, my son ? "

" Rot," said Fairie.

But he sat up. There was that in the other's face which there was no mistaking.

" Fact," said Marlowe, leaning forward to ring the bell. " Of course, I know it's only dross, still . . . Have a ninepenny drink ? "

His brother-in-law regarded him.

" Is this the confidence trick ? " he said.

" Two winners," said Marlowe. " One at seven, the other at twenty. Thanks very much. Twenty. Think of it."

Fairie groaned.

" And you had——" he began.

" A fiver to win on both. Five times twenty-seven equals one-three-five. Am I right, sir ? "

" Good Heavens ! " said Fairie. " How did you spot them ? "

" Old Long gave me them."

" Jerry Long ? " cried Fairie. " Well, why the blazes didn't he let me know ? "

"I don't know," said Marlowe. "I tried to ring you up twice, as a matter of fact, but I couldn't get on. Any way, he sent me a wire from Cheltenham this morning, just giving the names. Where's a paper?"

He rose and crossed to a table, returning a moment later with an evening paper. Quickly he turned to the 'stop-press.' Then:

"Here you are," he said. "'2.30 Cheltenham, Peterill.'"

"Peterill!" gasped Fairie. "Peterill!"

"Yes," said Marlowe. "Queer name, isn't it? I've never heard——"

"One moment," said Fairie wildly. "Don't say the other was All Night."

"That's right," said his brother-in-law. "But——"

"'Peterill, All Night, Long,'" quoted Fairie, his voice broken with emotion. "What have I done to deserve this? Who am I, to be singled out to be the sport of——"

"What on earth's the matter with you?" said Marlowe.

"Go," said the other, covering his eyes with his hand. "Go, fat-head. Leave me alone. Pay for the drinks and go. I have been mocked, cozened, bewrayed."

"Drugged, you mean," said Marlowe coolly.

Fairie sat up and looked at him. Then:

"No," he said. "Not drugged, bewitched." Here he took a deep breath. "Yes," he added gravely, "bewitched. What you have just witnessed, brother, was a brain-storm. The air, however, is now clear again. Allow me to congratulate you upon your ill-gotten gains, and—oblige me by never referring to them again."

"The man's mad," said Marlowe. "This Rih stunt has deranged what little——"

"Listen," said Fairie. "I'm going to tell you a story, a good story, a true story. But, mark you, it's my tale—my own. Will you promise to respect my ownership, and never to tell it yourself?"

"All right," said Marlowe. "Go on."

"Thank you," said Fairie. "You see, I've bought the copyright. It cost me a hundred and thirty-five pounds."

Then he told him.

CHAPTER II

" OF course, this is silly," said Fairie.
"What is ?" said his wife.

"This mail stunt. They've been slinging correspondence into the hold for the last three quarters of an hour, and now another mail train's arrived."

"And we're late now."

"I know. We shall miss the ebb if we're not careful. Besides, paper's notoriously heavy. Where's Robin ?"

"Gone to find Fay. I wish they'd buck up. I want my tea awfully."

Mr. and Mrs. Fairie were standing upon the promenade-deck of the good ship *Castle Rising*, due to sail from Southampton that same afternoon. Southwards, too, over the high seas, out of the grey March weather into the warm sunshine, and so, presently, to fair waters, where the air is dry and gentle and there is no edge to the wind's blowing. As Fairie had predicted, the Brokes, brother and sister, were also aboard. At Rih the liner, herself bound for Cape Town, was to break her voyage. Except at this chosen island she would call nowhere.

There was only one gangway left now, and the crowd upon the quay had been roped back and to one side. Only the business of getting the mails aboard was progressing steadily. The stream of canvas bags seemed to be never-ending. On the fringe of the press of people a little photographer was exhorting those on board to avail themselves of the opportunity his camera held out to them. One or two took his advice and then bellowed addresses across the twelve feet of sea. No money passing, it seemed clear that he was a speculator. All things considered, so were his patrons. Despite a searching east wind and more than a tang of rain in the air, the crowd seemed in a good humour. One poor girl was crying a little, but by no means bitterly; now and again she smiled through her tears. There was no real distress anywhere. Odd messages and injunctions were shouted and heavy jokes cracked, but, for the most part, connected conversation being out of the question, friends and relatives upon the quay contented themselves with nods and becks and wreathed smiles without number. In the background one or two friends of first-class passengers lingered somewhat uncertainly.

It was not an exhilarating picture—very dull, really, and commonplace. Yet Bill Fairie and Betty, his wife, leaned comfortably on the broad rail, watching it all, a strange feeling of satisfaction in their hearts. The knowledge that they were for fresh fields and pleasant places, blue sky and shores dressed all with sunshine, invested the grey scene with a peculiar interest. For them even the black weather had lost its sting.

The Brokes appeared, making their way along the deck towards their cousins. As they came up:

"At last," said Betty. "Where have you been, you two?"

"You may well ask," said Robin aggrievedly.

Fay Broke leaned on her brother's shoulder and laughed helplessly.

" If you could have seen him, darling," she said.

" Oh, very comic, believe me," said Robin coldly.
" Quite side-splitting. When I say that it was in an
endeavour to unlock her cabin-trunk that I lay down
upon the floor——"

" But why didn't you make Falcon——"

" I'm coming to your handmaid in a minute," said
Robin. " It was she who was responsible for that
most droll of moments, when my head was jammed
between the trunk and the dressing-case by her sudden
opening of the door."

He stopped. Betty and Fay were shaking with
shameless laughter.

" Not her new dressing-case ? " said Fairie anxiously.

Broke regarded him scornfully. Then :

" Lubber (nautical)," he said.

" Well, Fay and I are going down to have tea,"
said Betty. " Are you coming ? "

" Tea ? " said her husband. " Certainly not. I'm
going to wait for the grog-tub. But don't let me keep
you. If you want me, I shall probably be on the
larboard tack, slightly abaft the main hatch. Of
course, that's assuming the mizzen-shrouds aren't—
er—shrouded. In that case——"

" I don't expect they will be," said Betty. " But
I think you'd both better come. Even if you don't
want tea, you can see the steward about where we're
going to sit."

The idea seemed a good one, and the four descended
to the saloon.

The straight charge which Fairie laid upon the chief
steward, that he should place them all four together
and with nice neighbours, was not forgotten. When,
one by one, they strolled—rather late and a little unsteadily—into the saloon for dinner, it was to find that

they had been allotted seats at one of the side-tables, and that their companions consisted of a good-looking girl with drop-earrings, and an eminent King's Counsel.

" I'm not at all sure I like this motion," said Betty, settling herself in her revolving chair.

" It won't last long," said her husband briskly. " The breeze is freshening."

" Yes," said Broke. " I expect the waves in the Bay'll be wonderful. By the way, Bill, I don't think those could have been rats you saw leaving the ship at Southampton."

" Will you be quiet ? " said Betty. " The Bay'll probably be like a mill-pond."

" You mustn't expect too startling a resemblance," said Fairie. " I mean, those of the passengers who are not unconscious can usually tell the difference."

" I wonder," said Fay suddenly, " I wonder if Lester remembered to pack my——" Here the liner lurched somewhat heavily to port. " O-oh ! That was a big one, wasn't it ? "

" Only dropping the pilot," said her brother. " What you felt was the recoil."

" Rubbish," said Betty. " It's getting rough."

" Rough," said Fairie. " You rave, woman ; this is nothing. Old salts would tell you we were becalmed. Isn't that so ? " he added pleasantly, appealing to the girl with the earrings.

" I think you're putting it rather high," she said, with a smile. " All the same—well, we haven't got the fiddles on, have we ? "

" I can see that you are a traveller," said Fairie. " My womenkind, poor fools, have lived such sheltered lives——"

" Do you mind kicking him for that ? " said Betty. " He's got a bruise just above the right ankle."

C

The girl laughed merrily, while the ship heaved slowly upwards and then rolled slowly to port and starboard in turn.

The man of law leaned forward.

" I trust," he said, addressing himself to Fairie, " that the statement which you made a few moments ago as to the breeze—er—freshening was without foundation."

" Wholly," said Fairie.

" That, of course," said the other, " is incredibly comforting. At the same time, assuming your friend's theory to be the correct one, I cannot forget that we have now discharged some four pilots, each apparently of a rather more ample habit of body than the one before."

" Unlike my wine," said Fairie, wiping his dinner-jacket with a napkin, " that circumstance had not escaped me. The burning question, therefore, would seem to be, how many pilots have we on board ? "

The lawyer nodded.

" And of what proportions," he said. " Are you going to Rih ? "

" I am," said Fairie, " and the others in my train."

The great man adjusted his eye-glass and looked round, beaming.

" Then perhaps I may take it that we are all pro-posing to illuminate the——"

The girl by his side shook her head.

" No," she said ; " I'm going on to Cape Town."

" Must you ? " said Broke. " I mean . . ."

The girl smiled.

" Afraid so," she said ; " thanks all the same. Besides, South Africa's a great place."

" I know," said Broke. " But is it anything else ? "

" Of course it is. Why, if you . . ." She plunged

into a recital of some of the qualities of her Canaan. Born and bred there, she was returning after an absence of five years—long ones, it seemed. Broke listened amusedly, protesting now and again. So the two slipped into a conversation of their own.

"This is our first visit to Rih," said Betty, addressing the King's Counsel.

"Indeed," said the latter. "With me Rih has become a habit, almost a matter of course—the Sunday morning sausage of my solar year."

"You like it so much?"—with a smile.

"It suits me."

"And it'll suit me," said Fairie. "I can see that. A man of simple tastes, give me a long day, a long chair, and a long drink, and I——"

"And a long wind," said Fay. "Oh, no. You've got that."

"It is an age of rudeness, is it not?" said Fairie, turning to the lawyer. "Now, when I was a child——"

"You needn't think you're going to lie in a chair all day," said Betty. "What are the tennis-balls for?"

"Sale, as far as I'm concerned," replied her husband. "What about my wasted tissues? Shall I not build them up?"

"Are you also a labourer?" said the man of law.

"You see in me," said Fairie, "a careworn drudge."

This was too much. With one accord Betty and Fay turned upon the miscreant and rent him. At length:

"I must apologize," said the former, turning to the King's Counsel, who was listening amusedly, "but there is a limit, isn't there? And when my husband starts——"

"On the contrary, my dear lady, your exposure of him is most opportune. The combination of hypocrisy and sloth is almost Cretian."

" Talking of activity," said the unabashed Fairie,
" the cheese I had at lunch——"

" Do you want to make me ill ? " said his wife
darkly.

" I agree," said the lawyer, waving away the horse-
radish sauce. " The reference was ill-timed. One
must eat, of course. At least, they say you should.
But there are occasions upon which the thoughts
should dwell upon food lightly, turning rather to
loftier things . . ."

" The high seas, for instance," said Fairie, as the
saloon soared sideways into the air after the manner
of a gigantic lift. " Is there a casino at Rih ? "

" There is—euphemistically known as The Strangers'
Club. In a sense it more resembles a hospital."

" A hospital ? "

" I mean that it is supported entirely by voluntary
contributions."

" I see," said Fairie. " Put a dollar on zero and
keep The Strangers' Club for 'alf a mo."

The K.C. nodded.

" That's the idea," he said. " Are you charitably
inclined ? "

" My beneficence," said Fairie, " is my undoing.
More than one such institution owes its open doors
to my generosity. The Monte Carlo Institute for the
Mentally Deficient has a ward called after me."

" A whole ward ? " said the man of law. " Now,
if you had said an operating table . . ." He paused
for a moment to join delightedly in the merriment.
" It is, indeed, a poor heart," he added, " that never
rejoices. And now "—he glanced at the menu—" I
wonder whether it would be madness to essay some
grouse."

     ✹   ✹   ✱   ✹   ✹

By half-past eleven o'clock it was really rough. They had run into the tail-end of a whole gale, and, seaworthy as she was, the liner pitched and rolled desperately.

The last of his party to turn in, Robin Broke—himself an excellent sailor—staggered along the deck, slithered down the companion, and ricocheted along the passage volubly. A dim light showed him his cabin's number. As he opened the door, a roll of the ship assisted him into the apartment anyhow. The washstand, however, brought him up sharp, and the next moment the vessel righted herself, and the door slammed to.

"Thanks very much," said Robin. "And now where the deuce do they keep the electric light?"

The operation of groping effectively about the cabin's sides was rendered difficult by the motion of the ship, but, after a little delay, his fingers closed about the porcelain switch, which was lurking beneath a pendent overcoat. With a sigh of triumph he turned the button. . . . He twisted it four times each way before giving up hope. Drowning men catch at straws. But there was nothing doing. The switch was out of order. Robin groaned.

"Of all the——"

"I say," said a voice, "are you sure this is your cabin?"

Robin stared into the darkness.

"Well, it was," he said; "when I was dressing for dinner, I mean."

"There now," said the voice. "I was half afraid, too. I'm most awfully sorry."

"That's—er—all right," said Robin uneasily. "I mean——"

"You see," said the voice, "I couldn't stand the

motion after a bit, and came to lie down. I wasn't
sure of the number, and, when the light wouldn't turn
up, I couldn't see if there were my things here or
somebody else's. I tried to feel about, and there was
a sponge just where——"

"Have you got a sponge, too?" said Robin.

"Idiot. And then the ship gave an awful roll, and
I felt so terribly ill, I just risked it and lay down.
I'm all right if I lie down, you know. Quite all right."

"I'm glad of that," said Robin heartily. "Very
glad."

"Yes, but—I mean, I'm awfully sorry. If you'll
give me a minute or two, I'll get up and make a dash
for it, somehow. I do hope you understand. You
see," the voice continued, " you're one of these good-
sailor people. You don't know what it is all of a
sudden not to care what happens or where you are,
so long as you can lie down. You don't know that
feeling."

"Forgive me," said Robin, " but it's—er—it's just
as well I don't, isn't it?"

"Oh "—the voice trembled with laughter—" I'm
so awfully sorry."

It was a nice voice. Clear-toned and merry—very
eloquent.

"I wish I could see you," said Robin suddenly.
"If only I'd got a match . . ."

He began to feel his pockets.

"I'm glad you can't," said the girl. "It makes
it a little better. I saw your face as you came in,"
she added.

"That ought to have restored you."

"It made me feel more easy. I was so frightened
when I heard you opening the door. Then I saw you,
and I thought you looked as if you'd understand."

"My dear," said Robin, "you were right. I do. Every time. So she mustn't worry. Besides, *mal de mer* covers a multitude of sins. All the same, this isn't a sin at all. It's a pleasure. Which reminds me, I'm not looking after you very well, am I ? "

"I think you're wonderful," said the girl.

"And I'm sure you're cold," said Robin, taking a light overcoat from one of the hooks. "Where are your small bare feet ? "

"Bare ? " cried the girl. "I'm fully dressed, just as I was for dinner. I told you I——"

"My mistake. Still, we'll cover them up. It isn't as if the light was on."

"For all you know they may be hideous. Darkness covers a multitude of——"

"Pleasures. I'm sure of it. That's what's so tantalizing. Besides," added Broke, spreading the coat carefully over my lady's limbs, "big feet and big eyes never go together."

"Another bow at a venture ? "

"Not at all, my dear. You see, you're only a dark horse. And I always put my shirt on a dark horse."

"You've put your coat on this one."

"And my shirt. Listen." He flicked a startling example of the shirtmaker's skill from another hook and laid it across her feet. "Now I've backed you both ways—a coat to win and a shirt for a place in your heart. Selah."

The girl broke into long laughter. At length :

"You are mad," she said. "But you're very kind ; and I'm going to make my dash in a minute. I think I've done enough trespassing."

"I never prosecute," said Robin.

"No ? Still . . ."

She hesitated.

" Go on," said Robin.

" Ships that pass in the night," she murmured dreamily. " That's what we are."

" Are we ? "

" Yes. Ships that pass. And that's why I must go."

" Aren't they ever becalmed ? "

" Never for long. When day comes, they're always out of sight."

" Not always."

" Invariably."

" I see," said Robin meditatively. " The difficulty here is that I am disabled. Lost my figure-head somewhere in the Channel. Won't you take me in tow as far as the Lost Property Office ? "

" No."

Robin sighed. Then ı

" I shall know you again, any way," he said. " Instinctively. Besides, the moment you open your mouth—oh, I'd love just one look at you. Mayn't I ? "

He could hear the girl shake her head. Then ı

" No," she said gently. " I hate to say it, when you've been so awfully good. But you see—besides, you're going to know me again any way, aren't you ? Instinctively, too." This in a grave tone, the faintest suggestion of mockery lurking behind it.

" You witch," said Robin. " You maddening, unprincipled witch."

A low ripple of merriment answered him. He set his teeth.

" That's right," he said bitterly. " Deride the helpless male. And now you've roused me. I will find you, if I have to scour the ship."

My lady stretched out what was a shapely arm, the hand groping its way towards her companion.

" Where is he ? " she said, her voice all uncertain

with laughter. " Oh, there you are." The fingers
closed about his sleeve. " No. Don't move. Perhaps you will find me. But that's for to-morrow.
At the present moment you shall look for somebody
else. There's a stewardesses' room place just across
this floor or deck—which ever you call it—a little
way down the other passage. Will you go and see
if there's one there ? She'll know where my cabin
is, and help me to get to it."

" But why can't I——"

The grip on his sleeve tightened.

" Please."

" Oh, all right," said Robin. " Are you sure one's
enough ? "

" I think so. And thank you once again for being
so good to another ship in distress."

As the fingers slipped away, Robin caught them.
Smooth, cool, pointed they were—he could feel that.
Ringless, too—it was her left hand—and their nails
polished. For a moment he held them.

" Wireless communication with the mainland has
its points," he said slowly. " Personally, I'd always
sooner be in touch with a sister ship."

" Even if she only passed in the night ? "

Robin lifted the fingers to his lips.

" Till to-morrow," he said.

The next moment he was in the passage. With
some difficulty he found the stewardesses' room, but
there was no one there. He went the length of both
passages, but apparently not a soul was abroad. So
he came again to his cabin, unevenly, for the liner
was still all over the place. They were getting a
dusting, certainly.

" I say," he said, as he opened the door, " there's
no one anywhere. It must be the dog-watch."

No answer.

" My dear," he said, leaning forward and stretching a hand towards the head of the bunk.

But where her shoulder should have been there was nothing. Save for its sheets and blankets, the bunk was empty. The ship had passed.

Robin Broke swore thoughtfully. Then he sat down on the edge of the bunk and began to laugh. . . .

Preparation for the night upon a ship which is wallowing in the midst of an angry sea is a business to be gone about circumspectly. The fact that his electric light was out of order hampered Robin considerably. For all his care, rails, corners, and similar excrescences, which at the more outrageous moments he essayed to grasp, eluded his groping fingers, and by the time he was ready to clamber into his bunk, he had sustained a whole series of bruises and a most painful abrasion of the left shin. It was while endeavouring to remove his trousers that he had been precipitated violently on to the floor. There and then he had dealt with the Atlantic Ocean. From one point of view his description of it was masterly.

As he was disposing the sheets, his hand encountered something hard and rough to the touch—almost sharp-edged, able to scratch. For a moment he fingered it curiously. Was it a brooch ? No. Yet . . . The next second he knew what it was. An earring. Instantly his thoughts flew to the fair South African. But it was of a different shape to those she had been wearing. Besides, it had not been her voice.

Broke forgot the Atlantic and his recent battery, even the abrasion upon his shin. With a smile he slipped the earring into the breast-pocket of his pyjamas.

"Lost," he murmured, "one dainty earring. The finder will be—ah, suitably rewarded. And this is going to save me a lot of trouble."

    *   *   *   *   *

"And may I ask," said Fairie, "if the arena of political life (*sic*) has never beckoned you?"

The eminent King's Counsel frowned.

"There are some invitations," he said, "which I disregard. One cannot be too careful of the company one keeps."

Sunday. The three men were sitting easily in the afternoon sun. It was good to rest a little after a heavy lunch. Already the air was appreciably warmer, while the wind had dropped to a stiff breeze. Somehow it was difficult to realize that it was not yet twenty-four hours since they had left Southampton. A fair sea was running, but it was not nearly so rough.

Broke rose to his feet, laughing.

"Where are you going?" said Fairie.

"To get some cigarettes."

"All right," said his cousin. "But how did you know I wanted one?"

But Broke was already out of earshot.

When he reached his cabin, he fastened the door back, took out his keys, and stooped to unlock his dressing-case. It was then that he noticed the envelope, lying upon his pillow, addressed to "— Broke, Esq." The note it contained was short enough in all conscience.

"DEAR SHIP,—Please, have you got my earring? I think it must have come unscrewed whilst I was lying down. If you have, will you leave it with the Purser? Please. Your Sister Ship. P.S.—You were very nice to me."

When he had read it twice, Robin slipped the note into his pocket, turned again to his case and extracted the cigarettes. Before rejoining his cousin and the man of law, he made his way to the writing-room. There he sat down and wrote his answer.

"SISTER SHIP DEAR,—Yes, I have. No, I will not leave it with the Purser. You shall ask for it nicely in person. You know me, and I want to know you. Thank you for saying I was nice. You were sweet. Your Ship. P.S.—I get off at Rih."

Then he went to the Purser's office.

"It's just this," he said. "If anyone should come and ask about a lost earring, this note's for the owner."

The Purser nodded.

"I'll see she gets it," he said.

Robin thanked him and made his way back to the others.

"You have been quick," said Fairie. "Did they have to move much luggage to get at yours? In the hold, I mean."

"I saw no reason to hurry," said Broke coolly. "You smoke too many cigarettes. I've had to speak to you about it before. By the way," he added, "did I tell you that when I went to turn in last night, my electric light wouldn't work?"

The lawyer gazed at him.

"Am I to understand," he said, "that you were therefore compelled to essay those preparations, which precede repose, in total darkness?"

"You are," said Broke.

"In that case, I fear you must have sustained several contused wounds."

" Yes," said Fairie. " Was it a darkness that could be felt, brother ? "

" I don't know about the darkness," said Broke. " The furniture was there all right."

" How incredibly chastening ! " mused the lawyer.

" It was, rather," said Broke. " What would you have done ? "

" And or said ? " said Fairie.

The K.C. rose to his feet before replying.

" I do not think," he replied, " that I should have hurried down the alphabet."

As he strolled leisurely away down the deck :

" Brother," said Broke to Fairie, " this man is a privilege."

" More," said Fairie. " I see in him The White Hope."

*   *   *   *   *

The weather continued to improve, making their path smooth, the voyage very pleasant. The Brokes and the Fairies made the most of their time. But then, so they did always. Besides The White Hope and the girl bound for South Africa, they came to know many people. The ship liked them. Fairie organized the ' sweep ' on the day's run, Broke helping him, so that the auction was successful beyond expectation. Even the smoking-room steward, a hardened veteran, was surprised at the bidding. That was on Monday. And an hour and a half's cricket in the afternoon served to pass the time. Not that it hung heavily. So far from mattering, the fact that there was little or nothing to do was very comfortable. So engaging may be the atmosphere of fresh surroundings. The voyage had not had time to begin to pall.

The hours slipped by, the ship's bells telling them ; yet the earring's owner did not make herself known.

Robin Broke had done nothing. His policy was to wait. Obviously, it was up to my lady to make the move. Of course, when opportunity offered, he had looked closely at three or four of his fellow-passengers who seemed to answer more or less roughly to the slight description he could have given. But it was very difficult. Once he made up his mind that he had discovered the girl. He had run into her on Monday morning at the top of the stairs. So pretty and graceful she was, with her small gloved hands and an innocent look on her face that was full of promise. Big-eyed, too, and wearing no earrings, though that was nothing to go by. Something about her seemed to suggest the identity he sought. Gravely he had asked if she would take tickets for the ' sweep,' almost sure of his ground. Almost . . . Then she had opened the red lips. Her he-American accent stung Broke like a lash. The ground crumbled away suddenly.

Broke wandered down to his cabin on Tuesday night a little uneasily. The liner would arrive at Rih early the next morning, and, even supposing my lady were herself going no further, it seemed awkward not to restore the earring before he left the ship. After all, it was her property, and if he could not find her on board, it was longer odds against his identifying her in Rih. Moreover, she might not know where he was going to stay. Looming always in the background was the possibility that she was going on to the Cape.

It was with something more than irritation that he discovered, on entering his cabin, that once again the electric switch would not answer to his touch. Robin let out a rugged oath.

" Hush," said my lady.

" Herself," said Robin.

" In person. And now, please, may I have my earring ? "

His reply was to twist the switch-button furiously. But it was no good—the light would not come on.

" This is the limit," groaned Robin. Then : " Come into the corridor," he added. " I'll give it to you there."

" No," said the girl. " I was to ask for it nicely in person. I've done so."

" I believe you're a shadow," said Robin ; " the Spirit of Darkness. Yet your fingers were firm," he added musingly, " and there was a faint scent ——"

" Ships that pass in the night," she said slowly. " In the night."

" Perhaps," said Robin. " But the fourth line says : ' Only a look and a voice, then . . .' "

" I had the look, ship. I saw you, you know."

" And you have the voice, my dear. The softest I ever heard. But you can't have everything. Where do I come in ? "

" Haven't you got the earring ? "

Broke shifted his ground.

" Why should we keep to the poem ? " he said. " It's a great mistake to sail too close to the wind, sister ship. Didn't you know that ? "

" Yes. And that's why you're going to give me my property and let me go."

" Do you ask that ? "

" I do."

In silence Broke drew the earring out of his waist-coat pocket.

" Give me your hand," he said.

Fingers brushed against his sleeve. Gently he took

the slight wrist and put the earring into the little palm. The fingers closed over it.

"Thank you," in a low voice.

"I say," said Robin.

"Well ? "

Still holding the one, he sought for and found another cool wrist.

"I think we ought to salute one another, sister ship."

"I've presented arms, haven't I ? "

"Charmingly. But at sea . . ."

He raised her wrists slowly and set them upon his shoulders. Then he released his hold. The soft arms might have slipped away. . . .

For a second she let him hold her. Then :

"I don't think the switch is out of order," she whispered, moving towards the door. "It was all right when I tried it. And—and you'll find the lamp in your bunk."

The next moment she was gone.

*   *   *   *   *

At seven o'clock the next morning the Brokes and the Fairies started to go ashore. And The White Hope with them. As Robin stepped on to the accommodation ladder, something impelled him to look up. Exactly above him, leaning upon the rail of the promenade deck, was the he-American girl he had encountered on Monday. She looked at him steadily, a faint smile on her lips, open merriment in the big brown eyes. For a moment Broke stared at her. Then he took off his hat. . . . Even a disinterested party must have remarked her earrings.

CHAPTER III

TO SEAT FOUR

" SHALL we rest here a minute ? " said The White Hope. " It's rather a climb, isn't it ? "

" Oh, but it is so lovely," said Betty, sinking on to a low stone seat, to gaze down and over the smiling bay. " Isn't this wonderful, Robin ? "

Her cousin deposited three heavy coats, two tennis rackets and a despatch-case upon the parapet before replying. Then :

" Glorious," he said.

A ripple of laughter floated up from the curling flight of steps they had just ascended. The next moment Fay Broke stumbled into view, her fresh young face alight with merriment.

" Oh," she cried, " Bill's being so awfully funny about your bag, darling. He says—— Oh, I say how lovely ! Look at the sun on the mountains."

The prospect was very pleasing.

The terrace was set upon the edge of the cliff, down whose side steps had been built and fashioned in odd curving flights to the dark rocks below. Here was a rough-hewn landing-place, to which a launch belonging to the hotel was used to bring visitors from the liners in the bay. So it had brought the Fairies, Betty, and Bill, at half-past seven o'clock that fair March morning. The Brokes, too, and the man of law.

49   D

The latter had constituted himself their guide. Had he not been to Rih before—many times ?

Rih. From islands set in the midst of shifting ocean, you have almost a right to expect something. Perilous seas and faery lands seem to go together—the one but the toll-bar to the other. Rih.

Far at the back, high mountains stood up against the sky, their steep heights thickly wooded, the line of them broken now and again by a sheer gorge, for all the world as if the ridge had started asunder at some mighty shock, suffered when Time was young. Very fair, these timbered heights, very arresting ; but the mighty sweep of the mountains away and down into the glistening sea—that was the thing. A sweep miles long, steep at the first and then growing ever more gentle, its warm slopes rich with wood and sward and plantation and, presently, with flower-gardens, yet never losing the line of its grand curve, till the ribbon of surf in the bay cut it across, noisily marking the place where land slipped under water. All about the sides of the bay hung the little town of Starra, its white-walled houses clustering thick by the water's edge and thence scrambling creeper-wise up the long slopes, to lose their fellows and at last themselves in the deep gardens and the woods above. The blue of the sea itself was wonderful, and the great sky matched it. The hue was almost that of the Mediterranean. On the horizon, straight ahead, two shadowy forms seemed to float upon the face of the waters—baby islands, these. Except for them, beyond the bay itself, there was no land, no sail, nothing. Miles away a faint wisp of smoke betrayed the whereabouts of some liner, herself hulled down behind the vast spaces of the Atlantic, which appeared to stretch endlessly into the distance, about it an air of such superb immensity

that all talk of mastery and subjection, ruling the
waves, and the like, seemed on a sudden impertinent,
vain, very ridiculous. Over all, the sun blazed out of
the heaven, crowning beauty with splendour, making
the blue sea brilliant, the grand sweep of the mountains
glorious indeed.

The prospect was very pleasing.

Fairie's head appeared above the topmost step.
For a moment he stood regarding the others, who
were gazing over the sunlit bay. Then :

" If I were to drop this bag," he said, " it would
imbed itself in the rock."

" It isn't really heavy," said Broke, looking round.
" The trouble is, you're not carrying enough in the
other hand. If you were, you wouldn't notice it.
All a matter of balance, you know," he added airily.

Fairie looked at him.

" Would you rather die now, or after breakfast ? "
he said. " I mean to say, it doesn't matter to me.
The bears are waiting on the tennis-court." He
nodded towards where the wire-netting rose high
among the bushes on the right. " Within call. You
see, you shouldn't have mocked me."

" Poor old boy," said Betty. " But you gave me
the bag, didn't you ? "

" I didn't fill it with ingots," returned her husband,
heaving himself up the remaining steps on to the
terrace. " Incidentally, if Fay's bag's half as heavy
as this, Falcon'll never get up these steps alive. However." He set the offending receptacle down gingerly.
" Not another inch," he added defiantly.

" But you can't leave it here," cried Betty.

" Can't I ? " said Bill. " Well, I'm going to have a
devilish good try. And when we get up to the hotel,
I'll send some men down with a truck and ropes and

things. I don't know why you didn't bring the safe. It would have taken your hats easily. Did I tell you that the hideous strain has displaced several of my organs ? "

" This manual labour," murmured The White Hope. " Well, well," he added, " I think Mrs. Fairie's fears are groundless. The bag will be all right here. So will the garments and sporting requisites at present embarrassing your left arm. The porters can bring them."

With a sigh of relief Fairie laid four coats and two rackets upon the stone seat.

" I am in your debt," he said. " And now, I take it that we are now in the hotel's 'unrivalled garden ' ? "

" Yes," said the lawyer, " and this is one of the ' extensive views.' " With a sweep of his hand he indicated the bay of Starra and its surroundings. " Is it to your liking ? "

" Every time," said Fairie. " But breakfast would be more."

" Shame," said Robin. " The air is champagne, this prospect a meal in itself."

" Good for you," said Betty.

" Perhaps," said Fairie. " But not for me. That's just it. Alas, my diet does not include air, and prospects, like pork, are poison to me."

" Fool ! " said his wife.

" That's right," said Fairie. " Revile the hungry sage. Personally, I'm not used to doing weight-lifting stunts on an empty——"

" As a matter of fact," said the man of law, " the view from the hotel's verandah is rather finer than this, so that, if we were to continue our progress, our differing appetites might be respectively indulged.

Incidentally, the various fruits peculiar to Rih are very toothsome."

" At once rare and refreshing ? " said Fairie.

" More," said The White Hope. " They are tangible."

Slowly they passed up through the fair garden, over the cobbled paths. Some new wonder of blossoms met them at every step, gladdening their eyes with colour, filling the morning air with perfume. Here was a riot of roses, and here luxuriant honeysuckle scrambling beside them. Here again were thick-growing daisies, the gentle blue of plumbago bushes rising in their white midst, while there, at a bend of the pathway, flamed a deep mass of bougainvillea, which, like nothing so much as some red tumbling torrent, streamed down over a pillared arbour, drenching the white walls with scarlet, and magically arrested, somehow stayed in its fall, spell-bound, perhaps, at its own loveliness. Everywhere rose up great palms : shady junipers, too, and trees, fragrant and flowering, without number. Now the path was shadowed, and now again all open to the sun, but for the most part its reaches lay in a shade, splashed here and there with sunlight, odd rents in the protecting screen of foliage just suffering the great fellow to plant rude badges of glory by the way, lest you should think he was not shining and so the spring morning the poorer for his loss.

Through all this matchless beauty passed the five wayfarers, fascinated and, for a little space, speech-less, lizards darting at their approach on every sunlit wall, canaries innumerable leaping and singing in the boughs above. It was a royal progress indeed.

This, then, was Rih. Of a truth the entering in of the island was a thing to remember.

Suddenly:

" Listen to the birds," said Betty, turning to throw a reproving glance in the direction of her spouse. " They aren't worrying about breakfast."

" Rot ! " replied that gentleman. " They had theirs at cock-crow."

" How d'you know ? " said Fay. " I believe they started singing directly they woke up, and it's all so lovely they haven't had the heart to stop."

The White Hope looked round with a quiet smile.

" One might almost say ' Songs without Worms,' " he said.

*   *   *   *   *

Some two hours later Broke and Fairie were leaning upon the rail of the broad verandah, contemplating the bay of Starra, where the liner that had brought them to Rih rode easily, her burnished metal-work gleaming in the sunshine, boats of all shapes and sizes dancing about her great flanks. A slight haze of smoke drifted above her funnels, and, as they stood watching her, the breeze brought the faint sound of three bells to their ears. Half-past nine. Another hour and a half and she would sail.

" Aha," said Fairie, tilting his hat over his eyes. " This is what I call good. Now is the winter of our discontent made glorious summer by this sun of Rih."

Before his cousin could reply :

" That's right," said the K.C., who had come up behind them noiselessly in his rubber-soled shoes. Smilingly he tapped Broke on the shoulder. " Your bruised arms hang up for monuments," he added, referring to the latter's recent battery on shipboard. " Or was it the shins that suffered ? In that case you must put your feet up."

" Yes," said Fairie. " They'd make rather good monuments, wouldn't they ? Slabs always do."

" They'd be up now," said Broke, ignoring the offensive allusion, " only there don't seem to be any public chairs. All these are labelled with some visitor's name, and we're afraid to sit in them in case the owners turn up."

" It's the custom here to purchase your own chairs on arrival," explained the lawyer. " When you go, you take them to use on board. As I come every year, mine is kept for me. Are you going down into the town ? "

" We're only waiting for the girls. I understand the luggage won't be up before noon, so we may as well move round till it comes."

" Then I should get four chairs without delay. Insist upon their being delivered this afternoon. And here come the ladies."

Betty and Fay appeared on the verandah.

" At last," said Robin. " What have you been doing ? Having your hair washed ? "

" No," said his sister coolly. " We've been putting our gloves on."

" That admission," said Robin, " is in the nature of a gratuitous insult."

" Come along," said Fairie, moving towards the lounge. " I ordered a taxi twenty minutes ago."

The taxi proved to be a large open touring car, high-powered, too, and driven by a dark-eyed Portuguese, a shy smile on his merry face. He greeted the party with easy politeness, raising his peaked cap. But he could speak no English, so the concierge told him where to go—that was, just down Town, say, to the top of the Avenue Fayal. It seemed that there was a café there, " The Golden Gate " by name. This place was, as it were, the hub of Starra.

It was a pretty run, some ten minutes long.

The avenue led from the quay up to a broad place, full of noise and movement, all dazzling in the bright sun. Movement, mark you, not bustle. There is no hastening in Rih. Men go about their business as it were leisure. Often enough it is.

And there, at the corner of the place and the avenue, stood " The Golden Gate." In a sense the spot seemed a terminus, a bourn. In London, omnibuses would start from such a place instinctively. There would be no question about it. And we should call the site a circus. But here there were no police and no pavements, and the traffic went as it pleased. Motors and bullock-carts, some occupied, others awaiting that honour and so at rest by the low wall, men all in white, standing in groups, passing the time of day, black-haired girls in coloured stuffs, baskets upon their bare brown arms, lingering as they turned their steps marketwards, dogs asprawl on the cobbles, blinking sleepily in the hot sunshine, and little brown boys everywhere, now scrambling at play, now rushing to press tight-tied posies of wild flowers on such English visitors as passed by—these and their like made up the scene. Up the avenue a string of mules was slowly making its way, the poor beasts grateful for the shade of the tall plane-trees.

Betty and Fay were out of the car and across the avenue before Bill Fairie had paid the driver.

" What's the matter with them ? " said that gentleman.

" Embroidery," replied his cousin, with a bored air. " I don't suppose we shall get them away under five pounds."

" Leave it to me," said Bill.

Together they crossed over, to find the girls excitedly

examining large piles of exquisitely worked doilies, while a fat Portuguese stood benignantly by, supervising their inspection and smoking a cigar which was curved like a banana. A comfortable smile of anticipation had already spread over his countenance.

" More underwear ? " said Fairie pleasantly, as they came up. " I thought——"

" If you don't go and wait outside, I'll buy the lot," said his wife. " Oh, Fay dear, just look at this one."

The case seeming hopeless, the men retired to the doorway in some dudgeon. They were, indeed, on the point of crossing over to test the hospitality of " The Golden Gate," when there appeared two of their late fellow-passengers, who, bound for South Africa, were slowly returning to the quay laden with all manner of purchases and looking rather like freebooters who had had a good morning.

" Aha," cried Fairie. " The sack of Starra. Have you put many to the sword ? "

Mrs. Merrow laughed.

" It's we who've been bled," she cried, " or, rather, Denis. He hadn't been ashore a quarter of an hour before he'd gone and bought a hundred bananas and a hundred and fifty passion fruit. Says we must have some fruit on board. Of course, everybody thinks we're victualling the ship."

" I'm going to count them on the quay," said Denis. " That's why we're so early."

" While I go round with the tambourine ? " said his wife. " How much do you think we shall take ? "

" I for one would gladly contribute fourpence," said Fairie, " for the privilege of watching your husband tell over his fruit amid the plaudits of a helpful crowd. Friend," he added, turning to the culprit, " you are about to be stung. Of course, they'll give you short measure, and any idea of reckoning's out of the question."

" Yes," said Robin. " Each time you got going, some kid 'd roll up and badger you to buy his flowers or something, and by the time you'd told him off, you'd have lost your place in the produce."

Denis Merrow grinned.

" Any way," he said, " we shan't have scurvy."

Fairie and Broke bade them farewell, and stood watching them pass down the avenue towards the sea.

" Bill," said a voice.

They turned to see Betty standing in the doorway of the embroidery store, a delicate doily in either hand.

" Aren't these lovely ? " she said.

" Positively breath-removing," said Fairie.

" Idiot ! The only thing is, I think he's asking rather a lot. D'you think you could—I mean, I believe one ought to bargain, only I can't do it."

" Leave it to me," said Fairie. " I know my East. What does the merchant ask ? "

" Two pounds each."

In silence Bill took the embroidery and passed into the shop. The others followed a little uneasily and stood hesitatingly in the background. The stout Portuguese, a fresh cigar in his mouth, was hanging affectionately over his stuffs, carefully restoring order among such as had been inspected by the two girls. Fairie raised his hat. Then :

" You speak English ? " he said.

" A little," said the other, raising his hat in return.

" Right-o," said Fairie. He held up the doilies. " These aren't so bad. How much d'you want for them ? "

" Two pounds each," said the Portuguese.

Fairie shook his head.

"You mistake my meaning," he said. "I'm not asking what you pay for your cigars."

"Two pounds each," said the other.

Fairie raised his eyebrows.

"That is too much," he said coolly. "I'll give you three-and-sixpence for the two."

A perfect shriek of horror and dismay went up from Fay and Betty, while, with a choking sound, the Portuguese leaned forward and snatched his precious embroideries from Fairie's hand. The next moment the two girls bore down upon the latter and hurried him protesting from the shop. Robin, red with shame, remained behind, fumbling nervously with his cigarette-case, endeavouring to apologize to the indignant shopkeeper and explaining, in his anxiety in bad French, that his friend was not normal and had had sunstroke before.

Once outside :

"I was a fool," said Betty. "I was a fool to ask you. I might have known. Three-and-sixpence ! I wonder the man didn't try and murder you."

"My dear," said her husband, "to the ignorant the haggler's art seems almost——"

"Rubbish," said his wife.

"You didn't give me a chance," said Bill. "I was prepared to go up to two pounds. The beastly things cost him about six shillings each. He probably received them, knowing them to have been stolen."

"I wonder you didn't tell him so," said Betty.

Her husband shook his head.

"No," he said gravely. "That might have annoyed him."

Fay broke into peals of merriment, and Robin emerged from the shop. As he came up :

"There are your wretched non-skids," he said, handing a small package to Betty.

There was something irresistibly ludicrous about his demeanour.

"Oh, Robin dear," said Betty, her voice trembling with laughter.

"I hope the rude man did not overcharge you, brother," said Fairie.

"As for you," said Robin, "you owe me four pounds and your life. Call it four guineas."

For a while they wandered about the little town, exploring its winding streets. It was when they were making their way back to the hub of Starra that Fairie stopped suddenly and announced his intention of having his shoes cleaned.

"Nonsense," said Betty. "You've done enough harm for one day."

Critically her husband regarded his brown shoes.

"They've been through it on board," he said, "and a devilish good greasing is what they want. They'll never get it at the hotel."

He pointed to a tiny frontless shop, little more than a booth, where two chairs were standing upon a dais, the shoeblack's paraphernalia lying about them. On the threshold was lolling a little Portuguese, his arms folded, expectancy in his dark eyes.

"I'll have them done here," he said. "You go on and pick up a car. I shan't be five minutes."

With that, he entered the shop, ascended the dais, sank into a chair, and lighted a cigarette.

The others strolled on resignedly.

Ten minutes later Robin returned to the shop.

"What on earth——" he began.

"Hush," said his cousin. "Not a word. The professor is in his element. Never have I witnessed such shoe-cleaning. When I tell you that he has only just done one——"

" What ! " cried Robin.

" —to his satisfaction, you will appreciate——"

" Well, we're going, and you must come on in another car."

" That's a nice thing to do," said Bill. " You wait until——"

" Until we're fed up," said Robin. " It's getting on for eleven now. Will you have finished by lunch-time, or shall we begin ? So long."

With a sigh Fairie lighted his third cigarette.

The professor had just smeared his patron's left shoe with cream for the third time, when a dog's cry of pain rang out above the slight clamour of the street. A passionate lover of animals, Bill Fairie sat up. Again came the cry. The next instant he was out of the chair. As he stepped on to the pavement, a whirlwind of quick breath and perfume flashed past his face—a girl all in white, going as hard as she could. An instant later Fairie was by her side.

" Where's the dog ? " he cried.

" Over there," she panted, nodding towards the cathedral. " Oh, the brutes ! "

Under the shadow of the great church, close up against its very wall, a poor brown mongrel was shrinking from the attentions of two Portuguese. Whatever it was, the active cruelty had stopped, but the unhappy animal crouched there in obvious dread and terror of its tormentors. It dared not move, for it was in a corner where two walls met. To bolt would have meant to run the gauntlet.

The two youths were so engrossed in their occupation that Fairie's hands were upon them before they were aware of his approach. He brought their heads together with a shock that rattled round the open space in which the cathedral stood. The knees of one sagged under him, and he collapsed, holding his head and weeping like a child. The other tottered to the cathedral steps and sat there rocking himself to and fro, clasping his temples.

The whole affair was over so quickly that, before onlookers had recovered from their surprise, and those who had seen nothing had had time to inquire what was the matter, Fairie had picked up the trembling animal and was walking back with the girl towards " The Golden Gate."

" I'm so glad you were here," she said jerkily, for she was still out of breath. " I couldn't run properly because of this skirt."

" What skirt ? " said Fairie, staring. " That is—I mean I thought you went jolly well."

With a little laugh the girl put out a slim hand to stroke the mongrel, which was looking up at Fairie with wonder in his brown eyes.

" Poor old chap," she said soothingly. " I do hope he isn't much hurt. You were splendid," she added ; " the noise of their heads coming together made me feel sick."

Fairie laughed.

" It'll give them something to think about for twenty-four hours," he said. " Is there much cruelty in Rih ? "

" Practically none. I've been here for a month now, and this is the first I've seen. You see, the place is so English that the Society's practically wiped it out."

At this moment they were confronted by the professor, who, raising despairing hands, clearly implored his patron to let him complete the cleaning of his left shoe.

"Ah," said Bill, "I'd forgotten about my shoes. I was having them cleaned, you know." He turned to the Portuguese and pointed to the café, sixty paces away. "'Golden Gate,'" he said. "Bring your cloths along and finish them there."

The fellow appeared to understand, and turned again to his tiny shop. Fairie and his companion passed on.

Five minutes later they might have been seen sitting in wicker chairs outside the house in question, engaged in merry conversation, while their rough-coated protégé stood confidently between them, devouring a large portion of bread and meat. My lady was sipping a lemon squash, while on a table by Fairie's elbow stood a French vermuth and soda. The latter's left foot was poised upon the small portable dais peculiar to the shoeblack's art, once so familiar a sight, and yet to be observed, in the streets of London, and the professor, with the aid of a tin, two bottles, three cloths, and a toothbrush was working upon the leather with renewed energy.

"Fairly spreading himself, isn't he?" said Bill, pointing to the cleaner of shoes. "If he rubs it much longer, the leather'll catch fire. I wonder how I'm to pay him. By time or distan—I mean area?"

"Labour's cheap in Rih," said the girl, with a smile. "If you give him sixpence, he'll probably fall over himself."

She was a nice-looking girl, very natural and easy, say, twenty-one years old. Her soft straw hat was shading an eager face. This was distinguished by a pair of magnificent eyes, large, grey and steady, such eyes as, when a man meets them, make him lose the thread of his speech.

Her white silk shirt became her and might have been cut to show how well her head was set upon her shoulders. Beneath the broad brim of her hat was a promise of sweet-smelling hair, of which her straight, dark eyebrows offered a bewitching earnest. Her scrap of a skirt did her lithe figure full justice, calling up statues of Artemis and proving that there are still limbs to compare with those Praxiteles thought fit to reproduce.

" Is this your first day ? " said the girl. " I haven't seen you before."

Fairie nodded.

" Arrived with the dawn," he said. " Breakfasted before you'd had your bath. You're staying at ' The Bristol,' of course ? "

" Naturally. Everyone is. Are you alone ? "

" I have with me three children, two girls and a boy. They're not mine," he added hastily. " I'm just looking after them."

" Are you ? "

" Well, I was, but they cleared off just now, while I was having my shoes cleaned. I expect they'll find their way back to the hotel."

" Their absence doesn't seem to worry you."

" No," said Fairie. " Their presence does that."

" I believe," said the girl slowly, " I believe I saw them, just before we met, getting into a car. Was the —er—boy wearing a Zingari tie ? "

Fairie looked at her with a smile.

" I might have known from your eyes," he said, " that it was impossible to deceive you."

Over the munching mongrel the two became fast friends. It appeared that she was a cousin of Dorothy Lair's—they had been at school together. The news of the latter's engagement to ' Pip ' Marlowe went far to turn the acquaintance into a positive relation.

" How strange ! " said the girl.

"Yes," said Fairie. "Please don't add that the world's very small."

"I wasn't going to," laughed his companion. "But why?"

"Well, I've heard it said seven times in the last four days, and it annoys me. In the first place, it's a platitude; secondly, it is a grossly inaccurate statement. The world is, unlike your feet, extremely large."

"If you travel, you must put up with these things."

"I could put up with your feet for ever."

"Thank you, but I meant——"

"I know you did," said Bill. "Any way, there are compensations. You're one of them. And now, may I have the honour of driving you back to the hotel? I see that Orlando, who drove me down, is disengaged and ready for anything."

"Thank you very much," said the girl. "And we'll take the dog, too. One of the gardeners up there is a friend of mine. If I ask him, I think he'll give him a home."

"If you ask him," said Fairie.

They were just swinging out of the sunlit place, when the spectacle of a large store, crowded with wicker chairs of all sorts and descriptions, made Fairie remember the words of The White Hope. He cried to Orlando to stop, and turned to the girl.

"My dear," he said, "it's up to me to buy four chairs."

"For yourself and the children?"

"Got it in one," said Bill. "May I have——"

"The honour, etc., of my assistance? You may. You're very polite this morning, aren't you?"

"Always the same, believe me. Never a cross word."

E

" I thought you knew it was impossible to deceive me."

Fairie regarded her amusedly. Then :

" I wish you'd take off your hat," he said. " I want to see your hair."

The chairs were really quite inexpensive. For six or seven shillings you could purchase a very throne of luxury. After testing the resiliency of several seats, Fairie came to the conclusion that, so far as he was concerned, the choice lay between two triumphs of wickerwork.

" Hadn't you better have that one ? " said my lady, her voice trembling with laughter.

The chair she was indicating with a rosy forefinger, had a socket to take a tumbler by the side of its right arm.

Fairie shook his head.

" Attractive," he said, " but useless. Like all confirmed drunkards, I soak in secret."

He was on the point of ordering three others, similar to the one he had selected, when a miniature chair, in every respect like the others, but fashioned to fit a child, caught his eye. The girl's words flashed across his mind. " For yourself and the children," she had said. Quickly he turned to the man who was serving him.

" Have you two others like this ? "—pointing to the miniature chair.

" Oh, yes, sir."

" I'll have three, then. Send them up with the big one this afternoon."

" Oh," said the girl, and fell into long laughter.

At Fairie's dictation the man wrote the four names on luggage labels, and, to avoid all possibility of mistake, Bill tied his own label on to the big chair with his own hand. Then he paid for his purchases and cheerfully followed my lady out of the shop. The proprietor saw them to the door and watched their departure with every manifestation of respect. As the car disappeared, he sighed. A man of business, if not of humour, he could hardly have been expected to acquaint Fairie with the fact that, some thirty minutes before, two ladies and a gentleman had stopped at his emporium and chosen three large chairs and one baby one, giving the same four names and ordering them to be sent to the Bristol Hotel. The baby chair to be labelled " W. Fairie."

* * * * *

At seven o'clock that evening four large chairs stood in a row on the cobbled drive, close to the main entrance to the hotel. The Brokes and Betty saw them, as they came in to dress. They had all been at the Casino.

Their annoyance to notice that the chairs were all of the same size was intense. They were theirs, too ; the labels showed that.

Disappointedly they passed into the hotel.

Five minutes later Fairie appeared in the company of the King's Counsel.

" Are these your chairs ? " said the latter.

" They're not the ones I paid for," said Bill uneasily. Then he examined the labels.

" Well ? " said the man of law.

Fairie sighed.

" Your prayers," he said, " are desired for the fool who sent these chairs. He has not long to live."

* * * * *

They had nearly finished dinner, when :

" I see the chairs have come," said Fairie carelessly.

" Yes," said his wife. " Aren't you grateful to us for——"

" What d'you mean ? " said Fairie. " If it hadn't been for my providence——"

" Yours ? " cried Fay. " Why, you forgot all about them."

Fairie put down his glass and looked at her.

" If selecting, ordering, and paying for no less than four slumber-suggesting——"

" But we ordered them, too," said Robin.

" Then those are yours outside," said Fairie.

" We—er—thought, perhaps, they were yours," stammered Robin.

" No," said Fairie. " Mine were different. I mean——"

" So were ours," said Betty. " Those aren't the chairs we ordered."

For a moment they stared at one another. Then :

" Come along," said her husband. " We're about the last, as usual. We can thrash this out on the verandah."

With one consent they rose and passed out of the room, threading their way between the tables in single file.

In what was, perhaps, the most prominent place upon the great verandah stood four baby chairs, conspicuously and respectively labelled " Mrs. Fairie," " Miss Broke," " R. Broke," and " W. Fairie." Immediately opposite them, his back to the balustrade, lolled the King's Counsel, beaming over a long cigar and patently contemplating the ridiculous quartette with immense gratification. In the shadow of a tall pillar the lady of the mongrel was shaking with suppressed merriment. The dictates of good taste forbade steady and undisguised observation on the part of the other visitors, but there was on all sides an air of expectation and 'awaiting results,' and as the Brokes and the Fairies, all unsuspecting, emerged from the lounge, the interested smiles broadened and here and there the conversation died down. Discerning the long form of the lawyer twenty odd paces away, Betty, naturally enough, started towards him, and, that nothing might be wanting to fill their cup of confusion to the full—

" Any way," Fay was saying, " we may as well have the chairs put here, even if——"

A stifled cry from Betty made her look up, and the sentence died on her lips. She caught at her brother's arm.

" What's the matter ? " said Robin. " Good heavens ! "

The last to perceive the chairs was Fairie. For an instant his face lighted. The ones he had ordered, after all ! The next moment he saw there were four. He recoiled literally.

With an elaborate wave of his cigar, The White Hope indicated the row, the smile of smiles upon his legal face.

" The seats of the mighty," he drawled. " Won't you sit down ? "

Their sense of humour asserting itself, Betty and Fay began to laugh helplessly. Bill pulled himself together.

" I prefer to stand," he said simply. " Besides, I never take the chair."

" It is a mistake to confine yourself to biscuits," observed the lawyer. " Believe me, you would more than fill the position."

" The truth is," said Fairie, " I'm afraid it would cramp my style."

CHAPTER IV

LOVE THIRTY

"I HOPE you're not awfully good," said Miss Fettering, "because I'm——"

"But we are," said Fairie. "Our moral rectitude is almost staggering. When I tell you that our record includes four highest awards——"

"Oh, I know. I guessed that from your haloes. I meant, good at tennis."

"I see," said Fairie. "Of course, that's rather different. All the same, no champion has beaten me yet."

"Perhaps that's because you've never played one."

"Possibly. But a cousin of mine used to live at Wimbledon. For the others—Broke plays too much with the wood, while my wife's game is beneath contempt."

Miss Fettering threw back her head and laughed merrily.

"What's he saying about me?"

Robin Broke, walking ahead with Betty, flung the question over his shoulder.

"It's all right, brother," Fairie assured him. "I was only describing that wonderful racket shot of yours from the back line. The one that always finds the court, if the net's not too high."

His cousin sighed. Then :

" I feel in form to-day," he said. " Does your Accident policy cover you out of England ? "

Light-heartedly the four were making their way down through the garden, voices and the rustle of the two skirts alone marking their progress. There was no sound of footsteps, their rubber soles meeting the polished paths in silence. Fay Broke had insisted that she must write letters, a habit she had formed as a girl at school, and one of which the others, counting it vicious, had vainly endeavoured to break her time and again.

Among women the writing of letters is something akin to intemperance. Some go about it privily, in the seclusion of their apartment, and the silence of night. Others, more shameless, openly succumb to temptation, and, making no secret of the failing, indulge it brazenly. For such, temporarily, company and its calls may go by the board. When the fit is upon them, considerations of time and place weigh with them not at all. There and then the epistolary lust must be gratified at any price. After some hours they arise from the debauch dazedly, overdone, fatigued for the rest of the day. Reaction is bound to set in. The after effects must be slept off.

Fay, then, being engaged with her correspondence, Miss Fettering, Fairie's acquaintance and cousin of Dorothy Lair, had readily consented to make up the four. The girl seemed frankly glad of her new-found friends. Except for a ' companion,' who only appeared at meals, she was staying alone in the hotel.

They play much tennis in the island of Rih, and most of the courts are situate amid surroundings of great beauty. That for which the four were making was no exception to the rule.

Sunk deep in the heart of a fair flower-garden,

a smooth, white-lined sheet of asphalt stretched evenly from side to side, its spruce net dividing it half-way. The low grey walls that fenced the place about—netting like a faint gauze rising above them—were hung with living arras, ragged, maybe, but in fresh, gorgeous colouring beyond measure rich. Full thirty feet the flaming orange of a bignonia rioted over the stonework, scrambling to meet and mingle with the deep magenta of a mighty bougainvillea, whose blossoms stand for Royalty among the flowers of Rih. Far on the other side showed the pale purple of wistaria, looking like some soft silken drapery fallen from a goddess' tiring-room, which, floating slowly downward, had come to rest elegantly over a corner of the tennis-court—tattered a little, for, as it fell, odd boughs of overleaning trees seemed to have caught its edges. Little wonder that the delicate fabric could not bear the strain, but tore and ripped noiselessly as it settled down, leaving dainty trails to swing and droop gracefully from the branches above. A little of the court was shadowed by the tall trees standing about it, but for the most part it lay open to the hot sun.

Not much of a place for tennis, you will be saying. Perhaps. It would not do at Wimbledon. But then there are times when the game of tennis, like that of Life, need not be taken too seriously, when we can forgive the loss of a dropping ball against an improper background for the sake of the rare loveliness of which that same background is so irregularly made up.

" Of course," said Bill Fairie, " there are courts and courts. This is one of the latter."

" It makes me think of Omar Khayyám," said Betty dreamily.

" Yes," said Robin. " ' They say the Lion and the Lizard keep The Courts where Jamshýd gloried and

drank deep.' The very place. Only they're wrong
about the lion." He turned to Miss Fettering. " Jamshýd used to glory over by that side line, you know."

" Not really ? "

Broke nodded.

" A brass plate is to be let in there this autumn.
Not that they want anything to remember him by,
for the nets on this court are always tight. Here,"
he added suddenly, " when you've quite finished with
my racket . . ."

Fairie stopped whirling it to scrutinize the gut.
It might have been tauter, certainly. After a moment :

" You must forgive me," he said. " I thought it
was a landing-net."

" You needn't swank," said Robin, pointing to the
scarf about his cousin's waist. " You're not the
only member of the Cyclists' Touring Club."

" Wrong again," said Bill. " These are the colours
of the Post Office Telephone Subscribers Protection
Society. Arms : A conversation couped, between
an oath imbrued issuant, az. and a blasted trunk
charged on the nail, or. Crest : A line engaged proper.
Motto : Fair Exchange is No Robbery."

He stopped. Miss Fettering was laughing helplessly. With difficulty stifling a desire to join in her
merriment, Betty and Broke exchanged significant
glances.

" Thinks he's back at the Poplar Empire," said
Broke. " Let's pretend not to notice it."

A slim brown boy, perhaps eleven years old, slid
shyly out of the bushes and stepped down on to the
asphalt. Barefoot, he stood leaning against the
creepered wall, one finger to his white teeth. For an
instant he looked at the four, making ready to play ;

then he dropped his dark eyes, smiling a little. It was his naïve way of offering his services.

" Aha," said Fairie, " a gatherer of balls errant. A seeker of lost spheres. Almost an astronomer. 'Tis well. Consider yourself engaged, my lad. The play, I may say, will be fast, possibly furious. Don't say I didn't warn you."

" How shall we play ? " said Betty. " I think Miss Fettering and you'd better take on Robin and me."

" Every time, m'dear," replied her husband. " And now—— Hullo ! " He stopped to wave with his racket in the direction of a large size in German Jews, who had strolled on to the court, and was standing apparently wrapped in proud contemplation of his own faculty of perspiration. " To one side, O Israel. What's the German for ' Get out or get under ' ? "

" Try *achtung*," said Miss Fettering.

Bill tried it with some success. With a grunt the trespasser retired ponderously. A moment later the game had begun.

*　　*　　*　　*　　*

By the time that Fay Broke had written her letters it was getting on for noon. She strolled down into the garden, but the others had apparently had their fill of tennis, for they were nowhere to be seen. The court itself was occupied by two people. One was a lady visitor, who might well have been taken for thirty-five, had she not been behaving as if she were fifteen ; the other, a young man, who, because he had struck a bad opponent, seemed to think himself rather good, but was endeavouring politely to look as if he were having the game of his life. It occurred to Fay that, allowing for his Oxford manner, it was a rather creditable attempt. On a long stone seat four players waited amusedly for the conclusion of the set.

Thoughtfully Fay strolled back to the hotel. Inquiry at the office showed that the Fairies had sent for a taxi, and, with the Fettering girl and Robin, had gone down town; so she fetched a novel and once more descended into the garden. Five minutes later she was lying easily in somebody else's chair—her own was up on the verandah—on a tiny retired terrace, little more than a ledge set upon the edge of the cliff. It was so hidden that you might pass the path that led to it—and no further—a score of times, nor even dream that, if you followed it, your curiosity would be so well repaid.

The novel was not very interesting, but the air was warm and gentle, while the sea was making a lazy noise a long way below. Moreover, remember, Fay had been writing letters. On the whole, it would have been almost surprising if she had not fallen asleep.

A quarter of an hour later she opened her eyes. The first thing they rested upon was a good-looking man of about thirty summers, clean-shaven and very brown, clad in a plain white flannel suit. His grey hat lay on the curving seat beside him, and there was an unlighted cigarette between his lips. He sat with an arm on the parapet, gazing over the sea. The next second he turned to look at her.

"She's awake," he said, with an easy smile, that came into his strong face so naturally that Fay found herself wondering if he could ever look hard or cold-hearted. "And now"—for a moment he hesitated—"excuse me, but you don't happen to be my sister, do you?"

For a moment Fay stared at him. Then:

"Not that I know of," she said.

The man regarded her with an air of amused disappointment. Then:

"I am sorry," he said. "I suppose you're quite sure about it."

"Absolutely. But I oughtn't to have to tell you that, ought I? Don't you know your own sister when you see her?"

Her companion shook his head.

"That's the trouble," he said. "I know she's in Rih, and staying at 'The Bristol,' but that's all. I've been looking for her ever since I landed, nearly an hour ago. I made sure you were her," he added musingly, "directly I saw you. To tell you the truth, I very nearly kissed you, I felt so certain about it."

"Did you though?"

"Fact," said the other coolly. "Only it seemed a shame to wake you. That's why I didn't strike a match. May I smoke, please?"

"I don't suppose the manager will mind."

"I don't care if he does. Do you?"

"It doesn't matter about me," said Fay. "I'm going."

With that she picked up her novel.

The other was on his feet in an instant.

"Don't dream of moving," he said. "For one thing, you look so lovely like that. Besides, I'm just going to leave you, only I'd rather like to explain first. That is if you'll let me."

Fay regarded him steadily. Then she laid down the book.

"Well?" she said.

It was all simple enough.

He had not set eyes upon his sister for seven years. And she had been barely fourteen, and young for her age, when he had been sent straight from Oxford to enter the Indian house of a great English firm.

" My uncle's, you see. The idea was, I was to come home after two years. And I would have, too, only the head of the Indian house died a week before I was to have sailed. I had to take control—at twenty-five. There was no one else. . . . I loved it, but it meant another five years. I nearly came home once, but there was trouble in the air, and—I didn't."

He paused, meditatively regarding his cigarette.

" Well ? " said Fay, this time a note of interest in her voice.

" Well, now the old chap's retiring, and I'm home to manage the English house. His sons, my cousins, have taken on my job. They've been out there under me for the last three years. And I've come a month earlier than I was going to. They never knew at home till I was well on my way, and in Paris I got a letter saying the child was at Rih, so I cleared out to Lisbon right away and took the first boat across. We've no people, you know, she and I."

" I see," said Fay gently.

" When I landed I came straight to the hotel and asked for her. They said she was here all right, and, they thought, in the garden. So I'm just looking."

" And making shots ? "

" That's it. Of course, I ought to have sent her a cable. She'll have changed, naturally. When I saw her last, she had her hair down. Let's see, fourteen and seven's twenty-one. You must be just about her age."

" Twenty-three."

" Grey-eyed, too," he added musingly, " and the same lovely hair. Oh, I am sorry you're not her. I'm afraid she won't be half as beautiful. I only wish——"

" What ? " said Fay, smiling.

"I wish I hadn't been so particular. About not waking you, I mean."

"That'll do," said Fay. "As a matter of fact, I rather think your sister's gone into Starra, but she'll be back for lunch."

Surrey Fettering opened his mouth suddenly. Then :

"You know her ? " he said. "But how——"

"Of course, I may be wrong," said Fay dreamily, gazing with half-closed eyes over the dazzling sea.

"Which means, you know you're not," said the other. "When a woman admits she may be wrong, it means she knows she's right."

A faint smile crept into Fay Broke's face. Also she raised her eyebrows a little. But she still looked ahead and away over the dancing sea. The man regarded her pleasedly. Then :

"Yes," he said, "my name is Fettering." The smile deepened and the brows went a shade higher. "Of course, you had something to go on, and your instinct made you sure. Wonderful thing, instinct," he added musingly. "Will you have a cigarette ? "

Instinct. Of that strange subtle sense, which only women have, we are wont to speak over-lightly. It is no mean asset, if you please, this ability to peer, perhaps unconsciously, into a man's brain. In a war of wits the man knows what he is going to say. Often enough not so the woman. But, what is much more important, she, too, knows what the man is going to say. To tell the truth, he might as well lay his cards upon the table. Nearly always she knows what they are. If they be good ones, steady, relentless play may wear her down, may . . . And he need not be too sure about his victory even then. As often as not it is a defeat which she has tricked up, till he is deceived altogether. The battle is not always to the strong hand.

In a silence that was big with laughter, Fay Broke accepted a cigarette. After lighting it for her, Fettering resumed his seat on the low slab built into the curling wall.

"But don't you think you ought to begin looking again?" said Fay. "For your sister, I mean."

Fettering shook his head.

"She'll be back for lunch, you said," he reminded her. "Besides, my next mistake mightn't be such a happy one, Grey Eyes. And now," he added, "tell me about England. Is it the same dear place?"

"Yes," said Fay reflectively. "On the whole, it is. Only there are heaps of cars now everywhere, and strikes have come in, and cocktails. I suppose London's changed in a way, but it's really rather difficult to remember what it was like seven years ago. It still rains a lot, you know."

"I shan't mind that," said Fettering. "What about the country? Is that all right? Not spoiled, I mean."

"The real country's as priceless as ever. Of course, they're building a bit, making villages into towns, and giving towns suburbs, but, when you get right into the country, it's all right. Streams and woodland and deep meadows, and——"

"And the old, old elms, with their green jackets about their trunks. I know. It'll be very good to see it all again."

"It's just as well you didn't go straight home," said Fay. "England was hardly looking her best when we left her, about a week ago."

"Unlike yourself, Grey Eyes. At least, I take it you are. I think you must be."

" I don't think any girl can look her best lying in a chair with——"

" It's largely a matter of limbs," asserted Surrey Fettering. " A long chair, like yours, shows them off —all four of them. And if they're perfect, my lady looks her best in a long chair with her small white feet up. Very well, then."

Fay regarded him with a faint smile, something of scorn in it, then :

" And he's known me about twenty minutes," she said slowly. Mention of time made her glance at her wrist-watch. Before he could reply, " A quarter to one," she announced, sitting upright. " I must go up. I'll introduce you to your sister, if you like," she added. " I suppose she'll believe you."

Fettering smiled.

" When I say I'm her brother ? I think so. If the worst came to the worst, I could remind her of a certain summer Sunday morning about eight years ago, when she cantered straight into the Rectory crowd, who were coming home from church across our meadows. When I say that she was riding Blue Boy bareback at the time . . . I shall never forget the scene. The Rector said it was an outrage, Phyllis said it was pure bad luck, and everyone else said it was just like her—except the second gardener, that is."

" What did he say ? " said Fay, laughing.

" Oh, he said that Mrs. Rector's expression would have soured a bucket of cream at fifty yards. Several people thought her face would never go back."

Fay got up, took two steps forward, uttered a cry of pain, and sat down suddenly on the stone seat.

" What on earth——" began Fettering.

" Sorry," said Fay, whipping off a small buckskin slipper, " but there's a nail, or something, hurting like anything. Funny, I never felt it before." She slipped her fingers into the toe of the shoe. " I've got it," she added. " I say, it is sharp ! I don't wonder——"

"Let me feel," said Fettering.

In silence Fay handed him the slipper—Betty's, as a matter of fact. Finding her own uncleaned, she had sent for Falcon and borrowed a pair of her cousin's to wear till luncheon.

For a moment he felt gropingly, probing the pointed toe with a finger curiously. The next instant he withdrew it with a sharp exclamation of pain. Fay, who had been waiting for this, broke into a peal of merriment.

" Nail ! " said Surrey, regarding his second digit in some dudgeon. " Nail ? Barbed wire's more like it ! And don't hurt yourself, Grey Eyes. Keep some laughter for the blood ; it's just coming."

" I can't help it," sobbed Fay. " Your face when you——"

" I know—must have been a scream. But—— By Jove ! " he added suddenly, turning the shoe upside down. " Look at it. No wonder you couldn't walk ! I fancy a fakir'd think twice before he settled down to four miles an hour on that."

" O-oh," said Fay weakly.

Firmly embedded in the sole of the slipper was a brass-headed drawing-pin.

" But why did I only just feel it ? " said Fay, big-eyed.

" Probably because you've only just collected it," said her companion. " I expect some fool's been drawing here and dropped it, and you stepped on it as you got out of the chair. Is the foot bleeding, Grey Eyes ? "

" I don't expect so."

Fettering raised his eyebrows. Then 1

" No ? " he said.

With that, he stepped in front of her, stooped down, and put a hand for the white-stockinged foot. The next moment a warm heel was resting in his palm.

Exactly how it had got there Fay was never quite sure.

" It is bleeding a little," said Fettering. " I was afraid it must be."

" Is it ? " said Fay carelessly.

By way of answer, the other drew a handkerchief from his pocket and pressed it gently against her toes. When he took it away, there was a faint red stain on the cambric.

" You see ? " he said, holding it up.

" How awful l " said Fay. " D'you think I shall swoon ? "

Surrey set down the small foot tenderly before replying.

" I hope not," he said, smiling. " It's not half as easy to carry a dead weight."

" If you think I'm going to let you carry me up," said Fay, " you're wrong."

Surrey Fettering stood upright and looked at her.

" Well, you can't walk up barefoot," he said. " The most zealous penitent would shy at these paths. Besides, with that wound in your foot——"

" It is an ugly gash, isn't it ? " said Fay cheerfully. " Think they'll be able to stitch it up all right ? I admit the situation's pretty desperate," she went on thoughtfully. " But, as a last resort, don't you think we might take the pin out of the shoe ? "

" How stupid of me l " said Fettering, sitting down

LOVE THIRTY 83

and picking up the slipper. "I apologize. Will you shake it out, or shall I?"

"Idiot!" said Fay, laughing in spite of herself. "Haven't you got a knife, or anything?"

Fettering shook his head.

"Not in these trousers."

They wasted another five minutes endeavouring to press the drawing-pin out with a coin, but all their efforts to dislodge it proved unavailing.

When he had pricked himself for the third time Surrey Fettering raised his eyes to heaven, swore and rose to his feet.

"What are you going to do?" wailed Fay, weak with laughter.

"Take it to the nearest forge," he said bitterly. "This is a blacksmith's job. I don't suppose they've got any anvils at the hotel."

"Not in every room, any way," rejoined Fay, pulling herself together. "But if you ask at the office, they'll probably give you a pair of scissors."

Surrey stood reflectively drumming with his finger-tips upon the slipper's sole.

"And all this comes of having small pink feet the size of a baby's," he said dreamily. "If I'd been able to get more than one finger at a time into the toe, I could have got it out." He paused to lick the blood off his forefinger. "Grey Eyes, I have bled for you. How will you ever repay me?"

"If you're very quick," said Fay darkly, "I will hold my tongue."

*   *   *   *   *

While the girls in the office were searching for a pair of scissors, Fettering seized the opportunity of changing a five-pound note at the bureau on the other side of the entrance to the hotel. Just when he was

in the throes of his first struggle to reduce pounds to
reis, and trying literally to think in thousands, Bill
Fairie and Betty entered the hall. Even if they had
not stopped to inquire for letters, they could hardly
have missed the shoe, which was reposing in solitary
state on the mahogany before the office window.
Betty looked at it curiously, remarking that it was
of the same shape as her own. Then she looked at
it closely, exclaimed, and picked it up.

"What are you doing?" said Bill. "Put it down,
Bet—it's not your shoe!"

"But it is," said Betty, staring round the hall.
"I know it by this scrape on the leather. Besides, no
one else——"

"Where?" said her husband, taking it out of her
hand. "Are you sure?" he added, examining the
graze.

"Positive. But who on earth——"

"Ask them here, in the office," replied her husband.
"Perhaps Falcon——"

"Excuse me," said a quiet voice behind them,
"but that's—er—my shoe."

They swung round to find Surrey Fettering standing
with outstretched hand.

Instinctively, Fairie made as though he would hand
it over. Then he hesitated.

"I'm sure you'll forgive me," he said courteously.
"But—er—are you quite sure? I mean——"

"Perfectly," replied Fettering. "I've only just
laid it down."

"But it's mine!" cried Betty.

"Yours?" said Fettering. "But that's impossible.
I've only just——"

"I'm sure you have, if you say so," said Fairie.
"But that doesn't make it yours. And my wife has

identified it as her own. If you would say how you came by it," he added civilly, " I'm sure the mis-understanding———"

" I can only ask you to hand it to me at once," said Fettering stiffly. " I have to return it to a lady."

" But it isn't hers," said Betty indignantly, turning to her husband. " I tell you it's mine."

" I must insist on your giving it to me at once," said Fettering firmly. " The lady to whom it belongs———"

" Why, Surrey ! " said a gentle voice at his elbow. Fettering started and swung round.

" Phyllis ! "

Brother and sister embraced there and then in the sunlit hall. Robin Broke and the Fairies looked on open-mouthed. At length :

" Support me, somebody," said Fairie. " Support me at once. My breath is bated."

" Be quiet," said Betty. " This———"

" Be quiet ? Beware, you mean. This is a ruse. While the two are embracing, a third steals the shoe. I've read about it in *Chunks*."

" Er—this is my brother, Mr. Fairie," said Miss Fettering, flushing furiously. " I haven't seen him for seven years, and———"

" What did I say ? " said Bill excitedly. " He's only just out. Clearly a hardened criminal. Very glad to meet you," he added, shaking Fettering's hand. " And now, if we promise not to prosecute, you must tell us how in the world you got hold of my wife's shoe."

" Well, to begin with, a girl gave it me," said Surrey, laughing. " In the garden."

" But this is a shoe," said Fairie, holding up the slipper. " Not an apple."

*   *   *   *   *

Fay, mounting the cobbled paths delicately, limped round a corner to see The White Hope standing regarding critically the great pink blooms of a magnificent tassel tree. At the sight of her the look of appraisement faded from his face into a vast smile of greeting, which was in turn succeeded by a whimsical expression of surprise, as he observed her shoeless foot.

" Another harsh dictate of Fashion ? " he exclaimed. " Not content with the restriction of the kilt, does she demand——"

Fay interrupted him to explain. At length ı

" So you see," she concluded, " when he does come back, I shall be gone. It's his own fault for being so long."

The eminent lawyer smiled.

" Clearly an affair," he said. " Three centuries ago it would have been a glove. To-day it is a slipper. Your gallant has doubtless fastened it in his hat, and is probably at this moment engaged in murdering such well-intentioned pages and other members of the staff as have innocently presumed to draw his attention to the peculiarity of his headgear. When he has dispatched them, he will rejoin you."

" Well, he'll be too late, any way," said Fay, laughing. " And now——"

She stopped suddenly, and a light of excitement sprang into her grey eyes.

" What mischief——" began the K.C. intelligently.

Fay laid her hand on his arm and gurgled with delight.

" Oh, do," she said rapturously. " Do. It would be priceless. Just go and take my place where I was sitting. There's a chair by a seat in the wall, right on the edge of the cliff. And when he comes, he'll find you, and you can have him on beautifully."

She laughed softly in anticipation.

The lawyer's eyes twinkled.

" Show me the way," he said.

So she showed him the way, and then, smiling in anticipation of her swain's discomfiture, proceeded haltingly, by a circuitous route, through the fair garden up to the hotel.

*　　*　　*　　*　　*

Later that afternoon, amongst other sets, the Brokes took on the Fetterings, and were handsomely beaten. By the side of the court, shock-absorbing cushions received the weight of the K.C. gracefully. Through the drifting smoke of his cigar the lawyer followed the ebb and flow of the play with lazy eyes. In the course of one of the games, Fay Broke and Surrey Fettering met for a moment, each in quest of a ball, on opposite sides of the net.

" I shall never forgive you, Grey Eyes," said Surrey.

" You shouldn't have been so long," retorted Fay, with a dainty lift of her eyebrows. " And, as you feel like that, it's a very good thing I didn't happen to be your sister, isn't it ? "

Steadily Surrey regarded her. Then :

" I'm beginning to think it is, Grey Eyes," he said slowly.

" Come on, you two," called Robin, waiting to serve. " Love Thirty, isn't it ? "

" I wonder," said The White Hope to himself, watching Fay's face curiously, as she backed towards her place in the court. " I wonder." Then he thought of her age, glanced at Fettering, and smiled. " But it's pretty evident that it's Love Twenty-three."

CHAPTER V

FOR BETTER OR FOR WORSE

BILL FAIRIE leaned wearily against the doorway of the bathroom belonging to the suite.

"Any woman," he said, "who occupies the bath for more than thirty-five minutes, in her husband's teeth, is a desolation."

His wife, who had been invisible, made a sudden effort to sit upright. Eighteen inches of water reduced the endeavour to absurdity.

"I haven't been here a quarter of an hour yet," said Betty indignantly. "Have you shaved?"

"More," said Fairie bitterly. "I have removed all traces of the crime, perused the *Sportsman* we brought from England, and smoked a cigarette. Have I shaved!"

"Well, I shan't be long," said his wife. "I must wash, you know."

With a groan Fairie returned to the balcony and, leaning his arms upon the warm rail, prepared to abandon himself to a luxurious contemplation of his surroundings.

Half-past seven o'clock of an April morning may be a fair hour anywhere. In the Island of Rih it may be exquisite. There is a time for every place. The greenwood will look its best of a morning, so soon as the sun is up; this shadowed stream dreams on its way never so lazily as in the hot afternoon; your rolling moorland stretches into the purple distance, peerless at cock-crow, whilst at noontide deep meadows will blow most of all sweetly, the steady drone of insects hanging above them. Sundown, too, has a great following, Harlequin night and the moon's witchery, maybe, the greatest of all. But, then, show me the alley, never so mean, that will not take on a look of elegance, clothed in that famous livery of black and silver. There is a time for every place. Seven-thirty o'clock in the morning is Rih's time. At least, so you will maintain at half-past seven At any other hour of the day you will be less certain, so often is Rih all glorious.

Bill Fairie leaned there comfortably, awaiting his bath. Below him stretched the deep garden, heavy with the massed perfume of a thousand blossoms, which the first breeze of the day was beginning to dissipate. Beyond, the laughing bay and the ragged white of Starra glistened in the hot sun. Prospect and day alike were big with promise.

The sudden sight of Broke in breeches and leggings, strolling gingerly along one of the polished paths, set Fairie thinking. By the time his cousin was within range he was ready.

"Good morning, brother," he said pleasantly. Robin started, slipped on the even cobbles, recovered himself with an effort, and looked up. "Where's the meet?"

"On the pier," said Robin. "At half-past ten. Got your bicycle ready?"

Fairie looked at him for a moment before replying. Then:

"Seriously," he said, "what is it? Had some bad news this morning?"

Broke spread out his hands.

"To be frank," he said, "I propose to ride. To your blear eyes, I suppose, all horses look the same. As a matter of fact, the half-bred Arabs here are——"

"If you're going to be rude," said Bill, "I shan't lend you my pillion."

A quick rustle of silk, and there was Betty beside him on the balcony, all fresh and pink and white in a dainty kimono.

"O-oh!" she cried delightedly, clapping her hands. "Look at our horseman."

"Hush!" said her husband. "They're making a new film thing—'The Jockey's Sweetheart, or A Tale of the Turf.' That out there is the comic stable-boy." Here the soft sound of steps upon the path sent Betty flying into her bedroom. Making ready to follow her, Fairie nodded carelessly to his indignant cousin below. "Very well, Tom," he added, raising his voice, "have the mare round at ten o'clock, and see that that martingale's properly clean this morning."

As he disappeared, a ripple of laughter floated out of the room, and in its wake Betty's voice, crying:

"Never mind, Robin. You look very nice, and I envy you. Why didn't I bring my habit?"

"Probably for the same reason that induced your husband to leave his manners in England," said Broke acidly.

The next moment The White Hope was tapping him upon the shoulder.

"Perhaps he knew they wouldn't survive the Customs," he said.

It was the eminent lawyer's footsteps that they had heard approaching.

*   *   *   *   *

Half an hour later Fay Broke and her brother and Betty sat down to breakfast. Two tables away The

White Hope was already dissecting passion fruit with all the precision of the law. Beyond him again the Fetterings—brother and sister—were engaged in deep converse ; and Phyllis Fettering was wearing a fawn-coloured riding habit.

"Where's Bill ? " said Robin, as they took their places.

"Gone to buy the *Gazette*," said Betty, glancing out of one of the tall windows, which opened on to the cool courtyard and the sunlit road beyond. "There he is, talking to Get Out and Get Under. Aren't they dears ? "

Two bullocks, these if you please, that were used to draw a swaying sledge over the cobbles. In this one *carro* always the four drove after dinner to the Casino and home again. Fairie had marked down driver and animals at the first, and straightway retained them.

Fay nodded.

"I love their great patient eyes," she said.

"Give me their horns," said her brother. "So sympathetic."

"Dear idiot," said his sister, "where are you going to ride ? "

"Oh, just round about, I suppose, over the hills. And you ? What are you going to do ? "

"I don't see why we shouldn't go up the mountain," said Betty. "I dare say Surrey Fettering'll come," she added carelessly.

"Of course," said Robin. "Hullo, Bill, old pal. Had a good bath ? "

The gentleman so addressed laid a bunch of violets beside his wife's plate before replying. Then :

"Hush ! " he said. "That hideous incident is now closed. Let me share with you the two com-

pelling, if solitary, items of news with which the
English column of the *Rih Gazette* is this morning
bursting." He took his seat and spread the flimsy
sheet carefully in front of him. " In the first place,
you will be petrified to learn that, ' Bearing the Rams-
gate postmark, and dated September 9th, 1901, a
postcard from her mother has just been delivered to
a domestic servant at Wapping.' The second and
last sensation comes from New York. If we may
believe our eyes, ' The Newburn and Hatfield Railway
Company is shortly to be dissolved under the Anti-
Trust Law.' Now you know. I may add that I paid
fifty reis for this issue on the off-chance that some
distorted racing news might have wormed its way into
print."

" My dear," said Betty, " you don't seem to realize
that we are out of the world for a little, and it's no
use trying to keep in touch. Personally, I just don't
want to."

" Nor I," said Fay. " But I'm all for going up
the mountain to-day."

Fairie laid down his knife and looked at her.

" What new blasphemy is here ? " he said. " Go
up the mountain ? This isn't the Pentateuch."

" Just the day for it," said Broke, with a grin.
" If I wasn't riding——"

" Yes," said his cousin grimly. " Yes. I can just
see you climbing on a day like this. Always did make
a playground of the Alps, didn't you ? " He turned
to his wife. " My dear, you know that I can never
stand heights. That's why I never sit in the dress-
circle."

" Nonsense," said Betty. " You go up in a train
thing all the way and then toboggan down. They say
the view's lovely."

Her husband wiped his forehead before replying.

"At least," he said, "the *Gazette* will profit. The proceedings at the inquest should make absorbing reading." He turned to Robin. "You'll know this shirt again, won't you? I mean to say, you'll have to identify the bodies, and if my face isn't recognizable, or they can't find my head or anything——"

The White Hope stopped, on his way out, to pay his respects to Betty and Fay. With one consent they appealed for his support of their case. He heard them out gravely. Then:

"I am with you," he said simply. "Mr. Fairie's apprehension is baseless."

"But this tobogganing stunt?" said Bill.

"A mild affair, believe me, and rather delectable."

"See what you're going to miss," said Betty, turning to Broke.

The latter raised his eyebrows. Before he could reply:

"And yet," said the man of law, "were I twenty years younger, and some haughty barb fretting for me at the gates——"

"You'd give the mountain a miss," said Broke.

The White Hope glanced in the direction of Phyllis Fettering.

"Speaking impersonally," he said, "much would depend on whether anyone, and, if so, who, had brought a habit with them."

"That," said Bill, "is fair comment. Incidentally, we hope that you will dine with us to-night. Without prejudice, I mean."

The eminent K.C. beamed.

"It will be a privileged occasion," he said.

* * * * *

It was nine o'clock when Phyllis Fettering and

Broke rode out of the courtyard. Into Starra and up through the little town they passed, till there was more space between the dwellings, and the gardens spread wider and deeper behind their random walls.

Starra's ways are cobbled, every one of them. Not a back street, not an alley that is not paved with old black cobble-stones, small and close-set, worn smooth and polished by the traffic of many rolling years. There is no sound because of them, for of wheeled traffic there is none at all in the island, save only the panting cars, and they, on rubber tires, run quietly enough. For the rest, carts, wagons, and chaises alike sway to and fro on well-greased runners, sure-footed oxen drawing them. The pace is not of the hottest, but in Rih there is no hastening.

"Some of them would eat out of my hand," said Miss Fettering. "They would really."

They were talking about deer.

"Naturally," said Robin. "I myself would eat large quantities of food out of your hand. Afterwards I should lick——"

"Only dry bread, you know."

"Husks," said Robin laconically. "Out of your hand."

"He is tame, isn't he?" said Phyllis, with a maddening lift of her straight eyebrows. "And now——" She hesitated and reined up her horse. Clearly she was uncertain of the way. For a moment she glanced up a steep path rising between soft-coloured walls. "No," she murmured, "it wasn't that one. And yet——"

Broke's eyes never left her face. This was very thoughtful and grave for the moment, steady-eyed. The straight nose, the curve of her soft lips, her faultless chin, made up a profile to wonder at. Kissed of the sun, her delicate skin had taken on the look of health which that great lover alone can give his darlings—a favour precious indeed, though some will have none of it. Yet such kisses may be taken in all honour by royalty and ragamuffin alike, neither can they breed regrets nor any heartache, nor even an odd memory, which might not be there to smart, could we but call back Time.

" We'll try it, any way," said Phyllis suddenly, turning her horse's head to the path. " You'll have to forgive me if I'm wrong. By the way, you don't know where I'm taking you to yet, do you ? "

" I am in your hands," said Broke.

" I thought you were going to eat out of them."

" Ah," said Robin, " but I propose to rise to that occasion. Excuse me," he added, " but just look at the sunlight on that wall there, and then think of any English seaside resort at this moment. Of course, the grey light effects at Blackpool will be—er—effective. Lunch under the pier there on Easter Monday will be a festive meal. Wind E. to N.E. Some showers, some——"

" ' Oh, to be in England now that April's there,' " said Miss Fettering.

Broke frowned.

" A charming sentiment," he said. " But old Browning wasn't taking any himself. When he wrote that, he was in Italy. Enthusiasts would style that an accident ! I should call it a precaution."

Phyllis Fettering laughed. Then !

" Has he had much to make him cynical ? " she said.

" I protest," said Robin aggrievedly. " I do hereby protest. Mine is an approving nature. I'm always getting lost in Admiration."

" Where's that ? " said Phyllis.

" Where ? Why, in Thought. You must know the great city of Thought, with all her parishes, Memory, Wonderment, Melancholy, Awe, and the rest. Don't you ever go there ? "

" I think so. Tell me about it."

Broke shook his head.

" If you know it, there's nothing to tell. Only I'm rather fond of going there and wandering about its broad, silent streets. It has three great quarters, you know—Past, Present, Future and—and lots of parishes. Past I know well. Sometimes I lose my way though," he added reflectively. " It grows so quickly, you see, and if I'm looking for some special ——"

" Lost again ? You said just now you were always getting lost——"

" In Admiration, my dear. Same thing. Still, most of that parish lies in Present. For instance, I'm lost in present admiration of your throat. I love throats."

" From the way you speak anyone would think you collected them."

" So I do," said Robin. " Keep them in the south wing of a little gallery I have in Bond Street, Past, W. Yours will have a room to itself."

" Thanks awfully. I suppose you saw ' The Blue Bird ' ? "

" If you accuse me of plagiarism——"

" I am congratulating you upon your memory."

Broke glanced at her. She was looking straight between her horse's ears, her chin ever so slightly tilted and a faint smile on her lips. After a pause :

" Your name," he said, " is Mockery. Upon the hills of Rih you flout——"

" The dreamer who was kind and shared his dreams with a friend." She turned a glowing face to him, and for a second a little hand rested on his arm. " You mustn't take me too seriously."

" You darling," said Robin. As he spoke, her horse broke into a trot.

Five minutes later they halted before the high painted gates of a garden whose villa seemed to stand far back from the road.

Miss Fettering turned to Broke.

" This," she said, " is the Quinta Viola. No one lives here but an old gardener, who is given a trifle to keep the garden from becoming a wilderness. Would you like to see it ? "

" Please."

" Then put your hand up under that wistaria and ring the bell. The old man will know it's me, because no one else rings. You can't reach the bell unless you're mounted, because there's only an inch or two of the chain left."

Robin moved to the spot she indicated and felt under the purple tassels. The next moment the jangle of an old bell came faintly from the direction of the house.

In silence they sat waiting till they heard a shuffle of steps beyond the gates. Then one of these swung open, and an old man stood uncovered while they rode within. Under the shadow of tall trees about the drive, that swept to the villa's entrance, they dismounted, giving the reins to a bare-legged urchin, who received them with a shy smile. Then :

" This way," said Phyllis, stepping towards a broad path that clearly led into the depths of the garden.

Out of the tall trees' shadow they passed into the hot sunshine, a glowing riot of colour on either hand,

and so to where the path ran between the faded pillars of a long corridor. At the entrance to the latter Phyllis Fettering stopped.

" Isn't that beautiful ? " she said.

The corridor might have been hewn through a hill of living blossom. Here, not content to make a gorgeous canopy, a bougainvillea streamed down the sides of the pergola, staining with scarlet the snowy fabric of screens that clustering roses made, while further along the gaudy yellow of bignonias hung down beside a purple arras of wistaria, now in its full beauty. Framed in the far mouth of the corridor was a distant headland with the white surf beating about it, and a glimpse of the sparkling ocean beyond.

For a moment they stood looking at the picture. Then :

" Appearances," said Robin, " are deceptive. I thought the gate we came in by was made of wood. I now realize that it was made of ivory."

Beyond the corridor, steps led down to a little flagged terrace facing the sea, with white clumps of daisies and large-flowered violets all about it, while over an old stone seat leaned a great pink peach tree in full bloom, so that seat and terrace alike were littered with delicate peach-blossom.

With almost the air of a proprietress, Phyllis sat down. Pleasedly she watched Robin looking slowly about him. At length :

" What a wonderful place ! " he said. " I suppose this is my lady's bower, where she sighs and works tapestry on off-days. I can hardly believe I'm awake. Do you mind pinching my left ear—low down on the lobe ? "

Sitting down, he placed his head at a convenient

angle. With a smile Miss Fettering flicked his ear with her glove.

"Wake up," she said. "If this is my bower, I desire to be amused. Perhaps I'm asking too much."

"There was once," said Robin, "an old king, and he had one daughter, who was the apple——"

"Of his eye," said Miss Fettering. "I know this one."

"Not at all. She was the apple-women's delight, because she lived on apples. She and her father were very happy and proud of their home, which was full of beautiful things. They had a gold telephone and a cuckoo clock and one of the finest collections of picture postcards in the country.

"One day, just as they were finishing breakfast, the telephone went.

"'I'll answer it,' said the Princess, for the King had just put a large piece of trout into his mouth.

"When she asked who it was:

"'I'm the Chief of the Police,' said a man's voice. 'I want to speak to the King.'

"'I'm afraid you can't just now,' said the Princess. 'His mouth's full.'

"'What of?' said the voice.

"'Trout,' said the Princess. 'Can I give him a message?'

"'Take him by the throat at once,' said the voice. 'He mustn't swallow, whatever happens. That stuff is poisoned. Good-bye.'

"'Good-bye,' said the Princess. Then she replaced the gold receiver and took her father firmly by the throat.

"It took some time to make him understand the position, and several servants had to be called in to hold his arms and legs, but at length he began to realize that the trout was poisoned. After a very painful scene, order was restored. The King used up most of the mouth-wash in the castle before lunch, and the remains of the trout were given to the poor with the other scraps.

" The beggar who got the trout counted himself lucky, ate it, and was not one penny the worse. The King, however, expired at luncheon before he had emptied his tankard.

" The Chief of the Police, who had just arrived at the castle, expecting a knighthood, left ten years later without any ears, the golden telephone was disconnected, and the Princess let the palace and took the veil shortly afterwards.

" The only people well out of it were the beggar who got the trout and the King's physician, who had repeatedly advised His Majesty that ' stout was poison ' to a man of his corpulence."

Miss Fettering clapped her hands. " I like that," she said, smiling. " What's the moral ? "

Broke shook his head. " My tales," he said, " resemble my cousin Bill—they have no morals."

" But I love Mr. Fairie."

" He is a good chap, isn't he ? " said Broke meditatively. " Very offensive, though." He looked at her for a moment. Then : " I wonder if you realize what a lovely picture you make," he said simply.

" Another fairy tale ? " queried Miss Fettering.

" No. A true one this time."

Steady grey eyes met his. Broke regarded them thoughtfully. The thud of a heavy gun broke the silence suddenly. As the echoes rumbled into the hills, Robin stepped to the balustrade. The girl followed him.

Starra lay all before them, twinkling in the sunshine

about the bay, and, beyond, the dancing ocean stretched away till the sky met it.

"Never knew they fired off guns here," said Broke. "Never knew they had any to fire."

"Do they? Have they?"

Robin looked sharply at his companion.

"Didn't you hear that one, just this moment?" he said.

Phyllis Fettering shook her head.

"I heard a steamer give a long hoot," she said.

"Hoot!" cried Broke. "This was a gun. You must have heard it. No steamer has hooted since we've been here."

"One did a moment ago—just before you got up. Surely you heard it. It must have been that Castle liner." She indicated the great grey ship riding easily in the bay.

"The sound I heard was made by a gun," said Broke positively.

"If you ask me," said Phyllis, "I think this is another of your dreams."

"But you refuse to share it this time."

"You started for Thought without telling me."

"If I had told you, would you have come too?"

"I don't know."

Broke took a small bare hand into his own.

"Whether you would have or not doesn't matter now. In future you'll always be there. That is why I shall go. You are such stuff as dreams are made of, dear. You——"

The hand slipped from his. Miss Fettering turned suddenly and smiled into his eyes.

"Any way," she said, "I'm not going there with you now, because I'm going back to lunch. But don't let me take you out of your way. I know the ways of Starra just as well as you know those of Thought, though I'm afraid I haven't a gallery of throats here."

"Three quarters of an hour ago," said Broke, "a disastrous fire broke out in Bond Street, Past. No attempt was made to subdue the flames. Amongst other buildings the south wing of my gallery was almost completely destroyed."

"Oh !" said Phyllis.

"Yes," said Broke. "The only portion left standing was a room which had been recently added."

* * * * *

For the eleventh time Mrs. Fairie placed a florin on *impair*.

"It must turn up this time," she said.

After a tense moment :

"*Le vingt*," said the croupier.

"Bill," said his wife, "' even ' has turned up twelve times running."

"Then put your shirt on odd," said her husband shortly.

Betty choked.

"But I have," she said in a shaking voice.

"Do it again," said Fairie, standing up and covering most of the numbers below twenty-five.

Betty pinched him savagely. His involuntary cry of pain attracted some attention. A Frenchman on his right was courteously solicitous.

"A mere nothing," said Bill gravely. "A sudden brutal assault upon my person. That was all."

"*Le neuf*," announced the croupier.

"And I wasn't on," wailed Betty. "I can't stand any more. Let's go out into the garden. Come, Fay."

Rising, the two girls made their way to one of

the French windows, Broke and Fairie following them.

Night comes to Rih as a wizard, wand in hand. And Magic with her. Her very entrance is that of a sorcerer. There is no twilight at all. The shadows lengthen, but Rih knows no dusk. One minute it is yet evening—the quiet hour—and the next, night. In the twinkling of an eye the universe has shed her gay blue gown for one of violet, all glorious within, stiff with the broidery of myriad stars. From being an island, Rih has become an isle. Though there has been a breeze in the daytime, it will fall at sundown, so that from then till cock-crow Nature is very still. Not a leaf of all the foliage trembles, not a flower sways. It is as if a spell had been cast about the island, wrapping everything in the sleep of a fairy tale—an enchantment which only the caress of some destined lover's lips may unloose.

The four passed through the starlit garden to the edge of the low cliff, from the foot of which the leisurely lap of the waves rose to meet the languid dream-music which was floating out into the darkness from the Casino's ball-room. The white blossoms of an incense-tree loaded the soft air with perfume.

Bill Fairie seated himself on the broad stone parapet and lighted a cigarette.

"I'll tell you a funny thing," he said, turning to Robin.

" No," said Broke. " Not that. We can stand a good deal, but——"

" Now then, Polo," said his cousin, " I shan't buy those leggings if you aren't careful, and you'll have to advertise. Pair gent's riding-gaiters, size twelve, sell four shillings, or would exchange for fowls."

" What were you going to tell us ? " said The White Hope, who had joined them unobserved.

"Ah, there you are," said Betty. "We wondered where you had got to. I'm afraid the dinner——"

"Not at all," said the lawyer. "My digestion improved with every course, but the manner in which *rouge* persistently defied convention during the twenty minutes which I was so ill-advised as subsequently to spend at the tables was more than I could stomach. It was only your dainty tones that just now lured me from the dudgeon in which I have been labouring for the last half-hour. But let us have the humorous communication promised us by our friend."

"Sorry," said Bill, "but when I said 'funny' I meant 'strange.' This morning, when we were sitting in the garden of the restaurant on the mountain-top, a gun went off. Deuce of a big gun it was. Echoed like anything. Fettering'll bear me out. He heard it. You couldn't help hearing it. The funny thing is that, when I asked what it meant, Betty and Fay swore they hadn't heard any gun. Said they'd heard the hoot of a steamer. Well, no steamer had whistled for hours. We had quite a row about it. Fettering and I heard a gun, while the girls both heard the steamer. I confess it beats me."

"I heard that gun," said Robin.

"There you are," said Bill excitedly. "I knew ——"

"But Miss Fettering didn't." They all stared at him. "We had just the same argument. She insisted that she had heard a long hoot——"

"That's right," cried Betty. "It was a long hoot to begin with, and then the hills took it up. The echoes went on for a long time."

"I'll swear no steamer hooted just then," said Broke. "I didn't understand it at the time," he added slowly, "but your story makes it uncanny."

A silence fell upon the little group. Robin tossed the end of his cigarette over the cliff and strolled away into the darkness.

Betty shivered.

" I hate anything uncanny," she said. " I feel afraid, somehow."

But the White Hope laughed it off.

" Remember," he said, " you were upon an expedition, and alarms and excursions always go together."

As they strolled back to the Casino, Fairie and the man of law fell behind.

" Between you and me," said the former, " was that a gun we heard ? "

The White Hope shook his head.

" I will wager that no gun has to-day been fired within a hundred miles of Starra."

" Then what d'you make of it ? "

The other shrugged his shoulders.

" Occasionally Fate writes upon the wall," he said.

" You think it was a premonition ? "

" Who can say ? " said the lawyer. " I don't really believe in that sort of thing, but——"

He hesitated.

" Go on," said Bill.

" Well, if I were you, and I heard that gun again, for instance, just as I was going to enter a lift, I think I should walk down."

About this time Robin Broke was standing under a jackaranda tree, looking very hard at Phyllis Fettering.

" Give me your other hand," he said unsteadily. She gave it him.

" This morning," he said, " you told me I mustn't take you too seriously." Wondering grey eyes were raised to his. " I don't want to, dear. I want to take you for better or for worse."

The grey eyes fell. Then :

"I can hardly believe I'm awake," said Phyllis softly. "Do you mind—er—pinching my left ear ? "

* * * * *

The smell was very unpleasant, and the reek of the fumes made you cough. It was something, however, to have a whole throat to cough with.

Bill Fairie removed a large slab of mud from the side of his face, and turned to his Adjutant.

"Robin," he said, "that was extremely objectionable."

"I concur," said Robin. "It was also extremely dangerous. That gunner chap ought to be more careful." He turned to the Forward Officer, who was feverishly wiping the lenses of a pair of binoculars with a silk pocket-handkerchief. "Fettering," he said, "you witnessed that assault ? "

"I did," said Surrey.

"Then, for God's sake, tell your battery to knock that fellow out. He's no gentleman. Look out ! Here's another."

The shell fell to their right, but from the fragments that soared into the air it was clear that a direct hit on the trench had been scored.

"Gosh ! " said the Commanding Officer. " Anyone would think the swine knew we were going to attack."

"They probably do," said Broke bitterly. "They've never concentrated on us like this before."

His surmise was correct. The enemy was aware of what was toward. Also he knew the precise moment of time which had been appointed and called " zero." The information was a great help.

It was light enough to see now. The rain had ceased, but a piercing wind blew steadily. The Vardar wind does not blow in gusts, neither does it rise and fall. For more than a week now one long, continuous, withering blast had swept mercilessly, day and night, across Lake Doiran from the distant snows, laying a bitter curse upon life, turning red blood to ice in the veins, making men silent with pain and beasts indifferent and listless. There is an edge to the Vardar wind that no clothing will turn. Its cold iron enters into the soul.

The trench lay in the foot-hills below the heights to be assailed. Certain deep ravines running irregularly through No Man's Land made a formidable bit of country still less easy to negotiate.

"You'll have a topping good view from where we're going," said Fairie, looking at Fettering and taking out his watch. "Be able to give your fellows a treat for once. Three minutes to the barrage," he added quietly.

"Not there yet," said Broke grimly. "Yes ? " This to a signaller who had pushed his way up to the trench.

"From Major Dudley, sir. Shell fell right on top o' the trench. Six or seven killed and nine wounded. All 'A' squadron, sir. And he's having the wounded put in a dug-out."

"All right." He turned to the Commanding Officer. "Did you hear what he said, sir ? "

"I did," said Fairie. "Bad luck or fine shooting. Bit of both, I'm afraid. Doesn't seem to be going on, though, thank God. What a life ! " he added, with a sigh. "Never mind. It's a poor heart that never rejoices, *mes braves*. And after it's all over, Rih, my boy, and a long drink, and a hot sun, and a nimble dollar on old Zero o' nights, just for luck." And he slapped his cousin on the back.

Fettering looked up from his glasses with a smile.

" D'you remember——"

The sentence was never finished.

As he spoke, from the direction of the lake came the long hoot of a big steamer, and the words died on his lips. While the echoes rumbled into the hills, the three men stared at one another.

" But we're forty odd miles from the coast," cried Fettering, " and the lake——" He turned to the signaller by his side. " Did you hear that ? " he asked sharply.

" Yes, sir. Must be a new one, coming from over there." He nodded in the direction of the lake. " 'Eavy gun, too," he added reflectively.

A whine rose to a scream, which swelled into the rending tear of some tremendous fabric, culminating in a blinding crash, as a wrecked world staggered to meet the falling sky. The enemy gunner had scored again.

*   *   *   *   *

The remains of the Commanding Officer were identified by his servant, who recognized a fragment of the shirt his master was wearing. It was equally clear that the Forward Officer had been killed instantly. The Adjutant died that evening at the casualty clearing station. He rambled a little at the last.

" Can't think why I didn't ride up," he muttered. " Might have known I couldn't reach that bell. Under the wistaria ? I know. But I can't reach, I tell you. I can't reach. They took the horses away. Poor old regiment. They—— Why "—a great smile lighted up the poor quivering features—" the gate's open—open. Ah ! "

Then he died.

INTERLUDE

AND THE OTHER LEFT

"ANYBODY would think you were bored to find me here," said Bill Courtier.

"Would they? I simply didn't know you were coming. That's all."

"What's that to do with it? Why——"

"Oh, everything. And now, if you don't mean to go and fish, or anything, do be quiet and let me read."

With that, the Hon. Dolly Loan bent her fair head once more over her novel and turned over a page with an aggrieved air. The slight frown hanging about her straight brows suggested concentration, which had been disturbed once and really must not be disturbed again. Courtier started to fill a pipe thoughtfully.

Hitch a fortnight in Scotland on to the end of a London season, and you will swear by the simple life—till you are once again standing in the hall at the Carlton, considering the advisability of going on to a Night Club. It was the fourth day of August, and Dolly Loan and her companion were sitting on the verandah of the Flows' shooting-lodge at Yait. Forty-six miles from the nearest post office, all among woods and mountains and broken, scrambling waters, Yait is as retired a pleasance as ever was known. Half its charm lies in its inaccessibility. Once drift into the shelter Yait affords, and people simply cannot get at you. In these stressful days it is, as it were, sanctuary.

When his old friends, the Flows, had asked Bill

Courtier to make one of the small house-party, he
had been forced to refuse the invitation. They and
he were alike sorry, but it could not be helped. He
had promised to go to Dorset only the day before.
Then, at the last moment, his prospective hostess
had been taken suddenly ill, so he had wired joyfully
to the Flows to know if he might come to Yait, after
all. The text of his telegram was characteristic.

"Dorset stunt off have you a bed left I have
some nerve haven't I?"

So was their reply.

"No but you can sleep in the stable yes but
then you always had."

Which was how Bill Courtier came to be staying
at Yait, and why Dolly Loan was greatly surprised
to find him there, when she arrived two days later.

The two were old friends. At least, they had known
one another pretty intimately for three years. Dolly
was twenty-four and pretty enough to figure in one or
other of the weekly periodicals more or less frequently.
Sometimes she was described as "The Beautiful and
Talented Daughter of Lord Merlin," sometimes as "A
Society Favourite." Once her photograph had been
entitled "An English Rose." And it wasn't a bad
description either. For she was English to the tips
of her pointed fingers, and as fresh as a rose, new-
opened before the sun is high.

With eyes half closed, Courtier regarded her meditatively, sitting there, reading with a little air of severity
that he did not understand. This was a Dolly that
he had not seen before. He was one of the few who

had ever beheld her serious ; once he had seen her sad. Once, too, in his presence she had flashed out at staid Tag Ewing, a brother-subaltern.

The three had been sitting together at Ranelagh. Out of mischief Dolly had demanded a cigarette. As soon as it was alight, " I suppose you think I oughtn't to smoke, Mr. Ewing," she had said mockingly. Very gently, " Not here or now," he had answered. Dolly had gasped, and then turned on Ewing and rent him for an " impertinent preacher." The next moment she had flung the cigarette away, caught her offender by the arm and was crying : " I'm sorry, Tag. I know you're right, and I'm sorry. I'm just a child, Tag, aren't I ? " she added artlessly.

" Yes," said Tag solemnly.

So Courtier had seen her angry. But her demeanour this August afternoon was something quite new. And, since he believed he knew her better than anyone, he could not get over it. Possibly she was tired, for Yait was a hundred odd miles from her father's lodge in Argyll, and she had not long arrived, after motoring all the way. Possibly. Yet the soft colour of health springing in her cheeks, her easy, upright pose in her chair, her very absorption in her book, gave the lie direct to such a notion. Besides, she had just had a cold bath.

The eyes that Courtier was watching stole up and away from the page to gaze for a minute over the peaceful glen and the toss of the steep woods beyond. Then the faint frown died, and for an instant the lips moved ever so slightly. The next moment the Hon. Dolly shut her book with a bang.

" If the man isn't going to amuse me," she said, " I shall go for a walk."

And the tone was the tone of Dolly. If taken aback, Courtier was visibly relieved.

H

" I like that," he began. " You go and——"

" I dare say I do. Why shouldn't I ? I am Dolly."

" That's the devil of it."

" What I really want to know," said my lady, " is why my host and hostess were not here to receive me."

" Probably because, as you said, you are Dolly. By the way, did you bring a paper ? "

With a faint smile, his companion shook her head.

" I'm afraid not," she said slowly. " I'm so sorry. It's awful not having anything to read sometimes, isn't it ? Here," she added suddenly, picking up her novel, " you can have this. I'm going——"

" From bad to worse," said Courtier, taking the book, to send it skimming the length of the verandah. " Pretty rapidly, too. There are times when I almost fear for you."

" You don't ? " said Dolly with sudden interest. " How awfully exciting ! Do your knees knock together ? When you're fearing, I mean ? By the way, that novel cost six shillings, and now you've broken its back."

" Have you change for a sovereign ? " said Courtier, feeling in his pocket.

" No, but you can pay me to-morrow," said Dolly. " This is splendid. Isn't there anything else you can destroy ? I'm saving up for a new sponge, you know."

" I absolutely refuse to contribute towards your aquatic ventures," said Bill firmly. " To my great personal inconvenience, you have occupied bathrooms for an outrageous time all over England on more occasions than I like to remember. The six shillings must be spent upon another copy of the same novel. I have long wanted to see you turn over a new leaf."

" Good old Bill," said Dolly, laying a small hand upon his sleeve with a maddening smile. " And he's never said how he likes my nice new brogues."

" Who looks at the moon before sunset ? " said Courtier gallantly. " My eyes never get any further down than your ankles."

Dolly Loan broke into a little peal of laughter.

" A compliment ! " she cried delightedly. " When did he think it out ?   Oh, Bill, you'll be worthy of your name yet."

Courtier laughed.

" If you're like this at twenty-four, what'll you be in ten years' time ? " he said.

" Thirty-four," said Dolly pensively. " By that time I shall probably have one husband and two children, and instead of saying I'm pretty, they'll call me handsome. But that's a long way ahead. A long, long way. . . . So you got here on Sunday ? " she added suddenly.

The other nodded.

" After starting on Thursday, too. Nothing but trouble with the car after I crossed the border.   When Tag comes, I'll have the engine down."

" He'll be here to-morrow, won't he ? " said Dolly, gazing into the distance over the sunlit woods.

Courtier nodded.

" Complete with papers," he said.

" More papers "—musingly.

" Well, Doll, I haven't seen one for five days, and ——"

" Neither have I.   We only get two posts a week at Ferret.   And I didn't look at Saturday's lot when they came.   Somehow, I don't want papers when I'm up North.   I like to forget there's any news or any roar or bustle going on in the world."

"I'll be like that in a week," said Bill. "But the spirit of town life takes a little while to die."

He paused and let his eyes wander luxuriously over the prospect before them. The solemn peace over all lent the scene something more than dignity. Natural grandeur had taken on the majesty that is of silence alone. After a moment :

"It's wonderful to think the 'buses are still swinging down Piccadilly, isn't it?"

"They're not," said Dolly with conviction. "London's been a great dream. That's all. And now we've woken up."

"But they are," said Courtier. "And the traffic's writhing through the City, and the pavements of Regent Street are crammed, and taxis are crawling up Bond Street, and queues are beginning to form up for theatres and music-halls, and——"

> "'But I'm here,
> And you're here,
> So what do we care?'"

Dolly flung out the words of the song with inimitable *abandon*. She had a sweet voice. Bill Courtier joined in.

> "'Time and place
> Do not count. . . .'"

As they finished the chorus :

"As sung on the London—if you please—music-hall stage, Edison Bell Record," said Bill. "Much virtue in dreams."

A step on the verandah made them look round. The next moment a man-servant was at Courtier's side with a telegram.

"For me?" said Bill surprisedly.

"Yes, sir."

"A wire for someone at Yait!" yawned Dolly. "The population of seven will faint with excitement. How on earth did it come?"

As the servant opened his mouth to reply:

"My God!" said Bill quietly. And then "My God!" again.

Then he stood up quickly.

"Bill, what's the matter?" cried Dolly, laying hold on his sleeve. There was that in his face that frightened her.

Courtier turned to the servant.

"There's no answer," he said. "And I want my things packed at once."

"Yes, sir."

As the man left the verandah, Courtier handed Dolly the form.

It ran:

"Return instantly France and Germany at war England certain to declare on Germany to-night Tag."

"Oh, Bill!" breathed Dolly, rising.

For a moment the two stood looking at one another. Then Courtier broke into a light laugh and crossed to the balustrade.

"Quick work," he said, knocking out his pipe on the rail. "And now don't talk for a minute, Doll. I want to think."

Leisurely he began to fill his pipe, and a moment later he fell a-whistling the refrain whose words they had been singing together. Abstractedly, though, for his brain was working furiously. Dolly Loan never took her eyes from his face. He did not look at her at all.

When the pipe was filled, he pressed down the tobacco, folded his pouch very carefully, and slipped them both into his pocket. Then he turned to the girl.

" I shall go straight for Edinburgh," he said. " Will you lend me your car ? "

" Of course. In fact, I'll come——"

" No. You'll stop here. Your chauffeur can come to take the car back. If I can't get a train at Edinburgh, perhaps I'll go for Carlisle. And now may I tell him to get her ready ? "

" Yes."

He passed quickly across the verandah to the room behind. At the wide-open door he turned.

" So it's come at last," he said, with a great light in his eyes. " ' Made in Germany.' 'M ! They make a lot of rotten things there ; we'll see how they can make war." Here his glance met Dolly's. " Good little girl," he said gently. " I'll write to you on a drum. Don't go away. I'm coming back to say ' Good-bye.' "

Dolly stared after him. Then she sat down in a chair and tried to think. She read the telegram over again dazedly. All the time the lilt of the music-hall ditty danced in her head mercilessly. War ! Yes, of course. What of it ? There had been wars before. The war in South Africa, for instance. But this . . . not twenty hours from England. Perhaps not ten. And all among the places she knew. Rheims, Strassburg with its red roofs and its old cathedral, the one spire looking like some lonely twin ; Cologne and the curling Rhine ; Frankfurt with its proud Palm Garden ; Dresden, the dear sleepy place where she had been at school. Her thoughts leaped for a second to the cool house in Lessing Strasse, with the plane-trees along its front and the old stone fountain that never played.

War! Still, it was not the thought of the 'area' that wrought the catch in her breath. Familiarity with places made it exciting, rather. But . . . Courtier was her very good friend. He was—well, he was Bill—Bill Courtier. No, Bill. That was all; but it was a great deal. As for Tag . . .

She got up and leaned over the balustrade. 'So what do we care? Time and place do not count.' The mockery of the words blazed at her, while at the back of her brain the haunting number ramped tirelessly on. There rose and fell the sunlit landscape, calm and exquisite as ever, but not for her eyes, so black the magic of the flimsy form in her hand. Looking now, she found the sunlight brazen, the smile upon the face of Nature grim, the almighty peace of the place nought but a giant satire, bitter indeed. 'So what do we care? Time and place——'

"I like that man," said Courtier, stepping out of the smoking-room. "He uses his brain. Most servants would have started packing my trunk. He's pushed the things I'll want into a suit-case, and says he'll send the other luggage after me. Your chauffeur's a good sort, too. Simply spreading himself. As soon as he's ready, he's going to sound the horn. I've just about got time for a cigarette. One for you, Doll?"

Mechanically she took a cigarette from his case. When he had lighted it for her:

"Sorry I shan't see the others. Just show them the wire, and they'll understand."

She nodded.

"Don't look so serious, Doll," he said suddenly. "It's only going to be another dream, you know, and when it's all over we'll come back here and wake up."

She raised her eyes at that and swung round. So they stood facing one another.

"I can't laugh, Bill," she said quickly. "I don't believe you've appreciated it yet. Perhaps you never will. Soldiers are like that. Besides, it's—it's their show now. Only lookers-on. . . . And I think I've appreciated it—realized what it means—all at once. And it's awful."

For a moment Courtier looked at her—the thick dark hair parted above the left temple, sweeping over the right, and rippling as no *coiffeur* could ordain, the steady brown eyes strangely solemn for once, the lips that were made for laughter unnaturally set ; below them, the lift of the chin, very dainty, and the soft white throat standing for tenderness. Then he threw his cigarette away and laid his hands upon her shoulders.

"Doll," he said.

Her lips formed the word "Yes ? "

"Doll, I'm going away for a while, but I'm coming back, and then we'll have better times than ever we had before. And—oh, Doll, I love you better than anything in the world. I always have. And I want to marry you when I come back . . ." He stopped, dropped a hand from her shoulder, and turned to gaze at the woods and the glen and the sinking sun. And a great smile swept into his face, a boy's smile, the smile of a child. "There ! " he went on triumphantly. "I've wanted to say that for years, and somehow I never could."

He seemed to speak with pride, almost with defiance.

The Hon. Dolly Loan never moved.

"You've—wanted—to say that—for years," she repeated dully. "You've wanted . . . Oh, why ——" She checked the wail in her voice suddenly. "Bill, you mustn't speak to me like this. Not now, or ever again. You see, I just can't, Bill. Not marry

you. I'm awfully fond of you, but . . . It's difficult
to explain. I'll tell you one day, and then you'll—
you'll understand. I mean—oh, Bill, I'm so sorry."

The words came with a rush at the last, anyhow.

Courtier stood motionless, staring into the distance,
his one hand still on her shoulder. Then he took a
deep breath. She could feel him pull himself together.
A moment later the hand slipped away, and he turned.

" That's all right, Doll," he said simply.

" Oh, Bill."

He laughed easily.

" Any way," he said, smiling. " I'll write to her.
On a drum, too."

The gruff hoot of a motor-horn came from the other
side of the lodge.

Very gently he raised her slim right hand to his lips,
smiled and nodded. Then for a moment he held the
fingers tight.

" Good-bye, dear," he said.

As he turned :

" Bill," said Dolly.

" Yes, dear ? "

" I'd like you to kiss me, all—all the same."

He would have kissed her cheek, but she put up her
warm red mouth and slid her arms round his neck.

* * * * *

The stuff had to be fetched somehow. That was
clear. And there it was, waiting at Lence, twenty-
three kilometres away. Nitro-glycerine.

" Let me go, sir," said Courtier. " It's an officer's
job, and you can't ask a raw chauffeur chap to take
it on. Not that he wouldn't, every time. But . . .
And Ewing'll come with me. He's a better mechanic
than I am, supposing she did break down."

" My two Englishmen ? " said the French general.
" How should I spare you ? "

" For less than an hour and a half, sir."

" I would have sent Pierrefort," muttered the other.

But the daring driver lay face upwards in the white
moonlight, with one foot twisted under him and his
eyes wide and staring as never in life. Beside him
sprawled the ruin of a great automobile.

" We ought to go now, sir, if we're to get it to-night,"
said Ewing.

For a moment the general stared at the two young
Guardsmen who were attached to his staff. Then :

" After all," he said slowly, " it is Englishmen's
work. Listen. I am not sending you. Only I give
you the leave to go. But I bid you return safe. That
I command. Take Librand with you. He is a good
soldier, though he does not know the front from the
back of a car."

" Thank you, sir."

The Frenchman rose to his feet suddenly.

" After all, the good God is in heaven," he said.

*   *   *   *   *

The forty-horse-power Clement had seen better days
—merrier ones, any way. Once she had carried a great
touring body, rich in leather upholstery, its panels
gleaming, the sheen of its fittings matchless—a dream,
all blue and silver. Beauty had been handed out of
her doors. Gallantry had sat at her wheel. Laughter
and dainty voices had floated from under her hood.
More than once love had been made above her floor-
boards. At Biarritz she had been the car of her year.
So, for a while, she had flashed through life handsomely. To be exact, for some thirty months, and
miles without number. Thereafter she had been
purchased by a garage at Lyons. She had been given

a landaulette body, built for another car, and the syndicate hired her out, as and when she was wanted. That was often. Never silent, she had become noisy, but she still went like the wind. Sometimes she was greedy, but so long as they gave her her fill, she never went wrong. So, for two years. Then one day they put a van-body on her, and she went to the war.

" What about head-lights ? " said Courtier suddenly. " The moon——"

" May be able to do without them coming back," said Ewing, wiping his hands on a rag, " but going— no ; must have them. As for their attracting attention, they'd hear us, any way."

Courtier laughed.

" Right-o," he said. " And here's Librand." The man came up panting. " Sergeant," he added in French, " give me a hand with this petrol. No. Go and get some water in a can. We must give the old lady a drink."

Ten minutes later they swung out of a side-street on to the Lence road. Somewhere a clock struck the half-hour. Half-past three. Three minutes later they were clear of the little town.

If the French could hold Otto, as they were holding Lence, for another three days, all would be very well, and the allied forces would be up to and in possession of the twenty odd kilometres of country that lay between. At the moment the enemy were attacking both the towns vigorously, for they were seemingly more than reluctant to advance between them—though there was nothing to bar their way—till one of the two, at any rate, had been reduced. For the time being, therefore, the road from Otto to Lence was no man's land. In three days it would probably be in the hands of the Allies, any way. Till then there was nothing to prevent the enemy taking it, if they pleased. According to aviators, they had not pleased up to six the evening before—nine and a half hours ago.

It was awfully cold. That was thanks to the pace at which they were going, as much as the night air. Courtier was ' putting her along ' properly. By his side sat Ewing, his hands thrust deep into his great-coat pockets, his eyes fixed, like the other's, on the broad white ribbon of road ahead of them, straight for miles at a stretch. The sergeant sat on the foot-board, with his feet on the step. A strap had been buckled across to keep him in.

" Isn't it glorious ? " said Courtier suddenly. " Just the night for a joy ride. Wish I'd got some thicker gloves, though."

" Joy ride ? " said Ewing indignantly. " This is, without exception, the most horrifying experience I've ever had. I know you're supposed to be a good driver, but why—why exploit the backlash ? Why emulate the Gadarene swine ? For Heaven's sake, steady her for the corner, man."

" No corner, old chap. It's the shadow that cottage is throwing. See ? " They flashed by the white-washed walls. " And now don't make me laugh, Tag. We've got to get there, you know."

" That," said Ewing, " is exactly my point. Be-sides, it's all very well, but I came out here to be shot, not to have my neck broken. This isn't Coney Island, you know." Here they encountered a culvert, and the van leaped bodily into the air. " I warn you," he added severely, " that if you do that again, you may consider yourself under arrest."

He stopped. Courtier was shaking with a great silent laughter. Consciously or unconsciously his usually serious brother-officer was in form this night of the nights. At length :

" Oh, Tag," he gasped, " you are a fool. How's the sergeant getting on ? "

" Died of fright at the culvert," said Ewing gravely, " about three miles back. Thank Heaven, here's a bit of a rise."

They flew by cross roads and on up the long, slight gradient. It could not be called a hill.

" That's the main road to Very," said Courtier with a jerk of his head to the right. " I remember this part well. It's flat again in a moment for about half a mile. Road runs through a wood. There you are. Then there's a fairly steep hill with another wood at the top. There's a corner there, I know."

" Where ? " said Ewing.

" On top of the hill in the wood. Not this one. We're just about half way. Hullo ! "

The thud of a big gun sounded in the distance. For the first time Librand shifted in his place on the foot-board.

" Having another smack at Lence," said Ewing. " Or was it behind us ? "

Courtier shook his head.

" No. It was Lence way all right. Listen."

Two more thuds followed each other in quick succession. There was no doubt about the direction this time. The attack upon Lence had been renewed.

And now they were out of the wood and taking the hill with a rush. Half way up, Courtier slipped into third, and the van roared out of the moonlight and into the next wood grandly. The land lay exactly as he had said. As they rounded the corner, Librand shifted again and peered into the darkness beyond the scudding beam of the head-lights. He was looking a little towards the left.

" What is it, sergeant ? " said Ewing, speaking in French. " You're the wrong side for the Germans, you know."

" Ah ! My lieutenant will forgive me. I was not thinking of the enemy. There is somewhere here a sudden gap in the wood. In daylight one stands there and looks away down into the valley. There one can see a little farm. I have seen it so very often, but not now for thirty-seven years. It is the farm where I was born, my lieutenant," he added naïvely, as if everyone was born at some farm or other.

" Thirty-seven years, and now it's too dark," said Ewing. " What a shame ! You must look out for it on the way back." And he pointed to the grey look in the sky over towards the east.

" But no, my lieutenant," said the Frenchman. " It will be too dark still. Besides, I shall be on the other side then. It does not matter at all. I shall see it again one day. Two fortune-tellers have said this. I am to die there, where I was born. It is a good thing to know," he added contentedly.

For a moment there was silence. Then ᴉ

" So ? " said Courtier. " Thanks very much. I know you're not superstitious, Tag, but I rather think we look out for this precious wood on the way home."

" I hope you will," said Ewing. " That corner's just the place for a nasty skid."

The van fled on over the broad highway. Here, for a quarter of a mile, tall silent poplars lined it on either side, their shadows ribbing the pale road with darkness ; and here low, thick-growing bushes marked the edge of a stream that ran by their side for a while, and then curled capriciously off under their feet, so that the way rose and fell to suffer its passage. Now they swept through a village, whitewashed houses—deserted

—on either side. In the short street the steady mutter of the engine swelled into a snarl, that shore through the silence fiercely. By rights, dogs should have bayed the matter furiously. . . . And so again out into open country. Under the still moonlight the landscape slumbered very peacefully—untroubled slumber that even the dull thunder ahead could not ruffle.

Five miles later they slowed down for the Lence outposts.

As they ran into the town !

"Twenty-one minutes to the tick," said Ewing, looking at his watch. "And not a sight of a German all the way. If we don't strike the blighters on the way home, I shall ask for my money back."

* * * * *

By the time the van had been laden with its grim cargo, cock-crow had come and gone. A faint grey light had stolen into the sky, spoiling the moon of her splendour, lending to ways and buildings a look of dull reality in place of the illusive livery of black and silver they had worn before. Men and things were invested with a stern workmanlike air. Which was as it should be, for there was vital work to be done, and done quickly.

Smoking easily, Courtier and Ewing stood talking with three French officers, the better for the hot *café-au-lait* with which they had just been served. On the other side of the van, Librand was exchanging experiences with two or three comrades-in-arms. From time to time he applied a can of hot coffee to his lips with evident relish. Under the supervision of a sergeant, French soldiers were putting the finishing touches to their bestowal of the explosive. It was not the sort of stuff to have slipping and sliding about at every bend of the road.

At length the packing was over, two soldiers scrambled out of the van, and the sergeant closed and fastened the high back doors, lifting the crossbar into its place and thrusting the pin through the staple. The Clement was ready for the run of her life.

"The carriage waits," said Courtier, throwing away his cigarette. "Come along, brother, or we shall miss the curtain-raiser."

He spoke in French, and the three officers laughed wonderingly.

"You are brave fellows," said one of them. "It is not everyone who would escort Madame Nitro-Glycerine to the theatre."

"She is no worse than other women," said Courtier. "You take a girl to the theatre. If she does not like the play, she blows you up."

The next minute he had started the engine.

As he was settling himself at the wheel:

"Better let me have your revolver," said Ewing. "You wouldn't be able to use it any way."

With a sigh the other handed over the weapon.

"Now I really feel like a chauffeur," he said disgustedly. "Is the sergeant all right?"

"Yes."

Crying their good wishes, the French officers stepped back from the van. Courtier let in the clutch, and she began to move.

"*Au revoir. Bon voyage*," called the Frenchmen.

"*Au revoir.* So long," came the reply.

Then they swung out of the sentried yard into the cobbled street.

The firing had slackened a little. At one time, whilst they were waiting at Lence, it had been very heavy. The town's reply seemed to have silenced one of the enemy's guns, but, beyond a shattered searchlight, the defenders had suffered little or no damage.

"What's the time?" said Courtier suddenly.

"Five-and-twenty to five," said Ewing. "I didn't think the loading would have taken so long."

"Nor did I. However." They turned out of the market-place on to the Otto road. "S'pose I mustn't go all out now," he added gloomily. "Not with this soothing syrup on board."

"As long as you've got her in hand," said Ewing. Then : "Did you mark where the culverts came?"

The other nodded.

"Three, weren't there?" he said.

"Yes. I'll tell you when to stand by."

Two minutes later they were clear of the outposts.

Like the little town behind them, the road and the countryside had taken on a look of soberness. With the grey light of dawn, the shadows had fled. Fantasy, with all her shining train, was gone westward. The brave show the moonlight had made was over. The world about them seemed to be cleared for action.

As before, the sergeant sat on the foot-board at Ewing's feet. After a while he plucked a great revolver from under his coat, and held it ready for use in his right hand. With the left he laid hold of the strap that should keep him in. Above him Ewing sat motionless, his hands deep as ever in the great pockets of his coat, his eyes never lifting from the pale road tapering into the distance. Courtier leaned comfortably against the short back of the seat, his chin lifted a little, smiling easily into the rush of the air that swept over the lower half of the wind-screen steadily, like a long, cold wave. He might have been driving up from Newmarket after a good day.

So presently they came to the silent village, and

I

the stream flowing beyond it, and the long ranks of poplars lining the way.

As they dropped into the wood, Ewing made as though he would draw his hands out of his pockets. Then he changed his mind suddenly, and let them stay where they were. A smile at his own impulse flickered over his face. But Courtier had seen the movement with the tail of his eye and laughed outright.

"'Just the place for a nasty skid,'" he quoted amusedly, taking out the clutch.

And it would have been, if the road had been at all greasy. All the same, they rounded the corner carefully—to see the German uniforms seventy paces away.

Infantry, about a hundred strong, marching towards them in a dense mass : all on the slope of the steep hill midway between the upper and the lower wood.

At one and the same moment they saw and were seen. For a fraction of a second they stared—the one at the other. Then, with a cry, Courtier let in the clutch and pressed the accelerator right down. . . .

It was their only chance, and slight as a hair at that. Death in front of them, death swaying behind them. . . . Put an odd bullet into the body of the van and all in Lence and Otto alike would know the fate of their nitro-glycerine.

The Clement leaped forward like a thing gone mad. The grey mass had halted, and an officer was shouting and fumbling at his holster. Ewing fired with his left hand, resting his wrist on the wind-screen ; his right arm lay across Courtier's shoulder. He would cover him on that side if he could. The sergeant was on his feet firing.

As the officer fell, the mass shivered and broke—

too late. Into and over the grey uniforms—that was the way of the van. Literally she ploughed her way through, heaving, rocking, leaping, hurling herself along, hoarse screams of agony and terror ringing her round. Courtier clung to the wheel desperately, helping her all he could. Ewing had lost his balance and lay on his side on the seat, his right arm stretched behind Courtier, blazing away over the Stepney wheel. The sergeant was leaning out at the side, wielding his empty revolver, roaring like one possessed, roaring, roaring. . . . Then a German officer fired full in his face, and he pitched forward heavily on to the broad highway.

It was the only shot the enemy fired. The miracle had happened, and they had come through—they and the death swaying behind them.

" Is she all right ? " said Ewing, meaning the van. The other nodded.

" I think so. Don't ask me why ? Thank God, it was foot," he added jerkily. " I couldn't have done it to horses to save my life."

" Bet there are more behind," said Ewing laconically, trying desperately to reload. The pace was against him. " Those chaps had come from Very."

" And turned at the cross roads ? "

" Exactly."

" We'll be there in a second now. If the others aren't up——"

" We can go as we please for the rest of the way to Otto. If they are . . ."

" She'll never stand it again," said Courtier. " The steering'll go. Besides—— That's done it," he added quietly.

They were out of the lower wood by now, and there, at the foot of the rise, was the head of a German column wheeling out of the road on the left-hand side —the road to Very. Only the head of a column, a bare handful of men—so far. But behind, beyond, blocking the road to Otto, utterly cutting them off, was drawn up a squadron of Uhlans, waiting to see the infantry over the cross roads.

"Straight at 'em," said Ewing. "And when we're well in, if they haven't plugged the nitro stuff, I'll do it mys—— No!" he roared suddenly. "No! Take the road on the right, Bill. Take the road on the right."

"I'll try," yelled Courtier. "She'll break in half, but I'll try."

It is a cool-headed fellow who will stand fast and take deliberate aim, full in the path of an onrushing car. Had they but known of the death that lay in the van, so easy to loose, it might have been otherwise. The few men that had wheeled stared and shrank back dazedly. Others, unseeing, came on out of the Very road, treading upon the heels of those in front. In a moment all was confusion. Some of them turned to fly, one tripped and fell in the road. And, behind, the front rank of the Uhlans shouted and raved impotently.

The Clement tore down the slope desperately. If she could take the corner, her way was fairly clear. The stumbling, shouting, frantic mass of men was writhing on the very cross of the roads. On two sides their comrades and the Uhlans blocked their chance of safety. A few had started to rush down the road on the right.

As they reached the cross roads, Courtier jammed on the foot-brake and wrenched the wheel round. With a rending noise of tires, the great body swung over, pivoting, as it were, on the front wheels and tilting terribly. Half way about, her side met the jam of men like a wall, flying. She just shuddered and swung on, sweeping the broken bodies against the whole behind, and then breaking them in turn. . . . Somebody fired.

It was all the work of a moment, for in the midst of her swing, Courtier straightened her up and let her go. As she leaped forward like a slipped hound, an officer, screaming in German, thrust out his left hand and fired point-blank over the near-side wing.

Courtier shook the blood out of his eyes and glanced at the seat by his side. Ewing was still there.

" My aunt ! " he said. Then : " I thought you were gone that time. I held myself in by the wheel."

" Put her along," said Ewing thickly.

Then the road curled, and they pelted into the shelter of a belt of trees. They were through.

Nevertheless, they fled along swiftly, watching and waiting for an odd road on the left. So they should come to Otto, or on to the Otto road. . . .

The level-crossing they struck after about seven kilometres came as a glad surprise. No trains running, they had forgotten the line. And now it was only a matter of raising the tall bar—there was the windlass at hand—and pounding along the railway track to Otto. They were as good as home.

Courtier slowed down wearily, for the fiftieth time brushing the trickle of blood away from his eyebrows. A bullet had whipped across his forehead, just cutting the skin.

As the van came to a standstill :

" Oh, Tag," he said, merriment trying to struggle into his voice, " what a life ! "

As if by way of answer, Ewing slid round sideways, with his chin on his chest. Just in time to catch him, Courtier realized with a shock why the screaming officer's bullet had not exploded the nitro-glycerine. . . .

He got him out and made him as comfortable as he could in the grass by the wayside. After a little he died quietly, as he had lived.

He spoke for a moment or two, just at the end— queer muttering words, with no brain behind them. "Doll . . . ." The other started ever so slightly. "Dolly girl . . . . always . . . . Love her long lashes and . . . . on the fifth, Doll. So we'll be at Yait together, and then . . . . I promise. Not even Bill, till the . . . ." He sighed contentedly. Then, " A marriage has been arran——"

The poor voice faded. There was a sharp struggle for breath, blood fighting with air in the lungs desperately. Courtier raised him a little, and the blood sank back beaten. But the effort had been too much. A moment later he sighed very wearily, settled his head in the crook of the other's arm, and just slipped out.

*   *   *   *   *

Fifty minutes later the Clement, her head-lights smashed and bloody, her wings stained and buckled, blood and hair on her steps and wheels and dumb irons, slowed down between the low platforms of Otto's railway station. And Courtier sat at her wheel listlessly, a dirty handkerchief bound about his forehead, and an old and stricken look in his strong young face. Behind him, the body of Ewing, which had shifted helplessly with every jolt of the van, came to rest easily, with its white face pressed against the packing of the carefully stowed explosive.

BOOK II

HOW OTHERS LEFT THE COURTS
ONLY TO RETURN

CHAPTER I

A BÉBÉ IN ARMS

"IT'S going to be priceless," said Daphne, her white arms stretched along the back of the sofa.

From the opposite side of the fireplace her husband regarded her. Then he turned to me.

"D'you hear that ? " he said.

"I know," said I. "I can't help it."

"But she's actually looking forward. She finds pleasure in anticipation."

"I know," said I. "It's painful."

"Painful ? " said Berry. "It's indecent. I'm not sure I oughtn't to forbid the banns."

"I wish you would," said I. "I don't want to be best man. If it goes on as it's begun, I shall be about thirty pounds down before we've finished. That's tips and taxis alone."

"And then there's the blackmail."

"I know," I said gloomily.

Daphne picked up an evening paper. Then :

"Listen to this," she said. " ' One of the prettiest weddings of the year will take place on Thursday the 29th, when Mr. Peter Lileigh will wed Lady Daffodil Malmorey at St. James's, Piccadilly. The bride-to-be is the youngest of the three beautiful daughters of——' "

"That decides me," said Berry. "Next Sunday I shall forbid the banns in clear, bell-like tones. Let the Press be informed."

" Why shouldn't they be married ? " said Jill, from her perch on the sofa's broad arm. " I think it's sweet of them."

" There you are," said Berry. " Thinks it sweet. She'll be wanting to do it next. So much for the force of example." He turned to the grey-eyed maiden. " My dear, I warn you that, if any man has the audacity to ask me for your little hand, I shall push his face."

Jill knitted her brows.

" I hope you won't," she said. " But then "—with a quick smile—" he might forget to ask you, mightn't he ? "

" Rude child ! " said my brother-in-law. " Now you shan't have the mechanical frog in your bath to-night. Is that nurse calling ? "

" I think I'm going to have a cold," said Daphne. Berry turned to me.

" Ring up Harley Street," he said. " And tell William to have some straw put down outside the house the first thing in the morning."

" Any time to-morrow will do," said his wife. " I've got to be at the dressmaker's at eleven, and I promised to lunch with Helena Rush."

" Jade ! " said Berry. " Behold the horrid result of matrimony. A woman mocks her lord." Here a footman entered with the drinks. " Ah, well. For me there is always the schnapps (Low German). I will immerse my misery in alcoholism (Pekingese)." He rose. " Beverage, Jonah ? "

" One of the small ones," said that worthy.

" Small ones," said Berry contemptuously. " If I gave you what I call a small one, you'd think it was lemonade. You fishing crowd. For myself, as a matter of fact, I'm not really drinking at all nowadays."

Jonah sat up.

" If you ate and drank, and talked a little less——"
he began.

" Talking of golf," said Daphne, " what do you
think I picked up this morning ? "

" I know," said Berry ; " a taxi. I did, too. I
wonder who they belong to."

" Idiot ! On the links."

" Probably a ball," said I. " Other than your own,
if I know you."

" A gold watch," said Daphne.

" Gent's gold timepiece ? " said her husband.

" Lady's," said my sister. " Such a pretty one,
with a blue enamel back and a diamond in the middle."

" Jewelled in one hole," said Berry. " How much
did you get on it ? "

" It's with the secretary. But it's given me an
idea. Daffodil's got four wrist-watches, but she's
always wanted one to—to pin on. You and I can
give her one like this—on a brooch."

" You seem to forget I'm going to forbid the banns."

" Don't forbid the wrong ones," said I. " They give
out stacks sometimes."

" Trust me," said Berry. " ' A tall, well-dressed
man, whose features proclaimed him to be one of the
aristocracy, rose and in clear, bell-like tones (what
did I say ?) said, " I forbid the last banns but two." ' "

Daphne sighed.

" Well, well," she said. " I think we'll buy one all
the same. If Daffodil doesn't have it, it'll do for
Jilly, won't it, dear ? "

The shot went home. Berry glared at his wife. Then :

" You made me love you," he said defiantly. " I
didn't want to do it."

Daphne blew him a kiss.

"Have another drink, old chap," said I.

Berry emptied his glass and handed it to me.

"At least," he said, "I have one friend left."

"As a matter of fact, he's not drinking at all nowadays," said Jonah.

       *   *   *

Tye Gordon lies close in a deep park in one of the south-west counties of England. Who knows no more than its whereabouts might search for a month and never find it, unless he were told the way. In summer-time especially. Then, most of all, the rolling country keeps the old place secret, wrapping it about with the greenwood, folding it in her fresh young arms, so that even the sudden storms of summer deal with Tye gently perforce, and the spent wind buffets its ancient gables with feeble fury.

I and the car found it, but then I had been shown the trick of the ways. Even so, it was past three when I stopped at the grey lodge-gates. I had hoped to be there by two. I was on business bent. Pleasant business, perhaps, but still business. In fact, I was bound for Tye Gordon in my capacity of best man.

A week before, Peter had started the hare. It seemed that years ago Daffodil had seen Tye Gordon. She had been staying with friends somewhere in the county—a child of twelve then—and had been driven over to lunch with an old, old gentleman whose name she could not remember. He had been kind to her and her fellows, shown them the beauties of the old house, and let them play through its chambers and run happily in the sun-shot park. That was ten years ago. Long ago the friends had left England, and there had been nothing to take her again to the neighbourhood. But she had never forgotten Tye. And often thereafter her memory would leap back to the summer afternoon, the low, grey building and the fair lawns, the curling avenue and the bracken springing under the oaks, and everywhere the great belt of woodland ringing the place about, keeping it out of the world, saving it from the march of time. More than once Peter had heard her speak of the spot with rapture, wondering if she would ever see it again. And now, quite by chance, it had come to his ears that a place of that name was coming into the market.

" No ? " said I.

" Fact," said Peter. He mentioned the name of a firm. " It's in their hands. Get an order-to-view, old chap, and have a look at it. I'd go myself, only I don't want Daffodil to know."

I stared at him.

" You don't mean——" I began.

" Yes, I do," he said, grinning. " If it's all right, and the owners don't want the earth, I'll buy it at once and give her the title-deeds for a wedding present."

I always said Peter had more money than brains. However.

" We can't push the whole deal through in ten days," said I. " Besides, it mayn't even be the right place, or, if it is, it may have changed altogether."

" The place she drove over from was called Mills Brayling, so if it's near there, you'll know it's the right place. As to whether it's changed, you know a nice place when you see one."

" Yes, but I'm not going to take the responsibility of landing you for several thousand pounds, when you've never even set eyes——"

" Well, get the order and have a look at the place. There's a good fellow. If you do, I'll let you kiss Daffodil in the vestry."

" That's no consideration," said I. " I'm going to do that, any way. Still, if you really think she'll appreciate——"

There was no doubt about it being the right place. I had passed through Mills Brayling an hour and a quarter before. I looked at the lodge. White curtains in the windows showed that it was inhabited. But the gates were padlocked. Clearly I must leave the car where it was.

I stopped the engine and sat for a moment looking up the avenue. It promised well, certainly. And it did curl. Of course, if the park and the old house really were as exquisite as Daffodil painted them, it would be nice to . . . Then I thought of the responsibility and shook my head. A pity. I should have loved to see her eyes light. . . .

" They won't let you in," said a voice.

" What'll you bet me ? " said I.

" Unless you've got an order."

I swung round and looked at the speaker. Then I took off my cap. A slim girl in a fawn-coloured dress leaning against a five-barred gate, her elbows behind her on the top bar, one slight foot on the ground, the other above it on one of the lower bars. Her attitude was easy, reposeful. The open neck of the dress showed her white throat, and under a *bébé* bonnet I could see the thick brown hair. A nose ever so slightly tilted, and grave brown eyes. So grave. But the mouth was merry and told of gaiety in the air.

" All fawn," said I. " Down to her little shoes. I never realized what a becoming colour it was. But it's rather elusive. You might be a battleship going into action. No one would see you at forty paces ; you'd just melt into the road. I suppose that's why I missed——"

" Oh, no. You were craning your neck to get a glimpse of Tye. What do you know of the old place ? "

" Nothing, Bébé. That's why I'm here."

" Well, they won't——"

" Complete with order."

She sighed. Then :

" Years ago," she said, " a girl told me of Tye Gordon. And ever since she told me, I've wanted to see it. She never even said where it was, but the name stuck in my head, and I saw it last night, marked on a local map, when we were looking out the way to Mills Brayling. And now I've given up a party and walked two miles to be told I haven't an order-to-view. And I knew that when I started. However."

" A girl told her of Tye," I said musingly.

She nodded.

" The best friend I have. And I'm losing her next week."

Daffodil.

" Is she going to be married ? " I said carelessly, getting out of the car.

" Yes "—moodily.

" I was afraid so from your tone. These marriages."

" Run along in with your order," she said suddenly. " I'll look after your car. The others aren't picking me up at Pell Corner till five o'clock, so I've nothing to do."

I gave her a look. After a long moment the brown eyes fell.

" Do I look that sort of man ? " I said stiffly.

" No." She spoke so low that I could hardly hear her.

" Then why——"

" I beg your pardon," she said simply.

I handed her the order with a grave smile.

" I have come far," I said, " and it is important that I should see Tye to-day. That is my excuse for asking if I may accompany you."

Her eyes flashed.

" Why whip me ? " she said. " I've said I'm sorry."

For a moment we stood facing each other. Then I

" Curtain," said I. " Well, that's a jolly good scene. If the second act's half as good. . . ."

She broke into reluctant laughter. The situation was saved.

I took off my coat and flung it into the car. To-gether we walked to the door of the lodge. The keeper, who admitted us, promised to watch the car, and a minute later we were walking down the avenue.

It was the first real summer's day we'd had. Right at the end of May. Up to now the weather had been unpleasantly cold. The country was looking wonderful.

" So she's to be married next week," said I ; " your friend."

The girl nodded.

" Shall you attend the obsequies ? "

" As bridesmaid. The only one, too. Oh ! " She caught at my arm. " Isn't that lovely ? ".

It was. At a bend of the avenue the house had come into view. It stood fair on the slope of a hill, long and low, its grey stone mellowed by many a summer sun, wistaria drooping about its lattices, a broad flagged terrace running along its front. From the terrace wide steps of living turf led to a great greensward, which stretched on one side to the avenue and on the other to the fringe of the park itself. The timber was a great glory, oaks and elms and beeches of grave antiquity. On the sward itself towered a magnificent cedar. In the distance, rising and falling, the line of the famous woods stood up against the sky. The afternoon sun was striking the old place slantwise, making the windows flame and the trees fling long shadows across the grass.

" Glorious ! " I exclaimed. " I wonder which room Queen Elizabeth had."

" What a shame ! " she said, laughing. " It's much too sweet to make fun of. Just faery."

" Well kept, too. That sward's perfect. And look at those grass steps."

" The practical man," said Bébé. " I wonder where they keep the lawn-mower."

" Not at all," said I. " Gardeners came in long before Tye Gordon was raised. What about ' Richard Two,' where the gardener says, ' Go, bind thou up yon dangling apricocks, which, like——' " I hesitated.

" Go on."

" ' Unruly children,' " said I. " You would have it, wouldn't you, Bébé ? "

She looked at me critically. Then :

" Your hair's very untidy," she said.

" I know. But then the pleasure of meeting you was unexpected. Besides, you can't talk. Your eyes are all over the place."

" You know you're an impossible person," she said, smiling.

" On the contrary," said I, " I am extremely probable. Put your money on little Archibald. And now let's go to the house. Perhaps the caretaker will lend me a comb."

The entrance lay at the west side of the building. Here the avenue led to a wide paved court, from which a flight of handsome stone stairs rose to the front door. About the balustrade sat pigeons, sleeking themselves in the hot sun. But for them the place was deserted. For a minute we stood watching them. Then came the quick barking of a dog and a moment later a man's deep voice.

Round the corner of the house stepped a coach-man, a Bedlington at his heels. A real coachman, spruce in his undress livery and bright jack boots, placid, pink-faced, well-liking. He welcomed us re-spectfully, glanced at the order and asked us to excuse him while he went back to the house. Then he would admit us by the front door. A minute or two later there was the noise of drawn bolts, and the door creaked on it hinges. Slowly we ascended the steps . . .

It was at the far end of an echoing gallery that Bébé put a hand to her head and swayed. I was just in time to catch her before she fell.

" Faint, sir ? " said the coachman quickly.

" Looks like it," said I. " We'd better take her outside. The air'll pull her round. D'you think you could find some cushions and bring them down to the lawn. I'll carry her down. And some water."

" Very good, sir. I'll set the front door open for you as I go. You can find your way, sir ? "

" Yes, thanks."

He hurried away, his boots clattering over the bare boards and down the great staircase. I followed with the girl in my arms. Half way across the hall she stirred and opened the grave eyes. Then she started and put a hand on my arm, as if she would sit up.

" It's all right, Bébé," said I. " Lie still."

She flung a bare arm across her eyes, turning her face to my shoulder. I saw the colour surge into the white face.

Under the shadow of the great cedar I set her down, but she was on her feet in an instant.

"I'm a fool," she said passionately. "A fool. But I'm all right now. I don't know when I've done such a silly——"

"If you don't sit down at once," I said, "I'll pick you up in my arms again."

"But I'm all——"

I picked her up again. She was so light.

"After all," I said encouragingly, "it's the right place for a Bébé, isn't it?"

"I'll sit down," she said with a half-laugh.

Once more I lowered her to the lawn. Then the coachman appeared, soft cushions and a great rug in his arms. Also he brought water.

The rug spread, she slipped on to it and sat sideways, the cushions piled under an elbow. She drank the water gratefully.

"Better?" said I.

She nodded. Then she turned to the coachman and thanked him charmingly. Again I filled her glass. Then:

"I think you should rest," said I. "If you are really better, I'm going to leave you alone for a little. Quite alone. If you call, I shall hear you. Otherwise I shall not come for a quarter of an hour."

Grave eyes thanked me, and the mouth smiled.

I turned to the coachman.

"I should like to see the stabling," I said.

When he had shown me the stables, I asked him of many things. All information he gave me readily. At the last:

"They won't sell me with the place, sir," he said sadly. "I only wish they would. I was born there, over the coach-house, forty-six years ago. Tye

Gordon's the only home I have. They'll have their cars, sir, them that takes the old place. I know that. But if, likin' the stables, they had some thought of keepin' an old trap for luggage or errands, and if you an' me lady didn't happen to have a man in view . . ."

His voice tailed off pathetically.

"If the price isn't too high," I said, "I think a friend of mine will buy the place. If he does, I shall advise him to take you into his service. The lady will also ask him. And I think he will do it."

"You're very good, sir."

I left him and passed round to the great lawn.

My lady lay at full length, the cushions behind her head. I came and stood at her feet.

"How is she now?" said I.

"Please don't talk about it. There's nothing the matter now. Will you help me up?"

She stretched out a slim hand, and I pulled her to her feet. Together we strolled over the sward.

"He's a good fellow," I said meditatively. "The coachman, I mean. Of course, I am, too, but ——"

"I think he's a dear," said Bébé. "The coachman, I mean. So attentive."

I stopped still. Then ।

"Shall I go and fetch him?" I said.

Bébé burst out laughing and slipped her arm through mine.

"That's better," said I. "And now, my dear, as to the house. Shall we have it or not? Of course the one we saw yesterday had four box-rooms, and the bicycle-shed was a dream, but the view from the servants' bathroom——"

"Was very poor. I know. But d'you think we

should get the piano into this drawing-room ? The door's very low-pitched, while the key——"

" You forget it's only a *bébé* grand, my love. And the what-not would go on the second landing wonderfully. I measured it whilst you were stepping the housemaid's sink. Besides, there's a lovely stillroom here, if you want to be quiet."

" That's nice," she said reflectively, stooping to regard a small foot, " and of course I like the sundial, but doesn't it seem rather a shame to turn the old place into a private asylum ? "

" I see your point," said I. " But then we're not certified. So no one would ever know. Besides, we might get all right again some day. However, if we don't take Tye, I expect Peter will."

" Peter ? "—surprisedly.

" Yes, for Daffodil. You know, your best friend. Only don't you say so. It's to be a complete surprise —if it comes off."

She slipped her arm out of mine and stared at me.

" What do you know of Daffodil ? " she said.

" Not very much, Bébé. I know she's the youngest of the three beautiful daughters of——"

" But how——"

I explained. I told her of my friendship with Peter and why I had come to Tye Gordon. I did not tell her that I was to be the best man.

When I had finished :

" I do hope they won't want too much for the old place," she said. " Dilly would love it so."

" If I told him you said that, I don't think Peter would worry about the price."

" Then do."

I pondered.

" I'm not sure I ought to," I said. " If Dilly's

your friend, Peter's mine, and I oughtn't to let him be rushed, just because he's in love."

" But he wants to give it her, doesn't he ? "

" Exactly. If somebody told him they'd heard she wanted Covent Garden or the Bakerloo Tube, he'd try to buy them before lunch. That's the state he's in."

" But they'd be much more expensive, and they're not half as nice."

" I'll tell you what I'll do," I said suddenly. " I'll have a talk with the best man. He's another old friend. Older than Peter. We were at school together. You'll meet him, of course. Such a good chap."

" Blow the best man," said Bébé. " What are you here for ? Give Peter my love and say that you and I——"

" Like Tye so much that if he doesn't take it, we shall."

" Think it's a priceless place and that—— Oh, just make him have it. You will, won't you ? "

She laid a hand on my shoulder and looked up at me with her great eyes. I gazed back steadily. Then :

" I don't know which I like best," I said, " your eyes or your mouth."

Bébé lowered the former and looked at the springing turf. " Of course," she said slowly, " if it's a question of commission——"

" But it isn't," said I. " It's a question of taste. Besides, I don't—er—take commissions."

" No ? "

" No, Bébé. Nor advantage either. And now I won't tease her any more. If I can do anything, and the price isn't wicked, Daffodil shall be mistress of Tye within the month."

She looked up quickly, an eager smile on her parted lips.

"Thank you," she said simply.

The fingers slipped from my shoulder. I took a deep breath. Then :

"End of the second act," said I.

She shot me a mischievous glance.

"How many acts are there ? " she said.

"Only three," said I.

We strolled back to the house. The coachman was in the forecourt, feeding the pigeons. I tipped him and made a note of his name. He was very grateful. Then we thanked him for his services and passed into the avenue. When the house disappeared, I turned to the girl.

"The third act," I said, "is very exciting. The scene is laid between here and the next bend. You can see the lodge from there."

"What a pity you'll have to play it alone ! " said Bébé.

I raised my eyebrows.

"I don't think the audience——" I began.

"Here and the next bend," murmured Bébé.

The next minute she was running like a hare. Frowning, I strove to remember that I was to be the best man. At the bend of the drive she stopped. I followed at a leisurely walk. As I came up :

"End of the third act," she said triumphantly.

I glanced down the avenue. The lodge was not in sight. Bébé was facing me. I took her by the shoulders and turned her round.

"Oh ! " she said.

"Yes," said I, "I made a mistake." I pointed over her shoulder. "That's the last bend. I'll carry you so far. You must be tired with your run."

She looked up out of my arms.

"You said there were only three acts," she said reproachfully.

"So there are," said I. "This is an epilogue."

At the end of the reach I set her down and looked at her.

"I know which I like best now," I said.

Thoughtfully she drew on a glove. Then:

"Which?" she said softly.

* * * * *

On Wednesday the twenty-eighth Peter purchased Tye Gordon.

At twelve o'clock on Thursday, complete with gardenia, I entered the room.

"Oh, he's dressed," said Jill.

"Yes," said Berry, "it's a new rule. Didn't you know? In future all bridegrooms' supporters must come clothed."

"Look at our new trouserings," said Jonah.

"They're not new," I said indignantly. "Speak for yourself. I don't have to buy a new outfit just because——"

"Going to take Peter to lunch, dear?" said Daphne.

I nodded.

"Just to steady him," said I. "Well, so long." I turned to the door. "Mind you're not late."

"You might meet us at the Circus," said Berry; "we shall be coming by Tube—number four lift. Don't leave your gloves at the A.B.C."

* * * * *

The bride looked very beautiful, but the bridesmaid's face was a picture, the eyes grave as ever. But the mouth . . . . After all . . .

CHAPTER II

CONTEMPT OF COURT

"DO you mean to tell me to-day's the twenty-ninth?" said Daphne.

"To be frank," said I, "I don't. To begin with, it's the thirtieth."

My sister sat back in her chair pondering, one white hand to her lips. Then :

"So it is," she said slowly. "How this month has gone! You know, I keep on thinking to-day's Sunday."

"Comes of changing your bath night," said her husband, pouring himself another glass of sherry. "After having it on Sundays all these years——"

"Bound to feel it, of course," said I. "At this time of life, I mean. I remember an old horsekeeper doing much the same thing. He used——"

Before I could catch it, the tangerine fell into Berry's finger-bowl, which was about equidistant from its owner and myself. Daphne and Jill squeaked with delight. Then :

"After that, the deluge," said my sister coolly.

"In the neck," said Jonah, from the other side of the table.

"Pardon me," said Berry, wiping the water out of his eyes. "Mostly in the left eye and ear. A certain amount inasmuch as, and the rest in blank. Highly dangerous. And me on the Grand Jury to-morrow."

"The marked decay of table manners," said I, smearing my chest with a napkin, "is as deplorable as it is manifest. I sat down to dinner in a shirt. Thanks to a loving sister's care, I shall arise in a compress. Death was due to heart failure, consequent upon a severe chill."

"Have some sherry wine, brother," said Berry sympathetically, pushing across the decanter. "If you approve, we'll have a whole bottle at your wake. Till then, let us ignore the rude behaviour. After all, the mockers are below the salted almonds."

"The incident then terminated," said Jonah.

"Jill and I are going in with you to-morrow," said Daphne. "Derry said he'd put us on the Bench for a little."

"These High Sheriffs," groaned her husband.

"I'm going in, any way," said I. "Jimmy Aylwin's the Judge's Marshal this time. He sent me a card asking me to roll up."

"I will not have this Court turned into a theatre," said Berry pompously. "The Bench isn't a stage. When you three and Derry and the Marshal get going, people'll think it's a Revue. Will the Victoria Girls be there?"

"I'm afraid not," said I, "but the Judge will. And what with the footmen——"

"To change the numbers. . . . Exactly. Well, don't come to me for bail if you're committed for Contempt of Court. That's all. You've never been over the gaol, have you?"

"I do hope I shall remember to say 'Rabbits' first to-morrow," said Jill suddenly.

We stared at her. Then:

"I suppose you must," said Berry. "Belgian hares wouldn't do, would they? Or French bustards,

or any little trifle like that ? It must be rabbits ? "

"Oh, yes, it must be rabbits," said Jill gravely.

"Dear, dear," said Berry.

"D'you think you could write it ? " said I.

"No, Boy, you've got to say it, or it doesn't count."

"Ah, well, that settles it," I sighed.

"Don't take any notice of the fools," said Daphne.
"What do you mean ' it doesn't count,' Jilly dear ? "

"Didn't I tell you ? " said Jill. "I heard it when
I was staying with the Scarlets. On the first day of
the month you have to say ' Rabbits.' If you say
it to me first, I have to give you a present, and if I
say it to you first, you have to give me a present.
It's just whichever says it first."

"I'm glad you told us," said Berry. "Otherwise
we should have been somewhat handicapped. I mean,
of course, one never knows. I might have quite
innocently chanced to say—er—' Rabbits.' Just like
that. ' Rabbits.' But it would have been a fluke.
It would have been because I had just observed in the
Sportsman that Kent were all out for twenty-seven,
or something like that. The odds are you'd have had
it all your own way."

"Well, you know now," said Jill. "And if I
remember to say it before you do, I want another
tennis-racket."

"Right you are, sweetheart. And should it first
occur to me to name the burrowing rodents, please
remember that I have long desired——"

He paused to select a piece of ginger. We waited
interestedly. At last :

"Go on," said Daphne. "The suspense is awful."

"A wherewithal," said her husband. "A really
good one."

Jill's grey eyes looked puzzled.

" A wherewithal ? " she said slowly. " Where does one get wherewithals ? "

" You might try the Stores," said I. " But they'd probably have to get it for you. Of course, there are so many different kinds." I turned to Berry. " For what purpose do you require the wherewithal, brother ? "

" I want the wherewithal to do penance for a wicked spouse," he said. " Things are come to a pretty pass when one has to humble one's own body to atone for the backsliding of those we love. But there you are." He looked across at his wife. " I suppose you know your name's going to be a hissing," he added.

" She'll be able to get the sort of wherewithal you want at the Stores," said Jonah. " In the Surgical Instruments Department."

Berry started.

" No, no," he said hurriedly. " In the Drapery. I was thinking of a hair shirt. So—er—appropriate."

* * * * *

The next morning I awoke to hear a servant drawing the blinds.

" What time is it, William ? " said I.

" A quarter past seven, sir," said the man, coming to the side of my bed. " And Mr. Pleydell's compliments, sir, and ' Rabbits.' "

" My compliments to Mr. Pleydell, and there's nothing doing, because he must say it himself."

" Very good, sir."

Whilst I was shaving an idea occurred to me. I opened my door and walked quickly to the bathroom Daphne and Jill use. There I stood listening. The lazy lap of water against the side of the bath told me that it was occupied. With a crafty smile I cleared my throat. Then :

" Jilly," I said anxiously.

" What's the matter, Boy ? " cried my victim, falling into the trap.

" Er—only—— "

" Rabbits," whispered Daphne over my shoulder, slipping a warm arm round my neck. " And it just serves you right, old chap, for trying to do Jilly down. Kiss me."

I obeyed in some dudgeon.

" You shall give me one of those old little Japanese cedars," she went on. " A nice gnarled one in a blue-and-white pot."

I groaned.

" They're awfully expensive," I began. " Surely there's some limit—— "

Suddenly, " O-o-oh ! " came from the bathroom. Followed the sound of troubled waters and the padding of bare feet on the floor. The next moment Jill was beating upon the door and crying :

" Rabbits, Boy, rabbits. I said it first."

My sister began to laugh softly. I took a deep breath. Then :

" What sort of a racket d'you want, dear ? " said I. " Tell me the worst."

After all, a racket couldn't cost much more than thirty shillings.

" Oh, Berry's going to give me the racket," cried Jill, audibly dancing with excitement. " I thought perhaps you'd give me a panorama camera."

" Don't hang back," said I. " Quite sure you wouldn't sooner have a gold-fitted dressing-case ? "

" I'll have that next month."

"Off Berry or Jonah, then," said I. "This 'Rabbits' stunt's a bit too thick for me. In future I shall clear out at the end of every month and——" Suddenly I thought of Berry and Jonah. My face cleared. "Any way," I added, "I'll fix the others all right. If I touch each of them for a fiver—that's fair enough—I'll get out about square."

The wariness with which, half an hour later, I entered the dining-room was worthy of a scout-master. But only the girls were there. I was in good time. All the same, I took the precaution of looking under the table. There was Jonah, reading the paper. We said the plural together. After some argument we agreed that it should be counted a dead heat. Berry remained. Not for long. Of course, I suppose I might have suspected something when William came and told me that the garage wanted me on the telephone. . . . Or, at any rate, when, after an idle question about the cars, the chauffeur asked me to hold the line. My sole consolation is that I was just able to eat all the mushrooms before Berry got back to the house.

An hour later we were all in the car, slipping along the curling ways to Brooch. It was a glorious day, this first of July. There had been rain in the night, but now the sky was cloudless, and the great sun blazed out of it, bleaching the wet brown roads, setting the stout hedgerows a-glitter, and lending to the countryside an air of health and gaiety and *joie de vivre* that got into the blood and made the heart light and merry.

We stopped a moment at Fell to drop Jonah, who was going fishing, and could not be persuaded to lose his pleasure by the promise of grave revelry at the Castle. Another twenty minutes, and we swept round the corner of Loose Thicket, to see Brooch lying, all warm and smiling, in the valley below.

Brooch is a place of memories, a cathedral city and a fair market town. Standards have floated from its castle's tower ; blood has run in its gutters. Kings' standards, men's blood. Great-hearted gentlemen have lain in its gaol, demoniac Roundheads have mouthed blasphemy in its cathedral, till the gaping clowns licked up the lust of havoc, splintered the precious panes they had been taught to wonder at, and battered down the glorious statuary Piety had set up. Savage days. Later a trembling mayor has mumbled the Riot Act in the market-place, the mob roaring before him, while two score of troopers sit steadily in the background, waiting grimly, rather contemptuously, but waiting. . . .

And now—Brooch is different now. Very peaceful, almost sleepy. Of course, it has its police sports once a year, and the city football team—colours, black and green—won two out of the three home matches last season ; but, on the whole, Brooch has become sleepy. Still, there remain its ways, its buildings, its memories. Memories of high things. The place has made history.

We set down Berry at the Castle that he might join his Fellows of the Grand Inquest, after which we slipped silently down to the old Close. We were for the Judge's lodgings. We left the car outside the old archway and strolled a while under the shadow of the great church. There was no one about, and, when the gorgeous coach lumbered into the Close and drew up before the low red building which houses His Majesty's Judges in Brooch, Time might have stepped back over a hundred years. Jill and Daphne watched as if fascinated. Even the appearance of Derry Bagot in blue and silver, with white silk stockings, did not shatter the illusion. The Sheriffs and the Chaplain entered the lodgings, while the footmen stalked to and fro in the sunshine, very pompous. The wigged coachman sat his hammercloth very solemnly. Presently the doors were opened again and a little procession came out. As before, the Sheriffs and the Chaplain, then the Judge in his scarlet, his Marshal following behind. Uncovered, the latter watched them into the coach. The door was shut, the footmen clambered stiffly to their perch, and the equipage rumbled away. My Lord was gone to be churched.

For a moment the Marshal stood watching the swaying vehicle. Then he pushed his hat to the back of his head, took out a cigarette-case and lighted a cigarette.

Sic transit.

I introduced Jimmy, and we took him up to the Castle in the car.

The subsequent appearance of Daphne and Jill upon the Bench caused quite a sensation—at any rate, amongst the junior members of the Bar. They certainly looked lovely, and Derry and the Marshal were most attentive. They proposed to stay about half an hour; but by the time I had heard two men plead guilty, one to the larceny of a garden-fork and the other to obtaining one shilling and eightpence of the moneys of somebody else by false pretences, I felt that I had got the hang of the thing, and retired to the cool of the corridor and the stone stairs.

It was rather dark in the corridor.

"I say, are you the Marshal?" said a voice.

"Well, not exactly," said I. "But I expect I'd do. Some people like me better."

A girl's laughter. Then:

"I rather want to see you," she said. "D'you think——"

" And I simply must see you," I said. " Let us assemble by the casement, shall not we ? There's one just round the corner, commanding an extensive view, and, incidentally, admitting such light as a blank wall three paces away allows of. You will observe from my diction that the dusty atmosphere of Legal Proceedings has already—— Oh, I forgot. Excuse me, but ' Rabbits.' "

My lady struggled with her merriment. Then :

" What do you know of ' Rabbits ' ? " she said.

" Well, thanks to them, so far I'm anything from ten to fifteen pounds down on the day. That's not counting this one."

" And do you think I'm going to give a present to a man I've never seen ? "

" I base my claim on custom," said I. " Besides, if you'll only come to the aforesaid casement——"

We made our way to the window and surveyed one another amusedly.

Wonderfully long lashes she had, and a proud, strong face that I seemed to have seen before somewhere. Recently, too. Warm brown eyes looked at me, while a quiet smile played on the small soft mouth. I marked the short upper lip and the promise of a broad forehead under the dark hair.

" And now," said she, " for the Marshal."

" He's engaged just now," said I. " He is, really. On the Bench. I've just left him."

A pause. Then :

" D'you want him very much ? " said I. " Because if——"

She laughed.

" I've never seen him in my life," she said. " I don't want him. I only want to know what time they'll rise for lunch."

L

" I can find out that for you," said I. " Will you wait here ? "

She nodded.

I slipped back on to the Bench. Jimmy was sitting with Jill and Daphne, obviously whispering information about the antique procedure. I came up behind them.

" What time does he lunch, Jimmy ? " This in the awful tone of one interested in the habits and customs of the mighty.

" Half-past one, as near as possible."

" Gentlemen of the Grand Jury," said an announcing voice.

Counsel, who was on his feet, stopped short in his recital of wickedness—larceny of two live fowls—the Judge laid down the depositions, and all eyes were turned upon the Grand Jury Box.

" O-oh, Boy, there's Berry," breathed Jill, catching my arm.

With preternatural solemnity my brother-in-law manipulated the mighty landing-net, in which by time-honoured custom Bills of Indictment are passed from the Grand Jury to the Clerk of Arraigns. Breathlessly we watched, while the net with its precious parchments—a most unwieldy instrument even in sober custody—swayed and danced by way of a Superintendent's bald head towards the Clerk's impatient fingers. Twice an officious constable essayed to grasp it. Each time it swayed gracefully out of his reach. The second time the zealot over-balanced and fell over the official shorthand writer, to the unconcealed delight of the public at the back of the Court. The pained look upon Berry's face as, a moment later, the net won home was indescribable.

I retired once more to the corridor.

" Well ? " said my lady.

" About half-past one," said I.   " Shall we go and choose the present ?   We've plenty of time."

She looked out of the window with a faint smile. Then :

" Good-bye," she said dreamily, putting out her hand.   " Thanks so much for finding out for me. As for the present, if you'll give me your address, I'll send you along a pair of gloves.   What size d'you take ? "

" Send me one of your own.   I have a weakness for dainty——"

" You're four centuries too late, sir," said the girl, turning to go.

" You wouldn't think so if you'd been in the Close this morning," said I.   " However, if you must be going, please let me see you off the premises."

Together we passed through the great dim hall and into the sunlit court outside.

" You spoke of the Close," she said suddenly. " Tell me the way there.   I'd like to see it.   I'm a stranger to Brooch," she added.   " I've only come for the day to see a friend."

" Let the glove go," said I.   " That, over there, is my car.   Make me a present of your company till the Court rises, though why that——"

" Should affect my life you can't understand.   I'm not surprised.   But, then, you see, my friend——"

" Is a friend at Court."

" Exactly.   Yes.   You shall drive me down to the Close."

The High Sheriff's car was standing close to ours. I knew his chauffeur well, and beckoned to him.   As he came up :

" Badger," said I, " if Mrs. Pleydell asks for me or

the car, tell her that I have been called away and shall
be back at half-past one."

" Very good, sir."

We rolled down to the Cathedral and its greensward. She agreed with me that, given the coach
and its splendour, the old-time atmosphere must be
wonderfully preserved.

" Of course," said I, " there was no one crying
bananas just then."

The lusty bellow of a hawker was arising from
neighbouring streets.

" I dare say they cried their fruit in the seventeenth
century."

" No doubt," said I. " But not bananas. Pome-
granates or medlars, perhaps. But not bananas. The
fame of Wolsey's orange is imperishable. Can you
believe that he would have risen to such dizzy heights
if he had sported a banana ?"

" Perhaps not," she laughed, " but, all the same,
I don't think oranges are so very romantic."

" But then he always had the best Denias," said
I. " And they were stuck with cloves."

When she was tired of the Close, I asked if she would
like a run in the country. Was there time ? An
hour and a half. Very well, please. As we crossed
to the gateway, she nodded towards the old red
house.

" The Judge's lodgings, you said. They look very
nice and comfortable."

" Rather," said I. " They do themselves all right,
these Judges."

" Is that so ? "

" My dear," said I, " you may take it from me.
Compared with them, fighting cocks eke out a bare
existence."

" I never knew that," she said simply.

" And the Marshal doesn't miss much either."

" No ? "

" No. I only once knew a Marshal miss anything really good."

" When was that ? "—curiously.

" This morning," said I.

She laughed pleasedly. Then :

" Perhaps he won't miss me next time. I mean at half-past one."

" Perhaps not. But I shall. All the afternoon. And now for the country. I'll take her towards White Ladies."

Some twenty miles from Brooch we struck the tiny village of Maple Brevet. Small wonder that my companion caught at my arm and cried how sweet it was. Set on the slope of a fair hill, its white-walled cottages all shining in the sun, its gardens thick with flowers, the brown thatch of its roofs thick and well cared for. Sleek ducks preened themselves by the edge of the village pond, knee-deep in which a great shire horse stood lazily, wet-nosed, appreciative. The golden-haired child on the animal's warm broad back turned himself round to see us, and touched his little forehead as the car went by. I returned his salute gravely.

" I say," said I, as we slid by the old forge, its walls and roof near hidden by wistaria, " are you thirsty ? Because, if you are, my dear, the grocer of Maple Brevet is famed for his draught ginger-beer. We always have his at home."

" I'd love some."

The shop stood back from the roadway, and in front was an old bench, set under lime trees. I brought the car alongside, and we got out.

" But why is there no one about ? " said the girl, taking her seat on the bench.

" The people are in the fields, for the most part, and the others keep house in the heat of the day. You're right in the old world at Maple Brevet."

" Putting the clock back again," she said. " I never met such a man."

" It's a hobby of mine," I explained. " Hitherto, owing to some unfortunate omission, my name has not figured in *Who's Who*. When it does, ' Putting the weight,' I mean ' clock,' will appear as one of my recreations."

" And the others ? "

" Smoking, London, and wondering why."

" I can understand the first."

I laughed.

" Oh, London's a wonderful pastime. Like nothing so much in the world as a great big fair, full of booths, and taverns, and peepshows, its ways alive with hucksters, customers, constables, its life made up of laughter, and bickering, and brawls. Its very Courts are Courts of Pypowders. A very healthy recreation, believe me. You ought to try it. And as to wondering why—well, I'll get your non-intoxicant first."

I brought her ginger-beer fresh from a cool stone jar. A glass also for myself. She thanked me with a smile.

" Mind you quaff it," I said, " just to preserve the atmosphere. They always quaff at Maple Brevet."

" I'll try. But you mustn't look, in case I were to drink by mistake. And now, aren't you going to sit down and smoke a cigarette ? "

Gravely I offered her my case. She shook her head.

" Not in Maple Brevet," she said.

For a little we sat silent. Then a bee came, drank

from her glass and flew away.   She broke into the old melody :

> " Where the bee sucks there suck **I** ;
> In a cowslip's bell I lie. . . ."

She sang charmingly.   When it was over ı

" Thank you very much," said I.   " Omar Khayyám's idea of Paradise is the correct one, though what in the world he wanted a book of verse for. . . . You know, were it not for the volume of circumstantial evidence to the contrary, I should be inclined to style the inclusion of the book of verse in his recipe for bliss as ungallant."

" I expect that was his poet's licence."

"Probably."

" And now tell me about your third recreation ? "

" Wondering why ? "

She nodded, her glass to her lips.

" I'm always wondering why," I said.   " Always. At the present moment I'm wondering why your lashes are so long.   Just now I was wondering why your feet were so small.   And ever since I saw them, I've been wondering why your ankles are so slender."

" I've been wondering too.   Wondering why I let you take me down to the Close, drive me to Maple Brevet, generally do what you've done."

" Yes," I said, " it is a strange thing, isn't it ? I mean it isn't as if I wasn't an obvious blighter. However, if you should think of the reason, you might——"

A little peal of laughter cut short my sentence. The next moment she was on her feet.

" Come along," she cried.   " I'm sure we ought to be going.   Somebody else'll be wondering why, if I'm not back at half-past one."

I followed her to the car somewhat moodily. I was all against this mysterious friend.

If the tire had not burst, we should have been at Brooch to time. And if the detachable wheel had not refused to come off for twenty-five minutes in the broiling sun, we should only have been five minutes late. As it was, the cathedral clock was striking two as we tore up to the Castle.

"Come," said my companion, and flung out of the car. She sped up the great hall, making straight for the steps and the corridor that led to the Bench. I followed a little uneasily, putting my faith in Jimmy. Holy ground that corridor, meet to be trodden delicately.

By the time I had gained the passage, my lady was out of sight. She had dashed past the window where I had seen her first, round into the gloom at the back of the Bench itself. Where on earth did the girl think. . . . I peered round the corner to see the passage flooded with light. The door of the Judge's private room was open. Also, momentarily, the one leading on to the Bench, to admit what I took to be the person of the Judge's butler. Fortunately he was half way through and did not see me. The door closed behind him. A quick step, and my companion appeared in the other doorway.

"I thought I'd lost you," she said coolly. "You are slow. Come along in. Why didn't you tell me there was this waiting-room when I was here this morning?"

"Waiting-room!" I gasped. "My dear girl, d'you know where you are?"

She stamped her foot.

"Will you come in?"

I looked at her helplessly, hesitated, and then

stepped into the room. On the table were the substantial remains of a handsome lunch.

I looked round apprehensively. Then :

" This is the Judge's private room," said I. " It's not a waiting-room at all. There'll be the very devil to pay if we're caught here. Come out of it, I beg you," I went on desperately. " Any moment the Judge might come back for his handkerchief or—or anything."

To my horror, she took her seat on the edge of the table, put her head on one side and smiled at me.

" He'd better go, if he's afraid," she said provokingly.

" Not at all," said I. " At least, that is, I only don't want us to be fired out ignominiously. We may be any minute, you know."

" They can't expect a girl to stand and wait in the corridor when there's a waiting-room——"

" Not ordinarily, I admit," said I. " But they're rather exacting behind here. No true democratic spirit in them. On their dignity all the time. Besides, you know, the fact that it isn't a waiting-room at all is against us. Gives them a sort of handle, as it were."

She fell into long low laughter, and, putting a slim hand behind her, accidentally pushed a glass off the table. It fell with a crash.

" Oh," said the girl.

I laughed bitterly.

" That's right," I said. " Having thrust into the holy of holies, we will now proceed to sack the place. Where do they keep the axe ? "

At this my companion laughed so immoderately that, fearful lest her merriment should penetrate to the Bench, I stepped to the door and closed it. Then I turned to her :

"May I ask," I said, "how long you propose to stay here and what you're waiting for?"

"Well, the Marshal'll probably look in presently, and I must——"

"If it's only Jimmy," I said, "I may be able to square him, but if——"

I broke off and began to rehearse nervously.

"My lord, it would not be proper to contend that *primâ facie* this intrusion is anything but unwarrantable. The truth is—er—we thought it was a waiting-room, until we saw your—er—your"—I looked round wildly—"er—unmistakable traces of your lordship. The fourpence on the table is for the broken tumbler."

Here the door was flung open, there was a quick rustle, and the Red Judge swept into the room.

"Hullo, dad," said the girl.

Then she put her hands on the great man's shoulders, stood a-tiptoe and kissed him.

"And now," said her father, "where——"

She laid a small hand on his lips.

"Listen," she said imperiously.

Quickly she told him of my kindness (*sic*) and the drive to Brevet and the burst tire.

"So you see, dad, it wasn't anyone's fault. And we did try."

The Judge turned to me with a smile and put out his hand.

"Anyone who successfully takes charge of my daughter for more than a quarter of an hour earns both my envy and my gratitude, Mr. . . ."

I told him my name.

"So," said he, "your father and I were old friends. For years we sat in the House together. He represented Shrewsbury, and I Oxford. Well, well. I must go back to the Bench. I'll deal with you both

later. If cutting a lunch with a Judge isn't Contempt,
I don't know what is. You may consider yourselves
imprisoned until the rising of the Court. I shan't
sit after three to-day, but that'll give you plenty of
time for lunch."

*   *   *   *   *

When we had finished, I pushed back my chair
and held up my cigarette-case.

"Not in Maple Brevet, I know," I said, "but——"

She nodded.

"Here's different," she said.

I came round and stood by her side.

"Not so very," said I. "I don't see a book of
verse anywhere. Incidentally, I suppose you're still
wondering why, aren't you? I only ask out of
curiosity."

Slowly she selected a cigarette. I watched the
pointed fingers.

"I always discourage curiosity," she said, putting
the cigarette between her lips. "But as you've been
very kind, and as you did say 'Rabbits' first, you
may give me a——"

She hesitated.

"Yes?" said I.

"A light," she whispered.

"What about our Contempt of Court?" I said.

"I expect we shall be committed."

"I don't think so," said I. "But we might easily
be attached."

CHAPTER III

BEAUTY REPEATS ITSELF

BEFORE we left Port Said, Jonah had sent a wire to Berry, with the result that, when we arrived at Cairo, Daphne and Jill were at the station to meet us.

I think we were much the same. I could still do with plenty of sleep, but the voyage, uncomfortable as it was, had set me up wonderfully, while Jonah was as sound as ever, except for a slight limp—he used to call it " a present from Cambrai "—which he will never lose.

Neither of us had seen the girls for nearly four years. Berry had sailed for Egypt in 1915, and when it appeared that he was likely to stay there, my sister had followed her husband to Cairo. Jill had accompanied her, naturally enough. After a while they had taken a house at Ghezireh, that fair island suburb where the English live, and there with Berry, who was steadily employed at G.H.Q., the two had made their home ever since.

When the armistice was declared, both Jonah and I happened to be in England—as a matter of fact, I had just left hospital and was on sick leave—and this, together with the fact that neither of us was fit for general service, no doubt contributed largely to our early demobilization. This was actually a *fait accompli* before the New Year. The very next day

172

I had received a letter from my brother-in-law stating that, while he had no desire to appear sanguine, he hoped to be permitted to return to civil life not later than the fall of 1921, and asking me whether I expected to be sent to Russia before the spring. To this I had replied by cable:

" Jonah and I demobilized aaa Make arrangements to send girls home forthwith aaa you brother will continue to carry on aaa congratulations on M.B.E. aaa report compliance."

It was Berry's reply which was responsible for our visit to Cairo.

" DEAR BROTHER,—As one to whom the contemplation of vice in any shape or form has always been repellent, I have no desire to learn the nature of the filthy and corrupt procedure to which you doubtless resorted to procure your release. This is a matter which I prefer to leave—not, however, without grave misgiving—to your ' conscience.' If you do not recognize the word, Jonah will explain what I mean.

" Your request for the return of my wife and your cousin is not understood. Since I rescued the former, at the price of my own freedom, from the sphere of your baleful influence, her outlook upon life has not unnaturally changed, and she has no desire to sever her association with a husband for whom she has an irresistible respect. In the same way little Jill proposes to falsify a somewhat indelicate proverb.

" Talking of dogs, I may say that the latter's latest acquisition is an animal of disgusting habits

which she insists is a marmoset. We call it 'Baal.'
Its disregard for certain of the conventions which
we, foolishly perhaps, are accustomed to observe is
distressing. Only this morning it savaged me with
every circumstance of brutality. Need I say that
the untoward incident appeared to afford Daphne
and Jill the maximum of amusement? The brute
remains a prisoner-at-large for the excellent reason
that no one is agile enough to put it under close
arrest. I am putting up a wound-stripe, and propose to change the creature's name to 'Moloch' by
deed-poll.

"But I digress.

"After considerable hesitation we have decided
that you and Jonah should proceed to join us by
the first available boat. Before the hot weather
begins I hope to have brought this campaign to a
close, so that we can all return together.

"If you have any trouble at the Passport Office
refer them to Scotland Yard, when they will immediately arrange for your deportation.

"To avoid attracting attention, I suggest that
you should travel 'steerage.' I enclose a cheque
for five thousand pounds towards your passage.
I don't suppose it will be honoured, but you can
try.

"The anxiety, which you have consistently
omitted to express, for my well-being is, alas, but
too well founded. Privation has left its mark.
The soda-water at the Turf Club is not what it
was in England, and you will find me greatly changed.
Indeed, I am so emaciated that, were your instincts
less depraved, I should allow two or three pints
of your blood to be transfused into my veins.
But I dare not imperil that sweet spirit of

innocence which is at once my shepherd and my crown.

"For your information and necessary action.

B. P.

"P.S.—You might bring a 'shaker' with you. I can't get one here for love or money."

Upon inquiry I found that a "shaker" is a contrivance in which you mix cocktails, and Jonah and I started for Egypt ten days later.

*   *   *   *   *

"My dear," said Daphne, "you've grown a moustache."

"Neither have you," said I. "I mean—— Is it too hot to kiss you, or ought we to pass right to right? When I'm in Rome, I like to do as Rome does."

Before she could reply, Jill left her brother and flung her arms round my neck.

"I don't know what they do in Rome," she said, "but in Cairo——"

"And now," said Jonah, "about the luggage."

It was certainly high time to do something.

We were surrounded by a rapidly increasing crowd of yelling natives of all sizes and shapes. Some sought to bear our baggage away piecemeal, others to dispossess us of the coats and rugs we held; a third school endeavoured to connect several pieces of luggage by means of a long strap. One of the latter had actually succeeded in completing his festoon, and had commenced to stagger away before he became the victim of an organized assault.

"This, I presume, is your Spartacus group," said I. "You didn't tell me that you'd got Bolshevism here, or I wouldn't have come."

"Choose one or two quickly, for goodness' sake," said my sister. "It's the only way."

"I'll have the cove with one eye," I said. "Now, Jonah, your pick."

Jonah instantly chose a fellow with a physiognomy suggestive of a familiarity with the more brutal forms of assassination.

"Crippen for ever," he said.

I had quite expected that we should have to maintain our selection by violence, but, to my surprise, the moment we had chosen our porters, the rest of the natives turned nonchalantly away, jabbering excitedly to one another, and laughing and jesting like a rabble of children.

"They don't seem much disappointed," said I. "A moment ago it might have been a matter of life and death."

"'For East is East,'" said Daphne shortly. "And now we'll have a couple of *arabiyas*."

"To tell you the truth," said I, "we had one on the train. Still —— All the same, I always thought you were supposed to wait till the sun went down."

"Idiot!" said my sister. "An *arabiya* is a victoria."

By this time Crippen and Cyclops had succeeded in concealing themselves beneath our baggage, and we moved off in the direction of the exit. Our appearance upon the steps was the signal for twelve drivers, all of whose animals were feeding, to take immediate action. What followed reminded me irresistibly of a freak event at a gymkhana. Twenty-four nose-bags were torn off, twenty-four ponies were bitted up, the drivers flung themselves upon their seats, twelve whips cracked, and, amid a hurricane of frenzied bellowing, twelve equipages were launched simultaneously towards us. The distance to be covered was only about forty yards, and at least nine of the vehicles arrived together. Collision was averted a score of times as by a miracle. Our two porters regarded the baying avalanche unmoved, merely glancing inquiringly at us, much as stewards might look towards the judge for his decision.

"For Heaven's sake put the numbers up," said Jonah. "My nerves aren't what they used to be."

I boldly selected two of the nine, when the unsuccessful competitors quietly withdrew with every appearance of satisfaction. There were no appeals—there was no discontent. The judge's decision was not only accepted—it was apparently approved.

As we drove through the streets, Daphne gave me my bearings.

"There's Shepheard's, Boy, on the right—this is the Sharia Kamel, you know—and those are the gardens."

"Yes," I said, "I thought they must be. I was going by the grass, you know."

"Be quiet. And this is the Continental we're coming to. And over there's the Opera House, where they're going to have the masked ball. That's the way you go to the Muski."

"I didn't catch the last word," said I. "Just as you were speaking a horse coughed."

"The Muski, dear."

I looked at her in some alarm.

"What you want," said I, "is a sea voyage."

"I'm just living for one," she smiled. "And now put your hat straight ; we're going to pass G.H.Q. This is the Sharia Kasr-el-Nil."

"I never heard such language in all my life," said

M

I. " How you remember the beastly words, I don't know."

" Hush," said Daphne, laughing and laying a hand on my arm. " There," she said reverently, nodding to the right, " that's G.H.Q.—where Berry works."

" G.H.Q., perhaps," said I. " Where Berry works, never. That edifice has yet to be erected."

* * * * *

A few minutes before luncheon Berry strolled on to the verandah, where Jonah and I were lounging in a couple of basket-chairs. His brass hat—he was now a major—was slightly on one side, and in addition to the ordinary staff badges he wore the G.H.Q. armlet. Beneath an excellent pair of breeches his highly-polished field-boots and spurs gleamed in the hot sunshine.

With one accord we scrambled to our feet and stood stiffly to attention.

Berry nodded carelessly.

" Sit down, please," he said easily, " sit down. Let's have an understanding right away. You need never get up when I come into the room." And with that he sank into the chair I had vacated.

Hurriedly Jonah resumed his seat. There were only two chairs.

Berry looked at me.

" Where would you like to sit ? " he said tenderly.

Jonah turned to me.

" I think he's fatter," he said.

" Not a doubt of it," said I. " And there's a coarser look about him."

Jonah nodded.

" See where the camel bit him ? " he said.

" Don't be silly," said I. " That's his mouth. What he drinks with."

My brother-in-law regarded us affectionately.

" It's like a breath from the slums to see you two again," he said. " Several of my cockles are already warm to the touch. The muscles of my throat——"

Daphne and Jill floated on to the verandah.

" Well, you three," said the former, " have you made friends ? "

" We have," said her husband. " I've just been forgiving them. Didn't you hear Jonah crying ? "

I slid my arm round Daphne's waist and drew her close to me.

" You're older, darling, though no one would know it, and I think you're more beautiful than ever. Little Jill is actually twenty-two. We're all older. One of us is older in sin." Here Berry groaned. " But we're all alive and well, thank God, and——"

I stooped to kiss her, for her eyes were shining.

" We're all to-together again," said Jill shakily. Then she gave an odd little laugh and burst into tears.

" My sweet," said Daphne, and flew to her.

Berry followed Jonah and me into the house. In the cool hall he seized one arm of each of us in a grip of iron.

" Bless your two ugly hearts," he said uncertainly. " Did you remember the shaker ? "

*   *   *   *   *

Six days later we were sitting at tea on the verandah of Shepheard's Hotel. The Sharia Kamel was flooded with brilliant sunshine, and, though we sat in the shade, the atmosphere was agreeably warm. The famous street below us was full of movement, and the ragged babel of sounds that rose and fell without ceasing made up a din that was not unpleasant.

There is no loitering in the roadways of Cairo.

Scurry is in the air. Cars slip through the crowded streets mostly at top speed; its Arab ponies rattle the *arabiya* along at a hand-gallop; even a porter's barrow is thrust on its way at five miles an hour. But opposite Shepheard's the way is none too wide, and the traffic is heavy, so that the most impatient driver must needs go gingerly till he is clear of the throng.

It was a remarkable scene.

Arabiyas, motor-cars, donkey-carts hustled one another for the right of way, and here and there a camel, almost completely hidden under its tremendous load, swayed indifferently along the gutter. There was a mounted orderly of the A.I.F. side by side with a well-horsed brougham from the Sultan's stables. The sullen chamberlain upon the box-seat and a flutter of black and white at the closed window declared its occupants to be two of the royal harem. A funeral was passing—first the rude coffin, hoist on the shoulders of irreverent bearers, alternately chanting and jesting, as the mood took them; then the relatives, also afoot; afterwards a poor pony dragging a trolley crowded with professional wailers, whose thin song dominated for a moment all other clamour. Wearing the blue-and-white armlet of the Signal Service, a dispatch-rider straddled his motor-cycle in hobby-horse fashion as he sought to thread his way through the press. On the opposite side of the street a native policeman surveyed the stream of traffic with a bored air.

The pavements were swarming.

Here a British officer brushed by two Bedouin that might have stepped out of the pages of Holy Writ; there was a huckster of sticks pressing one or other of his varied collection upon the passers-by; here a man crying cakes, and there again a vendor of silks and stuffs displaying his wares to any that would throw them a glance. Little brown boys darted along selling papers. British soldiers on pass strolled by in pairs, looking about them curiously. White *abbas*, green *abbas*, *abbas* of all hues, glowed in the bright light. Some of the poorer natives wore theirs looped up and kilted about their thin brown knees. All but the latter were girt with gay-coloured sashes, and wore the inevitable *tarbusch* upon the back of their heads. Only the women gave no colour to the picture; for all that, there seemed to be as many abroad as there were men. Some of them bore loads upon their heads, others perambulated, plainly but taking the air; but all were sombrely dressed in black, wrapped every one in the voluminous *haik* and shrouded close with her heavy *yashmak*. A few went barefoot, with anklets clinking, but for the most part they were wearing stockings, that slipped into rucks and wrinkles as they walked, and shoes that were down at heel.

On the hotel steps a juggler was appealing against the decision of an under-porter who had been high with him and ruled against his admission. Three or four guides, soberly clad, regarded him with a sneaking sympathy which they were too wise to express. Every now and then a grave-faced urchin would thrust a bare arm under the balustrade and plead shrilly for *baksheesh* with the visitors of the hotel. His failure in no way discouraged his fellows—all well aware of the value of importunity.

" My brother—Miss Revel," said Daphne, by way of introduction.

I put out my hand.

" But we're old friends," said I. " Berry introduced us at the Club the day before yesterday."

Miss Revel shook hands with a quick smile.

" Did he ? " she said innocently.

" I regret," I said coldly, " that I should have made so light an impression that——"

" Oh, I kn—remember. Of course, you're the camel man."

I sat down beside her wearily.

" I thought I'd exploded that theory."

" But Major Pleydell——"

" Told you I was one of the greatest living authorities on camels," I said. " So you said on Tuesday. If you remember, I told you that my brother-in-law is not exactly famous for his veracity. I added that I knew rather less about camels than I do about Ahasuerus' private life. Since I saw you I've been approached by three different people in the Turf Club, all of them anxious to consult me about camels. They won't believe me when I say I know nothing about the beastly animals, and I'm getting so unpopular that I'm almost afraid to go inside the place. And now you start in again, just as if——"

I stopped. Miss Revel was shaking with laughter.

" I'm so sorry," she said. " I've got such a dreadful memory."

" Memory ! " I said. " You wicked child, you did it on purpose. I can see it in your left eye—the brown one."

" Whatever do you mean ? " said Miss Revel in a startled voice, turning two large soft eyes in my direction.

" Why, they're both brown," said I. " How silly —I mean, how beautiful ! "

For a moment dignity disputed with laughter the mastery of her lips. Then, before I could see which had won, she turned resolutely away, chin in air.

I watched her amusedly. Hers was that exquisite
colouring that will be found only with auburn hair
—that delicate dainty bloom which the sun will always
freckle, lest you should think it unnatural and not of
this world. Masses of coppery hair she had, lit with
a random lustre that leapt from tress to tress with
her every movement; well-arched eyebrows rose to
a smooth forehead and met above a small straight
nose, and below, a short upper lip gave a proud touch
to a face of more than ordinary beauty. She had very
long eyelashes.

" I didn't see you at the Continental last night,"
she said suddenly. " There was a dance, you
know."

" That was because I didn't know you were going,"
said I. " Besides, you wouldn't have known me, if
you had, would you ? "

" I expect I shall know you next time."

" I don't know," said I. " I'm a very ordinary
type."

" Perhaps you won't know me."

" Nonsense," said I. " Even if you wore a *yashmak*
and hid your hair, your lashes would give you away.
Placed end to end, they would reach from Grafton
Street to the Carlton Grill. I've just been working it
out."

" Can you be serious ? "

" Of course I can. Do you believe in zoology, or
are you Church of England ? "

After some hesitation Miss Revel decided not to
reply.

" If I were a man," she said irrelevantly, " do you
know what I should do ? "

" You'd probably save a lot of money," said I.
" For one thing, you'd wear socks instead of those

beautiful stockings. But it would be a great pity.
I hate to think of you in half-hose."

She eyed me severely. Then :

" I should go in for afforestation," she said.

I put up my right hand.

" I know, teacher," I said eagerly. " I know.
Growing oaks and things."

" I should have nurseries for the little ones, and——"

" Bound to do that," said I. " You can't have
them running all over the house. Besides——"

" I shan't talk to you any more," said Miss Revel
indignantly.

I sighed.

" I'm very anxious to see your arms," I said.

" My what ? "

" Arms, my dear. You know, sort of legs, only
higher up."

Miss Revel choked. Then :

" What on earth for ? " she said.

" Vaccination marks," said I simply. " I collect
them. Stamps never appealed to me, and brasses
are too big. But vaccination marks . . . I shall see
yours at the masked ball. And now what about
dances ? I should like numbers three to seven and
eight to twelve, please, inclusive. And supper."

" You can have four and five and nine and ten."

I groaned.

" Well, well, half the sofa's better than no bed,"
I said resignedly. " And supper."

" I don't know about supper," said Miss Revel.
" And now I must be getting back." She rose and
looked at me. " I should laugh if you didn't recognize
me," she added.

" Now is it likely ? "

She flung me a dazzling smile.

" I think," she said, " that it is more than probable."

*   *   *   *   *

" That animal," said Berry, serving himself with a second helping of buttered eggs, " makes my gorge rise."

Moloch (alias Baal) was perched upon the mantelpiece and engaged in a searching examination of the sole of his left foot. Every now and then he gibbered, as with excitement.

Jill made haste to swallow the coffee she was drinking. Then :

" He's a dear," she said indignantly. " You know he is. He's only bitten you once," she added reproachfully, " and then you asked for it."

" If trying to intimate to the brute that I was quite capable of conveying the quarters of a mandarin from my plate to my mouth without his assistance is asking for it, I must plead guilty."

" Perhaps he didn't like the way you eat," said I.

" Possibly," said Berry. " He has queer tastes. I trust, brother, that your peculiar method of imbibing has found favour in his eyes. If not——" He shook his head mournfully.

" Do you mean that he's likely to try to help me to drink ? " said I, glancing apprehensively, cup in hand, over my shoulder.

" It wouldn't be the first time," said Berry, " that he has engaged in a work of supererogation. Only a week ago he scoured Daphne for fleas for about ten minutes, and he must have known quite well that she'd had a bath that morning."

A roll sang past his ear. Berry reached for the marmalade.

" For devotion to duty," he said, " during a meal. This very gallant officer continued to attack his food with entire disregard for his own safety. He set a very high standard to those under him."

"Pig," said his wife.

"That's right," said Berry. "Liken your lawful husband to the lower animals. Compare him with swine." He raised his eyes to heaven. "And this is what I have fought for." He paused to gaze at a large piece of toast, which he had coated with butter. "D'you think that will go in, or shall I cut it in two?" he added miserably.

"Oh, easy," said Jonah. "Of course it's not everyone's mouthful, but for you . . . Hadn't you better have some more butter, though? I can see the toast showing through in one place."

Berry pushed away his plate.

"Now, I shan't eat it at all," he said. "Just to punish you. Is there any more coffee?"

"To-night's the night," said Daphne suddenly. "We may as well dine here, don't you think?"

For a moment I glanced at her questioningly. Then I remembered the masked ball.

"Much nicer," said Jill. "And we can just push off quietly at a quarter to ten."

"I shall go as a parade state," announced my brother-in-law. "I shall sit on a buff slip and be erroneous. Those who ask me the way to the bar I shall direct to the cloak-room. At times I shall be quite unintelligible."

"When you've quite finished," said Daphne, "I'll say that it's not a fancy-dress ball, but a *bal masqué.*"

"French!" said her husband rapturously. "The tongue of diplomats. Delivered with the famous Lyons accent. Who would think it, to look at her?"

"Fool," said his wife. "Are you playing polo this afternoon?" she added, turning to Jonah

" I am. You and Jill coming ? "

My sister shook her head.

" Our afternoon at the canteen," she said. " It's great fun, but I like the hospitals best."

" They cheer when they see her coming," said Jill.

" That'll do, Jill," said Daphne, " or I'll tell them about the letters you get."

Jill blushed furiously.

" They're a popular pair," said Berry. " Get more salutes in the street than the C.-in-C. I was with Daphne once outside the Turf Club, and an Australian happened to pass. I returned his salute, when the fellow stopped and came back. ' Excuse me,' he said, ' but I was saluting the lady.' "

I looked to my sister for confirmation.

" Quite true," she said, laughing.

" What on earth did you say ? " said I.

" Apologized, of course, and said I hoped he'd overlook it this time. The only way was to take the wind out of his sails." Rising to his feet, he consulted his wrist-watch. " A short ten minutes and I must be gone. Jonah, I'll trouble you for the paper."

Jonah passed him the *Gazette*, and he sauntered out of the room. I pushed my chair back, and Moloch alighted on my shoulder. For a moment I regarded him uneasily. Then he placed two small firm hands on my cheek and deliberately pushed my head round till he was out of my sight.

" He doesn't like being stared at," explained Jill, rippling with mirth.

" Have some more coffee," said Jonah eagerly.

" Wait till he's on your neck," said I. " Seriously, what should A do ? "

" A should humour B," said Jonah. " It's as plain as a pikestaff."

" You fool," said I. " How do I know——"

" Keep perfectly still. I'll tell you when he bites you."

I was afraid to throw anything at him, lest Moloch should misinterpret my movement. So I swallowed and sat very still. A disconcerting shriek of laughter from my companions increased my apprehension.

" I'm afraid he doesn't like your hairwash," said Jonah unsteadily.

This was more than I could bear, so I rose as quietly as I could and turned to look in the mirror behind me. I was just in time to witness the assault. With a squeal of rage Moloch braced his feet against my head, and, seizing my ear with both hands, strove to detach it from the scalp. With a yell I grabbed him by the body, when he bit me twice with the rapidity of a serpent, and took a flying leap on to the breakfast-table. A moment later he was turning over the dates with all the deliberation of a seasoned gourmand.

I said a most appropriate word under my breath. The others were all speechless with laughter.

Berry put his head round the door and watched me licking my finger.

" I suppose you asked for it," he said.

*　　*　　*　　*　　*

At a quarter to three that afternoon Miss Revel was driving a two-seater out of the Club gates. She missed me by six inches, and pulled up to apologize. I took off my hat.

" Now I shall want six and seven as well," said I.

She gave me a puzzled smile.

" Six and seven," she said. " What a funny sum ! I've heard of six and eight. Isn't that the lawyer's fee ? "

" I'm talking of dances," said I. " I was to have

four and five and nine and ten, wasn't I ? And supper."

Suddenly she seemed to understand.

" O-oh," she said. " How funny—I mean——All right, six and seven as well."

" Upon my soul," I said, " I believe you'd forgotten."

Miss Revel threw back her head and laughed. Then she gave me a mischievous glance.

" I swear I hadn't," she said. " So long."

" And supper."

" Perhaps." Then, instead of letting in the clutch, she pointed over my shoulder. " That a friend of yours ? "

I turned to see the marmoset regarding me wistfully about a horse's length away.

" Moloch ! " I said stupidly. " Moloch ! "

The animal whimpered a greeting. I turned to Miss Revel.

" He must have followed me," I said. " I don't like the look of it."

Hurriedly I told her the details of the morning's assault. When I had finished :

" I believe he's sorry," she said. " He's probably followed you to apologize."

" He might have chosen a better time," I said. " Now I shall have to take the little blighter home again."

Miss Revel opened the door of the car.

" Get in," she said, " both of you."

As we swung round the second corner, the door of one of the head-lights flew open. Miss Revel slowed up, and I got out to fasten it.

" You'll want two hands," said she ; " it's awfully stiff. I'll hold Moloch."

I handed him over. The next moment there was a shriek, and I whipped round to see the marmoset scudding up the drive which led to a private house.

If I had not slipped at the foot of the steps, I should have had him. As it was, I rose painfully to my feet to see the animal leering at me from the comparative safety of a tastefully furnished hall. Although the front door was wide open, there was no one in sight. I glanced at the windows, but all the shutters were drawn to. It was the hour of siesta.

Wondering what to do, I began to wipe the perspiration from my face. Should you wish to keep cool in Egypt, it is inadvisable to run, even in winter-time, until after sundown.

A step on the gravel, and there was Miss Revel beside me.

" Where's he gone ? " she whispered.

I indicated the marmoset with a shaking forefinger.

" There's the swine," I said bitterly.

Putting a small hand on my shoulder for support, Miss Revel bowed her head to a tempest of laughter.

" Hush," she sobbed. " I suppose it was my fault. Oh, I'm so dreadfully sorry."

" I beg your pardon," I said stiffly.

Miss Revel only covered her eyes and continued to shake with merriment. I glanced uneasily at the shuttered windows and began to rehearse a suitable explanation against the coming of the occupant of the house.

" Madam, I am extremely sorry, but . . . Yes, that behind the clock is our little marmoset. . . . I think the vase must have been riveted. He only just. . . . If I could have a pair of steps and some

dates. . . . I'm afraid my sister is a little over-
wrought. . . ."

Suddenly I turned to my companion.

" D'you know who lives here ? " I asked.

She shook her head.

I tried to consider what was the best thing to do.
Of course I could ring, but the summons was sure to
be answered by a black servant, who would not understand a word I said, and would probably make a
clumsy mess of things if he tried to catch the miscreant.
The noise would certainly bring the owner upon the
scene. If, however, we went to work scientifically,
there was more than a sporting chance of our catching
the creature and getting away without attracting
attention. After a moment's reflection I chose the
latter course.

" Look here," I said, " I'll just stroll in quietly,
without appearing to notice him, and then, when he
thinks I'm going by, I'll turn and pick him up. You
just stand at the door in case he makes a bolt that
way."

She nodded, and with a nonchalant air I walked up
the steps on tip-toe. To complete the illusion, I
uncovered and wiped my shoes on the mat before
beginning to saunter aimlessly in Moloch's direction.
With my gaze apparently riveted on the opposite wall,
I was careful to keep him in the tail of my eye.

I am prepared to swear that my pose was flawless,
but I had not allowed for instinct. I was still some
six yards from my objective, when, with a deliberation
as calculated as my own, he started on all fours to
walk towards the open door of what appeared to be
the drawing-room. His tail waved derisively to and
fro. At once I stood still where I was. So did Moloch.
But he did not sit down. He just turned his head to

look at me and see that I kept my distance. I watched the contemptuous gestures of his tail with rising indignation.

It was now clear that I must have assistance, and I turned to the front door. Curiosity had led my companion as far as the mat, from which point of vantage she could observe what took place. At the moment she was reeling against the wall in a paroxysm of silent laughter. Solemnly I beckoned her to my side.

"I daren't move," I said, when she had glided up to me. "So it's up to you to make an encircling movement and cut him off. For Heaven's sake, get between him and that door. Shut it if you can."

She nodded and began to move noiselessly in the direction I had indicated, when, clearly divining our tactics, Moloch, in a perfect ecstasy of impertinence, leapt into the air, spun into the caper of a demoniac, squealed, and hurled himself into the drawing-room.

What was left of my prudence I flung to the winds. After what had occurred I would have followed the sweep into a nunnery.

When we entered the room, the marmoset was investigating the contents of a bowl on the top of the piano. I fancy it was the look in my eyes that emphasized the discretion of a precipitate retreat to the nearest window-curtain. I saw the mistake he had made before he did, and turned excitedly to my companion.

"Now we've got him," I said. "He can't clear out, and he can't hang on indefinitely. You stand by the curtain to catch him if he tries to come down, and I'll harass him from the window-sill."

From his excited gibbering Moloch seemed to realize that his position was desperate. There was not room for him to sit on the pole and though he scrambled up to the curtain-rings, by dint of standing on the sill of the open window and holding on to the green shutters, I could reach to within three inches of him with my disengaged hand. It was only a question of time. Miss Revel and I regarded him expectantly.

"What's he done?" said a quiet voice.

Miss Revel gave a little cry, and we both swung round guiltily to see a good-looking man of about fifty regarding us with a grave smile. He was in khaki, but he had no coat on, and his sleeves were rolled up. His hands were in the pockets of his slacks. As I stepped gingerly down from the window, Moloch made good his escape.

For a moment we all stood looking at one another. Then:

"What ever must you think?" said Miss Revel weakly.

The soldier drew forward an easy chair.

"Won't you sit down?" he said courteously.

Taking a deep breath, I plunged into the sea of apology and explanation. When I paused:

"Trespass is bad enough," he said. "Happily I was just in time to save you from a worse crime." He stepped to the mantelpiece, where the marmoset sat watching us. "George," he said, "you wicked fellow, what have you been doing?" In silence the animal scrambled contentedly on to his shoulder and put a small arm round his neck. "You see, he's all right with me," he added, "but he's always a bit nervous of strangers."

"But you said it was Moloch," gasped Miss Revel, turning to me.

I opened my mouth, but at first no words came. At length:

N

"I—I thought it was," I stammered.

"They're all exactly alike," said the soldier. "It's a mistake anybody might make."

There was a dreadful silence. Then :

"D'you know any deep pools near here?" I said. "Where a man may drown undisturbed? The river's so public."

Our host rang the bell with a pleasant laugh.

"You must have some tea first," he said.

Of our united humble protests he would have none.

"I insist." He spoke as one having authority. "I think you have given me the right to choose your punishment," he added, with a quick smile.

With silent foot a native servant entered the room and stood awaiting his master's pleasure.

"Bring tea," said the latter. Then he turned to Miss Revel.

"You will hold me excused," he said, with a bow, "while I fetch my coat."

"Of course," murmured my companion.

When he re-entered the room, he was wearing the badges of rank of a lieutenant-general.

*   *   *   *   *

The fourth dance was a fox-trot. As we glided into the lilt of the tune :

"Shall we dance this?" I said to Miss Revel, "or shall we just jazz?"

"Jazz?"

"The new verb, my dear. You know. I jazz, thou just, he jad : we jammed, ye jabbed, they were extremely daring. You see, I knew you all right, didn't I."

"I'm not sure yet."

I stared at the little masked face so close to my own. There was a maddening smile on the red lips.

" There are times," I said, " when I don't understand you." My partner laughed. " However—I'm
more than pleased with your markings," I added,
critically inspecting the vaccination marks high up
on her right arm. " They will greatly add to the
distinction which already characterizes my collection."

" Don't mention it," said Miss Revel. " Can you
carry them in your head, or do you want to take an
impression ? "

" They are already graven upon my heart. You
can guess the name that's there, can't you ? "

" I've no idea."

" Moloch, of course. Queen Mary lost Calais. And
I thought I'd found Moloch."

" And who," said Miss Revel, " is Moloch ? "

I started violently, missed a step, trod on my partner's toes, apologized in a voice I hardly recognized
and then led her out of the dance. When we had
found a quiet corner :

" Do you mean to say you don't know who Moloch
is ? " I demanded.

" I don't seem to remember," she said slowly.

I looked at her very hard.

" I suppose you'll say we didn't have tea with a
General next ? "

" Did we ? " said Miss Revel.

Amazedly I regarded her. At length :

" Either you're pulling my leg," I said heavily, " or
else you ought to take up Mentalism."

" Seriously ? "

" I mean it," said I. " I knew a fellow who took
it up, and within a month he was a brigadier-general.
Of course he'd been a brigadier-general for years, but
I mean to say he retained his rank."

Towards the end of the interval between the fifth

and sixth dances she asked me to fetch her a glass of water. When I returned she was gone, and the music had already commenced before I saw her close to the entrance. I stepped to her side.

" I am quite prepared for you to deny that you asked me to fetch you some water," I said, handing her the glass.

She looked at me mischievously over the rim of the tumbler.

" I'm very glad of it," she said. " But I must admit I don't remember——"

I was getting frightened, and we danced the next dance in silence.

It was after the seventh, when we were seated half way up the grand staircase, that she turned to me with a smile.

" I shall never forget this afternoon," she said. " Your face, when the General called him ' George,' was the funniest—— What on earth's the matter ? "

With an effort I mastered a frantic desire to scream, kick somebody, and rush out of the building.

" Oh, nothing," I replied uncertainly. " One or other of us is mad. That's all. I don't know which yet. I'm beginning to think it's me. Let's talk of something else," I added hurriedly. " Vaccination marks, for instance."

" Vaccination marks ! " cried Miss Revel.

I laughed bitterly.

" Oh, you wouldn't remember," I said. " It must be quite half an hour since we discussed them. If you did, you'd recollect that I said yours were graven upon my heart."

I was sitting on her right, and, as I spoke, I glanced at her bare arm.

There were no marks on it at all.

I stared until I thought my eyes would fall out of my head. Then I looked about me dazedly, as one in a dream. Suddenly a wave swept surging into my brain.

"Have you a twin sister?" I said in a shaking voice.

"But how clever of him to find out," said Miss Revel, falling into silvery laughter.

For fully a minute we regarded one another in eloquent silence. Then I gave a long sigh of relief.

"I've had a wearing day, haven't I?" I said. "Chorus. First he mixed the marmosets and then he mixed the sisters."

"History repeats itself," said Miss Revel.

"I know. But I never knew that beauty did, too. Otherwise I might have guessed before."

"What we both want to know," said Miss Revel wickedly, "is which of us you want to take in to supper?"

"Shall I tell you?" said I.

"Yes."

"The one I had tea with," I said.

CHAPTER IV

THE DESERT AIR

" HOW d'you spell 'pyramids'?" said Daphne, looking up from the table at which she was writing.

"Which sort?" said Berry. "The game or the wonder of the world?"

"The ones at Mena," said his wife.

"With an 'h,'" said her husband glibly, turning over a page.

"Helpful ass," said Daphne. "Spell it, Jonah."

"What d'you want to spell them for?" said Berry, yawning. "I should leave them alone. Silly rotten things."

This irreverent allusion provoked a storm of abuse which beat about the culprit's head for several moments. As it subsided :

"Any way," said my brother-in-law, "the fools who say they were meant for tombs are simply talking through their hats."

"What were they, then?" said I.

"Air-raid shelters, obviously," said Berry. "Look at the bursting-course. I expect I shall be knighted for this. Can everyone spell 'noology'?"

"Be quiet," said Daphne. "I want to finish this note."

It was after dinner, and while my sister was writing, the rest of us were gathered about the fire, of which

we were all glad, for winter nights in Cairo are cold
indeed.

" You really think you'll get away in April," said
Jonah, looking at Berry.

" No one," replied my brother-in-law, " is indis-
pensable. My departure from G.H.Q. will, of course,
cause a certain amount of consternation. Consols
will fall a point or two, and Turkey will probably
consider the resumption of hostilities. But things
will gradually right themselves. Yes," he concluded,
" I'm inclined to think that the first week in April
should see us at Port Said."

" Hurray," said Jill. " I dreamed about White
Ladies last night."

" Comes of having your head washed on an empty
stomach," said Berry. " I well remember——"

" Thank you," said Daphne. " That'll do. Would
you like to hear what I've said to Adèle ? "

" Not in the least," said her husband. " To be
frank, such a recital would bore me to tears. I mean,
I want you to know."

" Who's Adèle ? " said I.

" She's an American girl," said Jill. " You'll love
her. She's got the sweetest accent."

" She's no accent at all," said Berry. " You know
it's an American speaking, and—and there you get off.
It's very peculiar—has to be heard to be believed.
And now shall we play halma ? Or would you rather
watch me recite ? "

Thus encouraged, my sister began to read :

" DEAR ADÈLE,—Friday's Berry's birthday.
They've given him a whole holiday at G.H.Q.,
and we're going to make a day of it. Come to
Sakkara with us. I know you've never been there,

and I want my brother to see it. Send a pony to Mena the night before, and we'll drive you down in the morning. We push off from the Pyramids at ten. Drill order.—Love, dear,

" DAPHNE.

" P.S.—He cried all last night because he thought you were angry with him. So you must come."

" Vulgar and offensive," said Berry. " I wonder where she gets it from. Did any of your family marry beneath them ? " he added, turning to me.

I shook my head.

" Daphne's the only one," said I.

" Give the gentleman a bag of nuts," said Jonah. Berry sighed.

" By the way," he said, " did I tell you that the bath won't run away ? "

" Nonsense," said Daphne.

" Well, it wouldn't when I tried to make it just before dinner."

Jonah turned to me.

" How do you make a bath bolt ? " he said.

" Feel the ' waste,' close both legs, and fetch it one with the loofah, I should think," I replied.

" Well, how am I to have my bath to-night ? " demanded my sister.

" I suppose it's a question of baling it out or using the same water," said her husband. " I should toss up."

" If the servants have gone to bed, you'll jolly well bale it out," replied his wife. " You filled it."

" You might have told us before," said Jill reproachfully.

" I came downstairs simply bursting with it," said Berry, " but the shock of finding the soup hot put it right out of my head."

" Are you sure you pulled the ' waste ' up ? " said Daphne.

" More. I even showed it a sausage by way of terrorism. I've never known that fail before. It gets wind up very easily—our bath does," he added by way of explanation.

With an indignant glance my sister stepped to the fireplace and rang the bell. A moment later a native servant stood in the doorway.

" What's the matter with the bath, Abdul ? "

The fellow grinned helplessly and spread out his hands.

" Water stay still," he said.

" Have you pulled up the ' waste ' ? "

" Yes, yes. No goo-ood. Finish bath. Yes."

" Nice, helpful crowd, aren't they ? " said Berry.

With the exception of the latter, we all proceeded to the bathroom to see for ourselves what was the matter. The mechanism was in order, but a very cursory investigation sufficed to show us that the pipe was faithfully obstructed by some foreign substance, which had apparently fallen down the shaft in which the " waste " operated. With the aid of an electric torch and a screw-driver, Jonah and I proceeded with the thankless task of removing the " waste." After a hectic twenty minutes, in the course of which Jonah swore twice, Jill dropped the torch into the bath, and I broke the glass of my wrist-watch against one of the taps, our efforts were successful. I don't think any one of us was surprised when, after a violent struggle, I extricated Berry's rubber sponge from the outlet pipe. Daphne, Jonah, and I regarded one another in awful silence, while Jill leaned against the wall, shaking with ill-suppressed merriment. The released water gurgled contentedly away. As I raised

my eyes to heaven, the strains of " Helen of Troy,"
rendered by the gramophone, floated up from the
drawing-room, and a peal of feminine laughter fell
upon our ears. For a moment we stared at one
another. Then, bursting with curiosity and indignation, we all flung out of the bathroom and down the
stairs. We tiptoed across the dimly-lighted hall, to
see my brother-in-law jazzing rather creditably, and
with every circumstance of hilarity, with a slim dark
girl in periwinkle blue. Her hair was short, and her
gay brown eyes full of laughter.

" They're all right, as a rule," Berry was saying,
" but every now and then they go off the deep end.
I only just happened to mention that the bath wasn't
quite in order, and off they all go to try their hand
at plumbing. Some people can't leave well alone.
They'll end by breaking something, and I shall have
to pay for the repairs."

" I can't see Daphne plumbing," said his partner.
The moment she opened her lips I knew who it was.

" Nor can anyone else," said Berry, " but so long
as she's pleased. . . . I live for that woman, you know.
The things I deny myself to make her happy. . . .
Lunch with me at Shepheard's Grill to-morrow, and
then come and help me buy her a little present. I
was thinking of a new string-bag. It's her birthday
on Friday, you know. I forget whether she's fifty or
fifty-one."

This was too much, and with a cry my sister snatched
the sponge from my hand and launched herself at her
husband. Jonah and I seized and held him while she
squeezed such cold water as the sponge was containing
down his neck. Jill and the fair American clung to
one another, helpless with laughter.

Our victim protested neither by words nor deeds,

although a series of involuntary shudders ran through his frame as the water coursed down his spinal column. He merely improved the occasion by introducing us.

"Adèle," he said, "allow me to introduce my brother-in-law "—here he nodded in my direction—" Miss Feste. Captain Mansel "—solemnly he nodded at Jonah—" Miss Feste. When they have finished with me, I expect they will bow. My wife, the vixen with the sponge that is, I think you know. She, too, will greet you in a moment. Frolicsome little things, aren't they ? "

Daphne gave a final squeeze before throwing the sponge into the fender. As Jonah and I released our victim, she turned to Miss Feste.

"The punishment of wickedness and vice," she explained. "We have to do this about once a month. Adèle, dear, I've just written to you. What a sweet frock ! "

Berry addressed his wife.

"I ought to go and change," he said meekly. "May I have one of your vests, dear heart ? You know, the thick flannel ones you're so fond of. Or would you rather stand your trial for manslaughter ? "

"No jury would ever convict," said Daphne.

Berry turned to Miss Feste and indicated Jonah and me with a wave of his hand.

"You must excuse their shirt-sleeves," he said. "They've just been running through a few conjuring tricks. The one on the left is quite good. Give him five piastres, and he'll take it to the Turf Club and turn it into a dry Martini at once. And now I'm going to bed. Adèle, my dear, I'm desolated to leave you, but I must get out of this shirt, and it's too late to dress again. Don't be late for lunch to-morrow."

He bowed over her hand, blew a kiss to his wife, and left the room singing a stave from ' The Gondoliers.'

Jonah and I retired to get into our dinner jackets and make ourselves more presentable. We had hardly returned to the drawing-room, and I was just suggesting that Miss Feste should return with us to Europe, when Berry, clad in gaily-striped pyjamas and an orange-hued silk dressing-gown, sauntered into the room.

" Hush," he said in response to the scandalized shriek which greeted him. " Don't wake me. I'm walking in my sleep. Has anybody seen anything of an expensive sponge ? I should be sorry to lose it. It's been in our family for years. They say it's the very one Doctor Johnson never used. Besides, I want to clean my teeth."

* * * * *

It was about half-past three on the following afternoon, and I had just crossed the Sharia el Maghrabi to look into the window of the saddler's shop, when Miss Feste came to the doorway with a wither-pad in her hand.

I raised my hat.

" What a funny sort of string-bag ! " said I. " Can't you get one with handles ? "

Miss Feste smiled.

" This," she said, " is a present for Pharaoh—I'm going to ride him on Friday. Shall I get two ? "

" I should," said I. " You can always use them for sleeping socks, if he doesn't like them."

Miss Feste retired to complete her purchase, and I followed her into the shop. When she had given the assistant her address :

" I'm just going to pick up a car," said I. " I'm going to Abbasiya. But I've plenty of time. Can I drive you anywhere first ? "

Miss Feste shook her head.

"No use, I'm afraid. I'm going further. Heliopolis. There's a girl at an hotel there who wants to sell a saddle, and I'm thinking of having a look at it. What are you going to Abbasiya for?"

"I'm hoping to get a joy-ride in a Handley-Page," said I. "A fellow I know in the Air Force——"

"You are lucky," said my companion. "I've never been up."

I looked at her.

"Would you like to go?"

"I should be thrilled to the core."

"I don't know whether they'll let you," said I. "I expect there are stacks of rules against it ; but Geoffrey Ross is a sportsman, and I'm sure he'll take you if he can. Will you come along?"

"What about the saddle?"

I looked at my watch.

"We can do that first, if we're quick," said I.

Five minutes later we were scudding along the road to Heliopolis.

"Have you thought any more about coming home with us?" I asked, as we slid by the station.

Miss Feste nodded.

"I have," she said. "D'you think it would be a wise move?"

"It would be mutually profitable. You're very sweet to look at, so we shall be able to feast our eyes, while you—— Well, I don't suppose you've ever travelled with a circus, have you? At any rate, you won't be dull. Besides, it would be a pretty compliment to the *entente* at present existing between the two countries."

"You know, I'd never have said you were English," rejoined Miss Feste irrelevantly.

"Let me know the worst," said I. "What do I look like? Siamese, or an advertisement for rolled oats?"

Miss Feste surveyed me critically.

"I think you've got rather a southern look," she mused. "Italy, perhaps. I don't know."

I sighed.

"Italians," I said, "fall into two classes. Either they purvey ice-cream or dance the tarantella. Would it be indiscreet to inquire into which of these categories——"

"It would," said Miss Feste. "Would you have known I was an American?"

"Every time," said I.

"Why?"

"By the grace which you lend the English language," I said.

Miss Feste gave a ripple of laughter.

"And you say you're an Englishman," she said, with raised eyebrows. "Well, well——"

"Believe me, I have that great honour."

"If you talk like that, I shall think you're German."

"Our hero took a deep breath," said I. "Seriously, I do wish you'd settle to come back with us. Then you can come down to White Ladies and see the family tree," I added thoughtfully. "We got it cheap during the sale at the College of Arms. I remember Rouge Dragon cracked the glass as he was doing it up, and Daphne made him take off another two shillings."

"For Heaven's sake——" said Miss Feste, laughing. "By the way," she added, nodding at the driver, "does he know where to go?"

"I don't know," said I. "I just said 'Heliopolis.' Just like that. 'Heliopolis.' I was quite frank about it. That, I take it, is the general idea. What's the special ? "

" The girl with the saddle is at Heliopolis House. I expect he's guessed. We'll be there in a moment."

We were certainly travelling, but the way was fine and broad, and, if there was plenty of traffic, there was room to spare. We flashed by a string of camels, fastened the one to the saddle of the other in front, then past three lumbering G.S. wagons full of stores. Natives trundling barrows of vegetables swerved to one side as we came. Here was a seedy *arabiya* crowded with native women staring about them. The busy clack of their tongues fell on our ears for a second as we swept by. There was a tender of the Royal Air Force leaving two M.T. lorries to rave and lurch on their way, as if they were standing still. As we sped past the barracks of native troops —gaudily clad sentinels at the gates—we met a squad of the Egyptian Labour Corps returning from work. Queer, rough-looking specimens, they wandered rather than marched, two by two, crocodile-fashion, most of them hand in hand and all of them chanting an idle stave more or less in unison, and with an air of such utter contentment and freedom from care as set you thinking.

A moment or two later the car came to rest at the foot of the steps leading to the terrace of the Heliopolis House Hotel. When I had handed her out, I addressed my companion.

" Don't be long," I said. " I want you to have that joy-ride."

" Not half as much as I do," she flung over her shoulder.

I re-entered the car and lighted a cigarette. On the opposite side of the road two white saddle-donkeys were discussing a little heap of green food, while their boys, dressed in white *abbas*, were squatting on the pavement, keeping a careful eye on the hotel on the look-out for custom. I watched them lazily.

It was, as ever in Egypt, a beautiful day. The sky was cloudless and the sun blazing. And this was but the end of February. I felt glad that we were going to leave before the summer. My watch showed me that it was just four o'clock. It seemed strange that in an hour or two it would be bitterly cold. Still, sundown was not yet.

My reflections were interrupted by the appearance of a porter bearing a good-looking hunting-saddle which he deposited by the side of the driver. Miss Feste followed him down the steps, and I got out of the car.

" I'm going to try it," she said. " If I like it, d'you think it's worth ten pounds ? "

I had a look at it and found the name of the maker.

" My opinion is valueless," I said, " but I should say it was dirt cheap. More. If you don't buy it, I will. And now for the aerodrome, or, at any rate, Abbasiya."

*   *   *   *   *

My apprehension was well founded. There were, it appeared, most stringent orders in force regarding the carrying of passengers on board His Majesty's 'planes.

" They'll wink at you," said Geoffrey pensively, " but a lady ! Gosh ! I should be dismembered if they got to know."

" Oh, then I mustn't," said Miss Feste. " I couldn't think of——"

" I'll tell you what," said he slowly. " D'you mind standing up and letting me see the length of your skirt."

Miss Feste stood obediently to attention. Solemnly Geoffrey nodded his head. I regarded them wonderingly.

"Look here, Miss Feste," he said, "you'll have to wear a cap and a coat and goggles, and that'll cover you up pretty well. The only trouble is your ankles. I've got a new pair of slacks I've never put on. If you like to wear them just anyhow—the top part doesn't matter, so long as they stick out under the coat."

He stopped, blushing furiously.

Miss Feste was shaking with laughter.

"Geoffrey," I said, "you surprise even me. When you are older, you will writhe with shame to remember—— Stop, I've got it. Never mind your new slacks. Have you got an old pair you don't want?"

"Stacks," said Geoffrey.

"And scissors and garters?"

"Garters? Will leather ones do?"

I nodded, and he ran out of the ante-room. Fortunately we had the place to ourselves. When he returned, I spread the slacks upon a table and proceeded to turn them into a pair of shorts by hacking off the legs above the knee.

"For Heaven's sake," cried Miss Feste, "what are you doing? The suspense is awful. Which part am I to wear?"

I turned to Geoffrey.

"Is the 'plane ready?" I asked.

He pointed out of the window. There we could see mechanics busy about a Handley-Page.

"I am supposed to be taking her up in ten minutes' time," he said, glancing at a clock on the mantelpiece.

"We'll leave you for fifty seconds," said I to Adèle. "Let me give you the recipe. Insert the foot delicately

o

into the cylinder of cloth." I pointed to the two trouser legs. " Then raise same slowly till the turn-up is on a level with the high heel. Make fast with garter below the hock. Keep cool and wear with a rich sauce. Will twenty-five seconds a leg be enough ? "

" I daren't," said Adèle, looking about her. " Supposing somebody were to come in ? "

" Not likely," said Geoffrey. " They're all at the sports."

The next moment I was outside the room, struggling into a leather coat. When we returned, Miss Feste was standing on a table, trying to see herself in the mirror above the fireplace. To all appearances she was wearing a filthy pair of slacks by way of panta-loons. It was sacrilege, but it gave the desired effect. When we had disguised her in leather coat, flying helmet, and goggles, nobody would have given her a second look. Only the little brown-shod feet looked smaller than ever.

While she and Geoffrey were strolling across the aerodrome, I deposited her bent straw hat in the car.

" Wait," I said to the chauffeur.

" Or-right, or-right."

*   *   *   *   *

If I had been sitting by the side of the pilot, instead of crouched on a petrol tin in the gunner's cockpit, I should have realized what was happening sooner than I did. As it was, of my simplicity I believed that Geoffrey was bringing us down so that we might have a closer view of the Pyramids, for at the time we were close to Mena. Only when we were about two hundred feet up and still descending did I look round. The first thing I noticed was the frown on the pilot's face. Geoffrey was looking as black as thunder. He was also peering disdainfully from side to side. Meeting my gaze, he raised his eyes to heaven and drew in his breath. Then he looked down very hard, and I saw the tip of his tongue appear between his teeth. As I glanced round and down, he made a beautiful forced landing. The great aeroplane alighted gingerly on a hard piece of desert, jolted over a stone or two, and came to rest easily a moment later in some looser sand.

"Well, that's that," said Geoffrey. "There will now be a short interval of twenty-four hours."

I stood up in the cockpit and faced him.

"I gather," said I, "that we owe you our lives."

Geoffrey sighed heavily.

"These laymen!" he said. "Give me a cigarette."

I felt for my case.

"You see?" said Miss Feste. "It hasn't fazed him at all. If I were let down in mid-air, I should probably lose my mind—try to get out, or something. But the law of gravity never enters his head. He just swears once—I heard him—and then slides out of the sky as though he were parking a car."

"Thank you, kind lady," said Geoffrey, "but I must hand it back. The most poisonous ass——"

"You were absolutely the most wonderful thing I've ever seen," said Miss Feste.

"Nonsense," said Geoffrey stoutly. "All I've done is to let you down badly. We can't get back, they don't keep cars out here, and you're about two miles from Mena House."

"What exactly happened?" said I. "That the pilot was forced to descend owing to engine trouble I know, but——"

"Let's get out of the old 'bus," said Geoffrey. "I'll tell you when we're down."

The mechanic, who had remained aft, was already

on the ground. He and I were just about to assist
Miss Feste to descend through the trap-door when
Geoffrey uttered a cry, leaned over the side of the
Handley-Page, and pointed towards the Great Pyramid.

" Good lord ! " he said. " The gilded staff ! "

Looking in the direction he indicated I saw five
horsemen trotting in our direction. Three were
riding together, while two followed behind. The brass
hats of two of the former were clearly visible.

" Quick," cried Geoffrey. " They mustn't find you
here—either of you. For Heaven's sake, push off !
Anywhere. Try the other side of that sand-hill, and,
if they see you, pretend you've nothing to do with
me. Looking for scarabs or something."

As he spoke, the approaching cavalcade disappeared
from view. Obviously it was crossing a patch of
' dead ' ground. Adèle half tumbled, half fell into
my arms. I helped her out of her coat and flung off
my own, and then, catching her by the hand, started
to struggle towards the sand-hill. The going was
hideous, for the sand was soft and loose. Mercifully
the staff were still out of sight. They were probably
considerably further away, when we first noticed them,
than I had imagined—so deceptive a thing is distance
in desert places.

As we were rounding the shoulder of the sand-
hill, I glanced back to see the head and shoulders of a
horseman come into view on the other side of the great
aeroplane. A moment later we were out of their
sight.

With her hand pressed to her side and panting
for breath, Miss Feste sank down on the sand.

" Don't look for a minute," she gasped. " I want
to take these wretched things off." She indicated
the ridiculous slacks with a shaking forefinger.

Obediently I turned away, mopping my face with
the spare handkerchief which the climate had taught
me to carry. The next moment:

"All right," she said.

When I turned round, she was shaking the sand
out of a small brown shoe. I folded up the trouserings, removed my helmet, and put the lot under my
arm. The garters I slid into my pocket.

"I shall have to keep this on," said Adèle, touching
her cap. "I can't walk about hatless. I must look
awful."

"As a matter of fact, you look lovely," said I.
"You do indeed."

Framed in the helmet, her merry face was most
attractive. Her brown eyes danced with excitement,
her red lips were parted in a smile, and the colour
had leapt into her cheeks as the result of her run.
But whilst I was streaming with perspiration, she was
comparatively cool. Tall and slim, her cream-coloured
frock of some soft fabric suited her admirably. Already
I had marked how the long coat, that fell to her knees,
set off the grace of her steps with every movement.
She made a goodly picture, sitting there on the
slope of the sand-hill, shoe in hand, her tiny unshod
foot resting upon the other's instep.

"I feel rather as if I was acting in a revue," she
said suddenly. "What comes next?"

"The comedian should really appear, complete
with garden roller and scythe, and start reclaiming
the desert or something. As it is, the first thing, so
far as I'm concerned, is to get cool. The second is to
find a means of transport for you as far as Mena.
You'll never get there in those shoes."

Adèle regarded her feet.

"I expect I shall have to try," she said.

" I wonder," I said reflectively, " what Crusoe would have done if he'd come across your footprint in the sand instead of his own ? "

" Lost his memory, I expect."

I shook my head.

" He'd probably have gone straight back to his cave to brush his hair. But we should never have known, for his diary would have come to an abrupt stop."

" And the world would have been the poorer."

" He would probably have turned out some excellent lyrics. You know, Adèle, I simply love your hair."

" That's a load off my mind," she flashed.

" Why did you cut it ? " I asked.

" To save trouble."

" I had mine taken off with the clippers three years ago for the same reason," said I, " but nobody said they loved what was left."

" You surprise me," said Adèle. " I'm sure you must have looked priceless."

" As a matter of fact, I looked about fifty-six. I suppose you keep your ears under the hair. D'you find they do well there ? After all, strawberries grow like anything under straw, don't they ? "

" As a matter of fact, they're most disappointing," said Adèle. " They simply won't grow."

" Heaven forbid that they should. Yours are specimens of the *aurium deliciæ* type, famous for their bloom. If it's anything like that on your cheeks, you ought to show them. To tell you the truth, I'm rather an authority on auriculture. Will you give me a private view one day ? "

" I'll give you anything if you'll get me back to Cairo by half-past six," said Adèle.

" Done," said I. " May I have anything on account ? "

For a moment she gazed into the distance, while the faintest of smiles hung hesitating in the midst of its mischievous dance about her lips. There was such a look on her face as makes a man catch his breath, and to this her raised eyebrows lent a puzzled yet inscrutable air that would have shaken the convictions of the most confirmed misogynist.

"Any more for the Sphinx?" I murmured.

Miss Feste flung me a dazzling smile and stretched out a slim hand to be helped to her feet.

"I never give anything on account," she said, "but I'll pay—in reason—when you deliver the goods."

A cautious glance over the top of the sand-hill showed us that the forced landing of the Handley-Page was affording the Staff considerable interest. Geoffrey was standing stiffly by the side of one whom I took to be an officer of some distinction, for his companions had fallen a little behind. The General —he could be no less—was pointing to the great aeroplane, and seemed to be asking a whole series of questions. The elder of the other two officers was not unlike Berry. I fell to wondering. . .

"Nothing doing there," I said, turning to Adèle. "We'd better try and work round their flank."

She nodded, and a moment later we had started on our circuitous route.

We saw the camels simultaneously. Unattended they were kneeling side by side in the shade of a sand dune. Both of them were saddled. With one accord Adèle and I stood still. The animals suspended the hideous process of mastication, upon which they were engaged, and favoured us with a supercilious stare.

I drew a deep breath.

"Luck," said I, "is with us. Behold our transport."

"Oh, but——"

" I can't help it. People shouldn't leave camels lying about. Besides, we can send them back from Mena. Seriously," I continued, " the moment we start backing them, you'll find their driver will roll up. They're always, as you would say, ' floating around,' just out of sight somewhere."

Neither of us had ever ridden or endeavoured to control a camel before, and several hectic minutes elapsed before we were mounted. Happily the animals had little choice in the matter, for, upon investigation, I found that their near forelegs were so strapped that they could not rise until the straps were unfastened. Against everything that we did, however, they protested with a series of uncouth snarls, which, in the circumstances, were rather trying to the nerves. But, for all their clamouring, no one appeared upon the scene.

It had occurred to neither of us that a camel rises to its feet, as it were, by numbers, and although I had established my companion firmly enough upon the brute's back, when it came, the double movement proved so exacting that she escaped a fall as by a miracle. I observed, moreover, that the embarrassment of its intending rider affords the camel great gratification, and that if by any means it can rise to its feet before he is ready, it is delighted to do so. It was therefore with some misgiving that I prepared to unstrap the foreleg of my own. However, it had to be done.

I loosened the strap, dived for the saddle, was flung on to the animal's neck, and was hurled backwards again in something under one second.

As I lugged at the cord attached to the brute's nose, I could hear Adèle sobbing with laughter. Solemnly I turned and regarded her.

" That's right," I said. " You have a good laugh. I'm not sensitive. But, if you do fall off, don't forget we're done. I'll never be able to get the swine to kneel down again. I've forgotten the password."

" I'm sorry," she wailed. " I'm sorry. But if you could have seen——" The merry voice trailed off into another gust of laughter. Helplessly I laughed with her.

We were nearing Mena, when the sound of voices made us look round. The three Staff officers, followed by their orderlies, were fifty paces behind us and coming up. We were just about to pass between two sand-hills, and if they were to keep on the level, they must ride close to us as they went by.

The General was talking to the Major upon his right. The latter was regarding us fixedly. It *was* Berry.

" Yes, I can see it isn't hers now ; but the camel my wife rides is very like that one on the right, and she said she might be taking the Professor out here this afternoon. He's rather an authority on excavation, you know."

With the tail of my eye I saw Adèle start violently at his words. I urged my mount to her side.

" Carry it off," I growled, " carry it off. They'll be by in a moment. Berry's there, but don't notice him."

She nodded.

I heard a horse snort, and the General laughed.

" Ah, Pleydell, your pony camel-shy ? Now, this old fellow of mine is a wonder. Never turns a hair. I believe you could run him in double harness with a camel and he wouldn't object. Any camel in the world, that is, except one. And that's the one I was speaking of—my wife's. D'you know, there's a sort of feeling between those two animals. Whenever he comes anywhere near it, the brute produces its water-bottle and gurgles at him. And he won't have it at any price. Squeals and kicks, and he's away if he's half a chance."

" 'Straordinary thing, sir," said Berry gravely.

They were only twenty paces behind us now, and the General pushed his mount into a trot to pass. As I have said, it was a narrow place. He made to overtake us on the right, and as he drew abreast of Adèle, her camel deliberately turned, opened its mouth, revealing a kind of bladder, and gave vent to a most offensive gurgle. The result was appalling. In less time than it takes to record the disaster, the General's horse squealed, lashed out like a wild animal, swung round, and streaked into the desert.

To say that the sudden swerve unsettled the General would be to understate what occurred. After travel-ling for about two hundred yards, seemingly crouched upon the near shoulder of his mount, that gallant officer appeared to succumb to the inevitable, for he slid slowly round its neck and took a first-class toss about fifty yards later.

The awful silence was broken by the A.D.C.

" Hurray ! He's off," observed that gentleman, with an indecent relish. Then he winked at Berry and galloped in the direction of his fallen chief, with the two orderlies thundering behind him. It was with relief that I noticed that the distant huddle of khaki and red was sitting up and looking about him.

Adèle and I pushed on.

" Can you beat it ? " said Berry. A glance showed me that he was riding as close behind us as his horse would permit. " Can you beat it ? First they pinch his wife's camels, and then they subscribe to one of the most unwarrantable outrages upon his person that I have ever witnessed. Most serious. Larceny of two live camels and grievous bodily harm by means of a trick. They won't be out for years. When charged, they made no reply. A long list of previous convictions against the male prisoner was proved by his brother-in-law, for whom great sympathy was felt. Police officers from New York identified his accomplice as Slipaway Doll, a notorious female crook, who was wanted for a daring jewel robbery in Philadelphia."

I looked over my shoulder.

" Go away," I said. " We found the camels straying, and are now in the act of restoring them to their rightful owners."

Berry continued to soliloquize.

" It is understood that a further indictment for perjury will be preferred, in view of the hideous lies with which the accused sought to palliate their abominable behaviour. The thanks of the community as a whole are due to Major Pleydell, but for whose prompt action and fearless sense of duty these desperate characters might still be at large. Seriously, if I wasn't here, you'd be for it, you two. I don't know what on earth you've been doing, but judging from Adèle's headgear, I associate you with that Handley-Page we were looking at. I must hear all about it at dinner. And now listen. It's a great deal more than you deserve, but my car's at Mena, as well as the General's. I'll ride on and tell the driver to expect you and to take you to Cairo just as quick as he can. Hand the camels over to one of those guide fellows on the right, and sprint for Mena House for all you're worth."

The next moment he was gone in a flurry of sand.

By this time we were under the shade of the Great Pyramid, and the ground was hard. I slid off somehow, and Adèle took a flying leap into my arms, as the natives to whom I had beckoned came running up. As we ran down the slope to Mena House, Berry met and passed us at the canter. By way of greeting he just raised his eyes to heaven.

A moment later we were in the car and stealing along the long straight road that leads to Giseh.

Carefully I wrapped the rugs about Adèle lest she should take cold.

*   *   *   *   *

Berry helped himself to another glass of port.

" The point," he said, " is this. Am I a *deus ex machina* or not ? "

" That," said I, " was your rôle this afternoon. But I wish you'd tell me what you told the General."

" Suffice it that I beguiled him."

I sighed.

" When you are secretive," I said, " I become uneasy. Any unusual action on your part is a sure sign of mischief. To take an extreme example, if you took to drinking water, I should leave the country."

My brother-in-law smiled.

" Since you press me," he said, with a yawn, " I told him the truth."

" You didn't ? "

He nodded.

" Names and all. Said you'd pinched the camels and ridden them, knowing them to have been stolen. I added that you suffered from delusions, and that this afternoon you thought you were Abraham. Adèle was acting under your coercion. He was rather wild at first, but he's mad on Bridge, and when I told him you were one of the best players in the United Kingdom, he got quite chirpy. You're going to make a four at the Turf Club to-morrow evening."

" I might have known," said I wearily. " You know I hate cards, and that I play Bridge about twice a year."

" Never mind," said Berry, piercing a cigar. " If you revoke more than once, put the blame on me, and say that I made a mistake, and it's Grab you're such a nut at—or draughts. If he tries to assault you, pretend that you think you're John Bunyan in a fit of religious terror. Has any gentleman got a lucifer match ? "

*   *   *   *   *

The train which was to bear us to Port Said, en route for England, was due to leave Cairo in less than a minute, and Jonah, Berry, and I were about to follow the girls into the corridor carriage, when a shriek from Adèle attracted our attention. We rushed down the corridor, to see the far door of the compartment open and Adèle swinging herself down on to the metals. Jill pointed excitedly to a native who was running as hard as he could with a green dressing-case in his hand.

As I passed Adèle I heard a whistle.

" Go back ! " she cried. " You'll lose the train. "

" And leave you behind ? Not likely."

A moment later the thief dropped his booty—for I was overtaking him fast—and started to leg it harder than ever. Recognizing the hopelessness of trying to catch him, now that he had shed his encumbrance, I contented myself with picking up the dressing-case, and turned to see the train gliding out of the station. Framed in the doorway of the compartment we had left were as much of Berry, Jonah, Daphne and Jill as its dimensions would admit. All four were waving and crying what I took to be instructions and advice. Thirty paces away stood Adèle—all among the points —waving frantically in response.

As the train roared into the distance, I began to pick my way across the rails to where my companion was standing. She spread out her hands with a little gesture of dismay.

" I'm so dreadfully sorry," she cried. " I've made you miss your train, and——"

" He made us miss our train," I corrected, nodding in the direction of the runaway thief. " It wasn't your fault. I only wish I could have caught the brute."

" I can never thank you enough. But what ever shall we do ? "

It was certainly awkward.

It was now half-past four. Another train would not leave for Port Said until ten the next morning and the boat by which we were sailing was expected to leave at noon on that day. Incidentally, with the exception of the contents of the dressing-case, neither of us had anything at all but the clothes we were wearing.

It is, however, the acute crisis which provokes the brain-wave.

As we left the line for the platform, I caught Adèle by the arm.

" Adèle, will you waste your sweetness on the desert air a second time ? In other words, if Geoffrey can fly us to Port Said, are you on ? "

" But of course ! "

The little group of curious officials who were stolidly regarding our approach were galvanized into action by my peremptory demand for a telephone, and I was conducted to the R.T.O.'s office without delay. As soon as the connection had been made, and I recognized Geoffrey's voice :

"I say, old fellow," said I, "have you got another pair of slacks you don't want ? "

"What—again ? " he cried. "Besides, I thought you'd gone."

I explained. When I had finished :

"There's a Handley-Page going to Ismailia in half an hour," he said. "I'm not taking her really, but I will. Can you do it ? She'll have to dress in my hut."

"Is Ismailia any good ? " I queried.

"The train you missed'll call there about nine."

"Prepare the slacks," said I. "We will be with you in fifteen minutes."

We were. And in another twenty we were off the ground and heading north-east.

*   *   *   *   *

Fifty minutes later we sighted Lake Timsah, and when we landed in a spacious aerodrome at Ismailia, it was barely an hour since we had left Cairo.

Fortunately our arrival occasioned no excitement, and, with the exception of a mechanic or two, nobody appeared as we taxied towards the hangars.

Geoffrey pointed to a shed in the distance.

"That's where they keep the cars and tenders," he said. "Just stroll over there, and I'll find the E.O. and get him to send you into the town right away."

He was as good as his word.

As we reached the garage, I heard a mechanic speaking upon the telephone.

"Very good, sir. To the station at once. Yes, quite ready. Good-bye, sir."

The next moment he was starting up a great touring car.

As we took our seats, Geoffrey came running up.
" Aren't you coming ? " said Adèle.

He shook his head.

" Might see you later at the Club, unless you take
an earlier train to Port Said. The one your party's
on won't fetch up there till about eleven. If you do,
just leave the coats at the Club. I'll have to dine in
the mess here to-night, any way. If I don't see you
again. . . ." He put out his hand.

Adèle caught that and the other in her own.

" I can't ever thank you enough," she said. " Come
to America one day, and I'll try and show you I'm
grateful. When I think of your beautiful trousers, I
feel so guilty. Two pairs ! "

" Cheap at the price," said Geoffrey gallantly.
" And so long as I have a pair to my back, they're
always at your service."

" Good-bye, St. Martin."

" So long, Geoffrey," said I. " You know what
I think of you. Come home soon."

Geoffrey nodded to the chauffeur, and the car slid
past a sentry and on to the white-brown track. We
turned and waved till we could see him no longer.

We stopped at the Club. Here I learned that the
station was five minutes' walk, and that a train left
for Port Said in a quarter of an hour.

After a hurried consultation we dismissed the car,
and, as we emerged from the garden entrance, no one
would have recognized the smart American girl and
her companion as the two muffled aviators who had
entered the Club from the street five minutes before.

To catch the down train was easy enough.

*   *   *   *   *

At eleven o'clock Adèle and I were still seated upon
the verandah of the Casino Palace Hotel, Port Said,

taking our ease. We had dined excellently, if a little late, and were feeling as fresh as paint. Except for a distant waiter and a party of French people at the other end of the verandah, we were alone.

"They'll be here any time now," said I, looking at my watch. "Keep calm."

Adèle gurgled delightedly.

"Berry'll have a fit when he sees us," she said. "I wouldn't miss his face for a thousand dollars."

"Which reminds me," said I. "You and I have an account to square."

My companion stopped laughing and sat very still. I turned to glance at her. She was leaning back in her bent-cane chair, looking straight ahead into the darkness over the sea, whose great rollers we could hear tumbling lazily towards us but a hundred paces away. As I looked, a puff of wind ruffled its way through her soft, dark hair. The light was dim, and I could not be sure whether that same faint ghost of a smile that once before had mocked me was haunting her red mouth. I continued :

"You were to give me anything, you remember, if I got you back to Cairo that evening by half-past six."

"In reason," whispered Adèle.

"Would you rather knit me a body-belt in the Guards' colours, or let me see your ears ? "

The ghost became a reality.

"Which you like," said Adèle.

"What's the American for ' darling ' ? " I said. "I want to address you."

As she paid her debt, the rattle of more than one approaching *arabiya* made itself heard. We settled ourselves nonchalantly, and began to discuss the situation in Poland.

"What a day ! " It was Berry's voice. "Nice

little journey hasn't it been ? I think I enjoyed that wait at Zagzig as much as anything. You know. Where the engine sprayed us with dirty water and we had to shut the windows."

" For goodness' sake, get out," said Daphne.

" Why ? " said her husband. " Listen to the thunder of the Atlantic on our left front. What was it Cowper said ? " He raised his voice, " Jonah ! "

" Hullo," came from the other *arabiya*.

" Do you say ' Coughper ' or ' Cooper ' ? Personally I always say ' Wordsworth.' "

" Will you get out ? " said Daphne fiercely.

A moment later, wearily she and Jonah ascended the steps. I could hear Jill laughing as Berry entrusted various articles of baggage—Adèle's and mine among them—to the porter's care.

Jonah saw us first.

" Good lord ! " he cried, standing still.

Then my sister saw us, and caught her breath.

" You are late," said I, stifling a yawn.

There was a shriek from Jill, and then she and Daphne flung themselves upon Adèle with every manifestation of amazement and delight. Jonah sank on to a chair, wide-eyed and shaking his head. I rose to my feet and took a step forward.

Berry came up the steps.

" What is it ? " he was saying. " Rabies, or have you met someone you know ? "

Then he saw me.

For fully a quarter of a minute we regarded one another in silence. Then he dropped everything he was carrying, and, stepping out of the havoc of wraps and sticks and dispatch-cases, walked round me on tip-toe. Presently he came up and felt me, then peered into my face.

" From the hooded (*sic*) look in your eyes and the unpleasant stench of spirits emanating from your person, I assume you have been the guest of the Royal Air Force. Did you have a nice flight ? "

" Lovely, thanks. Hope our luggage wasn't a nuisance ? "

" Don't mention it. I love working for you. Give me your room number, and I'll go and turn your bed down. You know, I'm not at all certain you didn't do it on purpose."

I clapped him on the back.

" I knew I could depend upon you," I said. " And there "—I pointed to a table—" is your reward."

" Don't say it's iced beer," said Berry. " I can't bear it."

" But it is," said Jonah, opening a bottle.

Berry turned to me, glass in hand.

" I'm not going to wish you luck," he said, " because you have more than your share already. But I am gratified to observe that, waster as you will always be, somewhere beneath that mass of corruption which you call your soul there are still stirring the instincts of humanity. And now I want a cigarette. You'll find some in your dispatch-case." He pointed to where he had dropped it. " By the way, I wish you wouldn't lock your things. Jonah and I had to borrow a ticket-punch from the conductor to get it open."

CHAPTER V

AS ROME DOES

SOLEMNLY we regarded the Colosseum.

"Reminds me of the Albert Hall with the lid off," said Berry. "But it does want doing up. Glad I haven't got it on a full repairing lease."

"Is anything sacred to you?" demanded Daphne.

"Yes," said her husband. "My appetite. That is why I venture for the second time to suggest that we should leave this relic of barbarity without delay. Besides, it revives painful memories."

"When were you here before?" said Jonah.

"In a previous existence. Joan of Arc was by no means my first incarnation. In A.D. 77 I was a comic gladiator. Used to fight with gorgonzolas which had been previously maddened by having Schiller read to them in the original tongue. They used to call me 'Sticking Plaster,' because I was always coming off."

"Of course you're spoiling the whole place for me," said his wife. "I came here——"

"They seem to have moved the cloak-room," continued Berry, looking about him. "It used to be over there just behind the mammoth-hutches."

This was too much for Jill and Adèle, who abandoned themselves to uncontrolled merriment. With a gesture of resignation, Daphne detached herself from the party and strolled out of earshot. Berry looked at me.

"I wonder if we can smoke," he said. "They used not to allow it before 1300 hours. Anyone who broke the rule was thrown to the bears. Not the ordinary ones, but the Camemberts. A shocking fate."

"Trajan altered all that," said I. "But, of course, that was after your death."

"Yes," said Berry. "I was flayed alive for trespass in 96. After that I became a sacred sucking-pig at Antioch. Thank you." He accepted a cigarette. "How many of these did we bring in all?"

"Adèle and I brought five hundred each," said Jill. "So did Daphne."

"Jonah and I a thousand," said I. "And you?"

Berry spread out his hands.

"Most unfortunately——"

I shut the case with a snap.

"Make the most of that one," said I. "It's the last you'll take off me. If I'd had the slightest idea you hadn't troubled, d'you think I'd have been financing you for the last ten days?"

"D'you mean to say you never brought any at all?" said Jonah.

"Fact," said Berry. "Look at those idle tiers. Do you know what they mean?"

Jonah turned to me.

"And I let him have a box of a hundred yesterday because he said he couldn't get at his."

I shrugged my shoulders.

"It was the truth," said Berry. "If they weren't there, I couldn't get at them. Obviously."

Jonah raised his eyes to heaven and turned to follow Daphne, who was alternately consulting a guide-book and scrutinizing the tremendous ruin.

"It is wonderful, isn't it?" said Adèle, looking about her. "How many did it hold?"

" Eighty thousand, I think," said I.   " Makes you
think, doesn't it ? "

She nodded.

" You ought to have seen it full," said Berry.
" Crammed.   And not a bit of paper in the house.
They used to have to put the orchestra in the arena
sometimes.   It didn't work, though.   They were
roped off, of course.   But the lions didn't see the rope
or something.   Any way——"

He stopped to light his cigarette.

" I'm afraid to ask anything else," said Adèle, with
such gravity as she could command, " and there are
such heaps of things I want to know."

" Come along," said I.   " This way.   My memory's
not like his, but one term I came out top in Roman
History."

As we moved away, my brother-in-law addressed
himself to Jill.

" My dear," he said, " let this be a lesson to you.
Never cast a silk purse before swine."

We were all on the way from Egypt to England.
We had come by Taranto, and had seized upon the
opportunity of spending a few days in Rome.   No
one of us had visited the city before.

It is not remarkable that we were all fascinated.
Even Berry, for all his ribaldry, was profoundly
impressed.   There was so much that was so venerable.
If Rome had been smaller—if we could have seen a
quarter at a time, perhaps it might have been otherwise.   But there was so much—and every yard of it
was hallowed ground.   We stood as pygmies beside
the mighty ghosts with which, for me, the streets were
thronged.   It was difficult to think that they, too, had
been men and women of like passions with us.   They
had been the Royalty of the world ; and so, for us,

Rome was a palace and her ways ' the presence strew'd.'
What manner of man had sunned himself at this
corner ? Maybe but a greasy-chopped scullion, a
coarse fellow, one-eyed, yet—a Roman. Small enough
fry while he lived, two thousand years have made his
shade that of a giant. So with their deeds and lives
and manners—Time has magnified them all, good and
evil alike, dressed them in purple dignity, so that the
venue of them is full of such tremendous memories,
the aged stocks and stones conjure up visions so not-
able, as make you fall silent with thinking on them.

But that was when we were grave.

Adèle Feste and I were fast friends. Indeed, we
all loved her, and the reflection that, when we reached
England, she was destined to leave us and continue her
journey to her home in the United States was already
painful, and one which we endeavoured to thrust aside
so often as it recurred.

Together she and I passed beneath one of the great
archways.

" Of course, I shall simply live to come here again,"
said Adèle, staring up at the great walls.

" May I come with you, when you do ? "

Adèle tilted her chin.

" If you still want to, and my husband doesn't
object."

" Your marriage would, of course, complicate
matters. I suppose you couldn't revisit Rome first
and marry afterwards ? "

Adèle looked thoughtful.

" Most American girls seem to get married between
their first and second visits to Europe," she said. " Of
course, I might be an exception. You never know."

" You're an exception to every rule I ever knew,"
said I. " Look at the way you move, for instance."

" But I can't."

" Nor you can. And you can't see yourself from behind, either. Or when you're dancing, or—— You do miss a lot, Adèle. D'you mind smiling for me ? Thank you."

She threw back her head and laughed.

" Don't flatter yourself," she said. " That wasn't for you. I smile for nobody."

I sighed.

" That's right. Break my heart. Throw it down and jump on it. You cracked it the first day I saw you. Now smash it up." I looked at her. " And when my sister taxes you with your carelessness, what shall you say ? "

" I shall tell her that it ' came in two in me 'and,' " replied Adèle. " And there's Jill waving. I expect they're thinking about lunch."

As we came up :

" To say," said Berry, " that I am an-hungered conveys nothing at all. My vitals are screaming for nourishment. My paunch——"

" Beast," said Daphne. " Vulgar beast."

" No coarseness, please," said her husband. " But I've been butchered to make one Roman holiday, and I'm not going to be starved to make another. Have you ever been flayed, Jonah ? "

" Very seldom."

" During my martyrdom," said Berry, " ' Bohême ' was played backwards to drown my cries. I don't suppose they gave you a band, did they ? "

Jonah shook his head.

" I suffered in silence," he said. " Same as I'm doing now."

" How rude ! " said my brother-in-law. " How very rude ! Never mind. I expect he wants his

lunch. I told you about my vitals, didn't I? Oh,
yes. If you remember, I was interrupted just as I
was saying that my——"

"This is sheer blackmail," said Daphne, turning
to Adèle. "It's a great mistake to give in to the
brute, but it's a question of being insulted or letting him have his way. We'll leave him behind to-
morrow."

As we set our faces towards the entrance:

"I shall begin with melon," said Berry.

*   *   *   *   *

Cultivate the siesta habit, and it is not so easy to
be rid of it again. Berry and Daphne and Jill had
been long enough in Egypt to become accustomed to
a rest after luncheon. This they were learning to
curtail, but they never left the hotel before four. Miss
Feste was more energetic. Besides, she had not been
in Egypt so long. Jonah had no excuse, and was
quite frank about it. "Sheer laziness," he would say.
"Sheer laziness. But a real sleep after lunch is to
my liking. Wish I'd thought of it before." And then
he would follow the others into the lift, and congratulate
them on "the contraction of a vice as wise as it is
beneficial."

Left to our own devices, Adèle and I usually went
for a stroll till tea-time. In this point the day on
which we had visited the Colosseum was not excep-
tional. When the other four had shamefacedly retired
to their respective rooms, I turned to Miss Feste.

"Shall we push off again? Shall we perambulate?
Or do you want to write letters?"

"I do not," said Adèle. "I ought to. It's scanda-
lous. Mother will be cabling to the Embassy about
me, if I don't take care. But I just can't sit here
with Rome at the door."

I rose to my feet.

" When I return," I said, " I shall have my headgear with me."

Ten minutes later we were abroad.

It was a brilliant afternoon. Not a cloud floated in the blue sky, there was no wind, and the sun blazed in the heaven, flooding the broad streets and open spaces with warmth and lustre, and lighting so faithfully the precious buildings that the eye need miss no jot or tittle of their beauty, fine and elusory though it might be.

Adèle and I went our way leisurely. As we turned the corner of a little alley tucked under the shadow of some great gallery, we almost collided with a dignitary of the Roman Catholic Church.

As I raised my hat :

" Why, Monseigneur ! " cried Adèle.

" My dear child ! "

The two shook hands.

" I am so glad to see you," said Adèle. Then she introduced me. " You're fellow-countrymen," she added, turning to me. " Monseigneur Forest lives in Rome, but he is still an Englishman."

" So I can see."

It was indeed a typically English face that was smiling from under the broad-brimmed hat. The features were fine and regular, the mouth kindly, the chin strong. A fresh colour was springing in his cheeks, and honesty sat in his blue eyes for all to see. Monseigneur was very tall and broad in proportion— fifty years old, perhaps, but I had never seen a finer man.

" And what are you doing here, my dear ? I wish I could believe that you were actually on your way to see me."

" I wasn't," said Adèle truthfully. " But I'll come gladly. We're on our way back from Egypt. . . ." Quickly she told him the circumstances of our visit. " Are you a cardinal yet ? " she added naïvely.

The prelate smiled.

" Not yet, not yet." He sighed. " And now I must go, or I shall be late. Come, both of you, to tea with me the day after to-morrow." He gave us his address. " It will make me so happy."

Gratefully we accepted.

The next moment he was gone.

As we walked, Adèle told me about him. They had been members of the same house-party in France in July, 1914. " And then the War came in the middle of it all, and we all left, and I didn't think I'd ever see him again. But I never forgot. He's just the finest gentleman that ever happened."

" He never forgot, either." Up went the chin. " And I shan't ever forget," I added. " That makes three. Had you cut your hair short when you met him ? "

Adèle shook her head, smiling.

" Ah. Then it must have been your brown eyes. Or your mouth. And yet I don't know. There's so much of you that's beautiful."

" For Heaven's sake," said Adèle, " leave something to the imagination."

" Don't blame me, my dear. You shouldn't be so attractive. Be thankful that I don't burst into song. I'm not at all sure I'm not going to intone, as it is. I shouldn't hesitate if I had a tuning-fork."

We had been strolling careless of our whereabouts, and as I spoke we entered a small sequestered square. Its houses were manifestly ancient, and on one side was towering the back wall of a church. The stained glass of a beautiful window flamed in the afternoon sun. Save for two men, the square was deserted. Doors and windows were open, but shutters were closed and blinds lowered. None of the occupants were in sight.

The two men were going in opposite directions. One moved heavily. Decently dressed, he might have been a merchant on his way to his office, wrapped in contemplation. The other was approaching us, so that we could see his face. This was very Italian, and there was a queer scared look in his eyes. His nose seemed to have been bent out of the straight. Whether he saw us or not I cannot say, but, as he passed the merchant, he turned, whipped his right hand from his pocket, and struck twice at the other's back. Without a cry the merchant spun round and fell heavily backwards on to the cobbles. In a flash his assailant had thrust his hand into his victim's breast, and was darting away in the direction from which he had come, cramming something into his pocket as he ran.

The whole thing was so sudden and unexpected that I was stupefied. Indeed, for the fraction of a second I wondered whether I had witnessed a vision, or imagination had played a mad trick upon my brain, but instantaneously the grim figure lying asprawl in the hot sunshine gave me the lie. Adèle gasped, shuddered, and caught at my arm, and the next moment I was across the little square in hot pursuit of the assassin.

The little silent street down which he had sped was tortuous, and though I was expecting to see him when I rounded a bend, the next reach of the alley was empty, and fifty paces further on the street curled again. Cursing my folly for not starting earlier in pursuit, I covered the fifty yards at a furious rate, only to find myself at a place where four ways met. Anxiously I stared down the little streets in turn. Here was a little traffic and a few passers-by, but there was no one that at all resembled the man of whom I was in chase.

I stood still, wondering what to do. Since I could not speak a word of Italian, I hesitated to accost the people that I saw about me. Vainly I scanned the streets for a policeman. Then I heard the sound of quick breathing behind me, and swung round, to see Adèle standing quite close to me, one little hand pressed to her side

" Gone ? "

She flung the question at me a little unsteadily.

I nodded.

" Not a sign of him," I said. " But I thought you'd stay——"

" He had a knife," she said slowly. " And you had nothing. I just couldn't have stayed. Besides, there was a man coming. I saw him."

I slid her arm into mine and held it.

" Dear little Adèle."

" We must go back," she said, in a low voice. " Oh, how cruel and treacherous it was ! That poor man. . . . What ghastly misery in some home to-night ! "

" He mayn't be dead," I said hopefully, as we turned to make our way back to the quiet square.

Adèle brushed a hand across her eyes.

" Yes," she said quietly. " He was dead. He was lying too still, too unnaturally. He was dead."

" I don't know what we'd better do," said I. " I suppose there'll be some police there by now, and I'd better give them my card and say where I'm staying. I don't want you to be mixed up in it, if we can help it, but I'd like to see justice done."

"I'm so afraid no one'll speak English. Would it be best to go straight back to the hotel and write a note to the Chief of the Police, saying you witnessed the murder and are willing to give them what information you can, if they communicate? They'll have to get an interpreter to translate it, and it'll show them you can't talk Italian. Or you could say so in the note."

"I think that would be best. But, all the same, I think I'll give one of the police my card right away. It might convey something to him. And then we'll go straight back to the hotel."

Two minutes later we were back in the little square. Save for two large pigeons, sleeking themselves in the sun, it was quite empty.

*   *   *   *   *

An hour or so later, when we were finishing tea, I drew up my chair and told the others exactly what we had seen. Adèle had gone to her room, and had not yet reappeared. When I had finished—

"Hallucination," said Berry shortly. "What you saw was a mirage."

"Don't be a fool," said I. "I want to know what to do."

"What did you drink for lunch?"

"All right. Ask Adèle. She drank nothing."

"I'd better go to her," said Daphne, rising. "I expect she's rather upset."

"My dear fellow," said Berry, "the effect of the sun upon alcoholism is notorious."

I turned to Jonah.

"You believe me?"

"I do. And I should leave it alone. They're a funny crowd, these Italians. Looks to me like the Camorra or something. And they simply hate being interfered with. After all, you did what you could."

"I'm not at all easy about it. I feel I ought to put my knowledge at the disposal of the police. It seems only fair to the wretched fellow who was done in."

"But he wasn't," said Berry.

"Well, somebody'd got him away, but, if he wasn't actually dead, it was a devilish near thing. He went down like an ox."

"No blood on the cobbles ? " said Berry.

I shook my head.

"Of course, he might have been bleeding internally. I confess it beats me. But there you are. I don't attempt to explain it."

"My advice is to sit tight and do nothing," said Jonah.

"I agree," said Berry, yawning. "If you've nothing better to tell the police than what you've told us, they'll detain you as an idiot."

"I expected this," I said bitterly. "I knew you'd ridicule the whole thing. I only wish you'd been there yourself."

"I remember," said Berry, "when I was in Antimacassar, a very similar experience. As I was returning from the club about midnight, a large skewbald goat stopped me and, speaking in broken Pekingese, asked if he could use the telephone. On my refusing, the animal burst into tears and changed into a mine-field."

This was too much. I rose with such dignity as I could command and, glancing sorrowfully at Jill and Jonah, both of whom were shaking with laughter, strolled out of the lounge.

As we sat down to dinner that evening—five of

us only, for Adèle was still resting—my brother-in-law handed me an unsealed letter.

"I'm afraid I was hasty this afternoon," he said. "By way of reparation I have drafted a letter for you to send to the Chief Constable or whatever they call him."

"Thank you," said I, giving it back. "Take it as read."

With a sigh Berry passed it to Jill.

In a shaking voice the latter read as follows :

"Sir,—I witnessed the murder which was not committed in the square this afternoon. Two men were concerned. The victim looked like a merchant, but fell like an ox. I cannot explain this. The victor had a scared look and a bent nose. For this the aroma of my cigar may have been responsible. In spite of the fact that he was well out of sight before I started to run after him, I failed to overtake him. I cannot explain this. When we got back to the square, the victim had disappeared. I am almost sure it was the same square, too.

"Hoping you are quite well,
"Yours, etc.
"P.S.—Wasn't it funny ? "

When the laughter had subsided :

"As a matter of fact," said Daphne, "you've omitted the best piece of evidence he's got."

"What's that ? " said Jonah.

"Adèle."

"What about her ? "

"She's so unlike herself that I've sent for a doctor."

*　　*　　*　　*　　*

After a good night's rest, Adèle was much better, but the impression created by the indisputable fact that she had experienced a severe shock of some kind was manifest.

Early the following morning Berry apologized for his scepticism, and desired me to conduct him to the scene of the tragedy. Jill stayed with Adèle, but Daphne and Jonah insisted upon accompanying my brother-in-law to the little square.

The crime was reconstructed, my pursuit of the assassin was re-enacted, and every aspect of the affair was scrutinized—all upon the very spot where the strange event had taken place.

Berry insisted on playing the part of the victim, and nothing would do but that I should push him in the back and bolt up the curling street. And Jonah was prevailed upon to run after me. Then Berry pushed Jonah, and I ran after him. Then Jonah pushed Daphne and bolted, and I told Berry when to start in pursuit. This last attempt at reconstruction proved not only abortive, but costly, for, on rounding the second bend of the alley, Jonah came into violent collision with a fat man who was pushing a perambulator full of vegetables, and brought them both down. He was in the act of assisting the indignant and tearful owner to get the perambulator upon its wheels, when Berry crashed into the trio, sending Jonah reeling into a doorway, the perambulator once more on to its side, and bringing the luckless Roman heavily to the ground for the second time. The latter was now thoroughly frightened and considerably hurt, while the inhuman but inevitable laughter into which his two aggressors subsided exasperated him to the point of madness. The more he wept and raved, the more helpless they became, and when Daphne and I arrived upon the scene, it was clear that between fright, suspicion, and rage, he was in some peril of losing his reason. A crowd was beginning to collect, when I thrust a note for fifty lire into his hand and hustled the others away.

" And that's that," said Daphne, as we hurried back the way we had come. " No more reconstruction for me. Silly stupid rot. I was a fool to come. I might have known——"

" Not at all," said Berry. " I count this a good morning's work. The solution of all great problems depends upon successful elimination. Just now I overtook Jonah. Why? Because his withdrawal was obstructed by a foreign body in the shape of a comic merchant complete with pram. That Boy did not overtake the assassin establishes the fact that the latter met with no such obstruction. We can therefore eliminate——"

" Valuable, no doubt," said I grimly, " but hardly worth fifty lire."

" More," said Berry. " We have this day forged such a link in the chain of evidence as shall never come unstuck. Frankly, I regard it as the second nail in the assailant's coffin."

" Fool," said Daphne. " What was the first ? "

" This," said her husband, drawing a button from his pocket. " It came off my trousers this morning, but I shall tell the bloodhounds I found it in the square."

*   *   *   *   *

Precisely at four o'clock on the following afternoon Adèle and I were standing upon the steps of Monseigneur Forest's house. The maid who opened the door seemed to be a little uncertain whether to admit us or no, and murmured something in Italian in response to the mention of her master's name. Doubtless the latter had few visitors. However, at a glance from me, Adèle stepped boldly into the cool hall, and a moment later we were ushered into a pleasant, sunny room, whose tall French windows opened directly on to a little flagged terrace overlooking the garden. The door closed, and we were alone.

Adèle sank into a chair, and I stood looking about me. The room was quietly furnished, but everything was in excellent taste and beautifully kept. The polished floor gleamed, the sheen of the silver candle-sticks was reflected by the rosewood table upon which they stood, and a slow wood fire was burning upon the well-swept hearth. Two or three old rugs were spread upon the parquet, and the rich blue curtains that swayed about the open windows made with the soft grey wall-paper a silent harmony that should still the restlessness of the most troubled mind. A grand piano stood at one end of the chamber, and, while there were no flowers, the air was charged with the magic of potpourri, that clean, sweet, rosy breath that instantly remembers long, low rooms, cool in the summer's heat, and the old quiet of English country, as can neither pen nor brush, charm they never so wisely.

" I like your Monseigneur," I said.

" I told you you would."

I nodded.

" By the way, what do I do when he comes in ? I mean, he's a big fellow, isn't he ? And if I ought to take off my boots, or squint, or kiss his wrist-watch— well, I'd like to do the right thing. When in Rome, you know——"

Miss Feste smiled.

" Strictly," she said, " you ought to keep your hat on and sing ' Tipperary ' in Latin as he approaches.

But he's not very particular, and I dare say he'll excuse you."

"Nonsense. I shall be charmed." I pointed to the piano. "D'you mind giving me B flat, or C sharp, or M for Mother, or something just to make sure I get off all right?"

Drawing off her gloves, Adèle stepped to the piano and took her seat on the wide stool. With her fingers upon the keys, she looked at me.

"I'll just have a run through first," she said, and with that she began to play.

The introductory chords rang out, faded, and up out of their cadence swelled the lullaby of an exquisite valse, rising and falling and sweeping so rarely that in a moment the quiet room was filled with melody.

It was manifest that Adèle Feste was no ordinary player of tunes.

I had never thought of her as a pianist, and I stood still, spell-bound, staring like a zany and thinking, too, how beautiful she was. And she sat there regardless, straight as an arrow, making me music fit for a king.

The valse faded, a brown eye glanced in my direction, a faint smile played about the red lips, and, with tuck of drum, the familiar pulse of "Come Over Here" came throbbing into audience. I crossed the room and sat down beside my lady on the broad seat.

The smile deepened.

"That wasn't an invitation," said Adèle.

"I know," said I. "It was a challenge. You wicked girl. May I talk to you, or is it badgering as well as sacrilege?"

"Carry on."

"Why didn't you tell me?"

"You never asked. Besides——"

I sighed.

" ' Orpheus with his lute made trees.' You are making most precious melody. And I am about to make love."

With a frown, Adèle threaded her way out of rag-time and into " The Soldiers' Chorus."

" No good," said I.   " And it isn't the music, either. It's the laughter in your eyes and the play of your lips and the sweep of your dark hair——" I stopped to gaze at the rosy, pointed fingers that fled so fast over the keys.   " I always loved your hands, and now I shall reverence them, too."

With a shrug of her dainty shoulders, Adèle stamped off the parade-ground and climbed into Montmartre. At the touch of those slender fingers the plaintive strains of " Bohême " rose up, hesitating and tremulous.

" You witch," I whispered.   " You Columbine. Adèle, I——"

" If you're going to be silly, I shall stop."

" That would be fatal.   The minute you stop I shall kiss you.   Your only hope is to go on playing till Monseigneur comes into the room."

Adèle raised her eyebrows and shot me a curious glance.   The next minute she tumbled out of opera and fell into rag-time again.

" Does she sing, too ? " said I.

" She has been known to.   But I think I've done enough harm for one day."

" Harm ? "

She nodded.

" You've given me the time of my life.   You've translated yourself.   You've expressed your charm in melody."

The tune faltered, recovered its rhythm, and then, drawing to a close, slowed down and—stopped.   But before its last notes had died away, the sensitive fingers had leaped again into life, and Adèle was floating into the valse of " The Lilac Domino."

I bit my lip.

With the tail of my eye I saw her mouth quiver with suppressed laughter.

The haunting melody flowed on, and I closed my eyes. She was playing very softly, so that we both heard the steps in the room above and a door bang.

" The siege is raised," said I. " Here comes the relieving force."

Then I stood up.

" I've just loved it," I said.

For a moment Adèle looked me in the face. Then she deliberately took her hands off the keys and examined her left palm.

" You know," she began, " I——"

When I touched her on the shoulder, she put up her face like a child.

The steps came to a stop in the hall outside, and the next moment the door opened and a man came in.

From his dress and manner I took him to be a valet. Standing by the door, he bowed and then spoke rapidly in broken English.

" If Signor and Signora 'ave come to see Monseigneur, I am afraid 'e will not come for some time. 'E was go to ze Vatican ago one 'alf-hour."

We stared at him in silence.

" I am very sorry," he added, spreading out his hands and inclining his head to one side. With shrugged shoulders he stood there, Apology personified.

I tried to mutter something, but no words came. I could hear Adèle's breath coming short and quick by my shoulder. And I knew that she was gazing,

as I was, at the man with the bent nose whom I had
chased so vainly two days before.

    *   *   *   *   *

We were all late for dinner that night, and it was
nearly a quarter to nine before we took our seats in
the restaurant of the hotel.

For more than an hour we had all been sitting in
Daphne's room, discussing the latest development of
the tragedy, and as yet we had arrived at no decision
regarding the steps we should take.

Meditatively Berry sipped his soup. Then he laid
down his spoon and addressed me.

" You're positive he didn't recognize you ? " he
said.

" Quite."

" Then I think you were wise not to collar him."

" I agree," said Jonah. " Now you know where
he is, you can lay your hand on him at any time. If
he'd tried to bolt when he saw you, that would have
been another matter."

" It's the most extraordinary thing I ever knew,"
said Daphne. " Weren't you frightened, Adèle ? "

Miss Feste shook her head.

" I just felt stupefied," she said. " To this moment
I don't know how I got out of the house."

" Nor do I," said I. " I know I tripped over everything and nearly took a toss down the front steps.
I was like a man in a dream."

" But what about Monseigneur Forest ? " said Jill.
" Oughtn't he to know ? "

" That's what worries me," said Adèle. " It's such
a terrible thing for him to have that awful man in his
service—waiting on him."

" And why wasn't he there when he asked you to
tea ? " said Daphne.

" Oh, I expect he'd forgotten all right. He's awfully vague. All the same——"

She broke off, knitting her smooth brows.

" Well, let's leave it alone for a bit, any way," said Berry. " We'll settle what's got to be done to-morrow morning. And now—what shall we drink ? "

The discussion of this new topic was cut short by the arrival of the wine-waiter with a magnum of champagne.

" My fault," said Berry, by way of explanation. " And two others are on the way, so please get down to it. To-day's my birthday."

" But you had one six weeks ago," said Adèle. " The day we went to Sakkara."

" I think I mentioned that I had had several lives. This is the anniversary of the birth of Titus Oates. In view of the proximity of the Vatican, I hardly like to give you ' No Popery,' but when I pass my glass across the asparagus, you'll know what I mean."

" I believe you were whipped at the cart's tail from High Holborn to Marble Arch," said Jonah. " Did it hurt ? "

My brother-in-law groaned.

" Don't talk about it," he said. " The driver lost his way and took us round by Victoria Street. And people were very rude. As much as fifteen and six was paid for a dead cat that afternoon." Mournfully he emptied his glass. " Why should this wine have appeared before a medical board ? "

" Why ? " said Jonah.

" Because it's only fit for light duty. However——"

" I think it's priceless," said Jill.

" Sweetheart," said Berry, " if I gave you corked ginger ale, I believe you'd say it was nectar. As a matter of fact, a woman's opinion about wine is rather less valuable than that of a gorilla on heraldry. They go by the colour, you know. Yellow for champagne, red for port, green for starboard."

" I confess I've never made drink a study," said Daphne, " if that's what you mean."

" It's not your fault, my dear. It's your upbringing. Now, when you were at the board school, they ought to have——"

" Whatever you do, Adèle," said my sister, " don't marry a wag."

" Anyone would think you two were deadly enemies," said Adèle, smiling.

" But we are," said Berry. " What makes you think otherwise ? "

Adèle glanced at the roses pinned to my sister's dress.

" He didn't see me, but I was in the shop when he bought them," she said slowly. " And I heard what he said."

" I protest," said my brother-in-law hastily, a tinge of red creeping into his brown cheeks.

" And I," said Jonah, " can explain the champagne." He smiled and nodded at Berry. " Seven years ago to-day I was his best man."

Daphne's face was transfigured, and when I slid my hand into hers under cover of the table-cloth, her fingers closed on it with a pressure that was more eloquent than the tenderest sonnet ever penned.

Dinner became a festive meal.

Just as I was lighting my second cigarette, some of the lights were lowered.

" Hullo," said Berry, " what are they doing ? "

" I know," cried Jill excitedly. " We're going to have some movies. Look. There's the screen going up."

" By Jove, she's right," said I. " I suppose they always do it on Saturdays. That's why the place is so full to-night."

A moment later the screen was in place and a great shaft of light leaped from between the curtains of a gallery at the opposite end of the *salon*. As the remaining lights were extinguished :

" I do hope we have Charlie Chaplin," said Jill. " I simply love him."

The next minute we were plunged into the mill-race which has been appropriately named ' Current Events.' His troops marched past the King of Italy at thirty miles an hour. Two British destroyers passed us doing seventy knots. A French general decorated and embraced eight of his officers in something under fifteen seconds. After a short breathing space, during which the lights were raised, we were regaled with an indifferent farce, in the course of which seven people followed one another unhesitatingly through a river, down a fire-escape, along some telegraph wires, and into a flour-mill.

" Shall we go or stay ? " said Berry, when the screen was empty again.

" Let's try one more," said his wife.

" Right-o."

" A Daughter of the Capitol " proved to be a melodrama of slight merit—so slight, indeed, that after two or three minutes I settled myself in my chair as comfortably as I could and made ready to sleep.

How long I dozed I do not know, but a stifled cry from Adèle sent my heaviness flying. I could just see that she was staring at the screen. Instinctively I followed her gaze. I was just in time to see a scared-looking man with a bent nose stab another viciously in the back. When he had robbed his victim, the assailant darted out of the picture. A moment later I saw myself sprinting across the square like one possessed, and in my wake a tall, slim girl, with the slenderest ankles, running like a deer.

The next minute there was a flicker, and the scene changed to a hospital ward.

But I had had enough.

As I groped my way to the door, a glance over my shoulder showed me that I was not alone. Five other shadowy forms were stealing in the same direction, threading their way between the tables.

When we had all emerged into the deserted lounge, we stood looking at one another, blinking in the strong light. Then Adèle abandoned herself to a tempest of laughter, buried her face in her hands, and leaned shaking against a pillar. Jonah tried to say something and broke down. Daphne and Jill fell upon my neck and sobbed.

" Featuring Miss Adèle Feste and—and—and friend," panted Berry. " Can—can you beat it ? "

He squirmed in an ecstasy of mirth.

" But—but I'll swear there was no camera," I stammered, beginning to laugh.

" In—in one of the ground-floor windows," stuttered my brother-in-law. " Or a doorway, or something. And the valet was making a little pocket-money in his spare time. What a pity you didn't collar him this afternoon ! " With an effort he pulled himself together. " Seriously, you know, you two are not to be trusted. Next time you go out on your own I shall follow you."

" I believe you're jealous."

Berry only grinned, but Daphne put her lips to my ear.

"I should be," she whispered, "if I were in love with Adèle."

CHAPTER VI

NEMESIS

THE gates, which it was obviously impossible to shut, were dragged to, those of my organs which had been displaced sank back into position, four bells rang, and the train plunged forward. There was just enough play between my face and a smart little velvet hat for the two to collide violently.

" Ow ! " said the owner.

" That was my nose," I said. " I hope it won't bleed."

" So do I," said the man immediately north-west of me.

Fifteen seconds later, without any warning, the train came to an abrupt stop.

" I'm sure it will bleed now," said I. " Nothing can stop it."

There was an uncomfortable silence. Then :

" I don't wish to jump to any hasty conclusion," said Berry, " but I think I saw a notice to the effect that there was more room in the rear of the train."

" You did," said I.

" Well, if that's true," said Berry, " they must be very crowded in front. You know," he added, " this is very nearly as bad as the Four Arts Ball."

" At least there was variety about that function," said the major half-left of my breast-bone. " People removed their feet from your insteps every now and then. I don't mean to say they didn't put them back, but it gave the circulation a chance."

"Force of will," said Berry, "can do anything. Let's all pretend we're waiting to see the Boat Race."

The velvet hat shook slightly.

"As a matter of fact," said I, "it reminds me irresistibly of Earl's Court."

The allusion proved unfortunate, and it took us all several seconds to convince a lady with four parcels, whose hat appeared to have been caught in the gates, that the train was in fact going to Warwick Avenue.

When the excitement had subsided:

"Why Earl's Court?" said the man immediately north-west of me.

"Because this is the sort of thing you used to pay for," said I. "If you remember, you could ruin a dress-suit there for sixpence, while with eighteenpence and a little judgment you could become a confirmed invalid. Of course," I added, "you can't expect so much for twopence halfpenny."

With a frightful jerk the train resumed its career.

The rearrangement consequent upon its arrival at Oxford Circus partook of the nature of a violent struggle for existence.

Under cover of the confusion I sought to recover a package which I had dropped at Piccadilly. My fingers encountered its surface, but when I tried to pick it up, it appeared to be attached to the floor. While I was digesting this phenomenon:

"Somebody appears to be trying to lift me into the air," said the major. "I may as well say at once that, in the circumstances, I believe such a feat to be beyond their strength."

Guiltily I wriggled the string of my package clear of his right spur.

Amid the frenzied bellowing of officials the train proceeded on its way. Two hundred yards further on it came to a dead stop.

Berry cleared his throat.

"It cannot be too widely known," he said, "that I propose to emerge at Regent's Park. The funny-looking man on my left will accompany me."

The ripple of amusement that greeted this remark was rudely terminated by a coarse laugh from the conductor.

"You'll 'ave to look sharp about it," he said. "We don't stop there."

There was a roar of merriment.

I addressed myself to the major.

"A walk," I said, "will do that vulgar fat man good. If he had walked more in the past, we should not now be suffering quite so much inconvenience."

"Before we break up," said Berry, "I should like to say how much I've enjoyed this. I've been assaulted more times than I can remember, my ticket has been knocked out of my hand, and I've lost my gent's umbrella. It only remains for me to be robbed."

"All right as long as you don't carry anything in your hip-pocket," I murmured thoughtlessly.

The effect of my words was electrical. Simultaneously every man within earshot sought to assure himself that his hip-pocket was inviolate. The fact that everyone was wearing an overcoat further complicated a gesture which demands more than ordinary elbow-room, and in a moment the utmost confusion prevailed.

Berry braced himself against the gate.

"May I suggest," he said, "that everybody feels in the hip-pocket of the neighbour immediately in front of him? In this way the investigation now afoot will be greatly simplified, and by an exchange of confidences . . ."

Somebody laughed hysterically. There were unmistakable signs of panic.

" The first 'and as feels in my 'ip-pocket'll get wot for," said an explosive voice.

The threat was launched inside the coach, and I felt glad we were on the platform.

Happily the train chose this moment to resume its journey.

The sudden burst of apologies, which succeeded its impulse, suggested that several hands which should have been straphanging were otherwise engaged.

The major spoke into my ear.

" I'm not a lawyer," he said, " but I should say that your friend has been guilty of a summary offence. Conduct more calculated to lead to a breach of the peace I never witnessed."

I screwed my head round.

" If I give you his address," I shouted, " will you promise to summon him ? "

The major blenched.

" God forbid ! " he said. " I'd rather go back to France."

*   *   *   *   *

As we were walking down Marylebone Road, Berry demanded a cigarette. Before proceeding to unbutton my overcoat, I eyed him suspiciously.

" Where are your own ? " said I.

" Probably still in my case," he said gloomily.

" Well, why——"

" And that," said Berry, " was in my hip-pocket."

THE END